202(P9-DHA-895

50690

Castleberry, Brian

Nine shiny objects : a novel

VALLEY COMMUNITY LIBRARY
739 RIVER STREET
PECKVILLE, PA 18452
(570) 489-1765
www.lclshome.org

7-21-20

NINE SHINY OBJECTS

BRIAN CASTLEBERRY

NINE SHINY OBJECTS

A Novel

CUSTOM
HOUSE

This is a work of fiction. Names, characters, places, and incidents are products of the author's imagination or are used fictitiously and are not to be construed as real. Any resemblance to actual events, locales, organizations, or persons, living or dead, is entirely coincidental.

NINE SHINY OBJECTS. Copyright © 2020 by Brian Castleberry. All rights reserved. Printed in the United States of America. No part of this book may be used or reproduced in any manner whatsoever without written permission except in the case of brief quotations embodied in critical articles and reviews. For information, address HarperCollins Publishers, 195 Broadway, New York, NY 10007.

HarperCollins books may be purchased for educational, business, or sales promotional use. For information, please email the Special Markets Department at SPsales@harpercollins.com.

FIRST EDITION

Designed by Neuwirth & Associates

Library of Congress Cataloging-in-Publication Data has been applied for.

ISBN 978-0-06-298439-5

20 21 22 23 24   LSC   10 9 8 7 6 5 4 3 2 1

For Steven Millhauser

You can jump into the fire

but you'll never be free.

—Harry Nilsson

NINE SHINY

OBJECTS

A LEAP

OLIVER DANVILLE—1947

Before he saw the paper that night, before he had inherited its wrinkled pages at an otherwise empty table in a cafeteria, Oliver had been a washed-up stage actor too tall and gangly to play the juvenile and too scrawny to play the heavy, without the talent to cover anything in between. He'd heard it said he was handsome, but lately his hairline wasn't doing him any favors at auditions, let alone his tongue tripping down a staircase every time he opened his mouth. Only that morning he'd flubbed the lines on a character without even a name. *Shoe Salesman.* A guy who would play foil to the romantic comedy banter of the two leads, marching in with a box to say, "Your ostrich-skin boots, madam," with a lisp meant to be funny. The director had kept him onstage alone, with only a cigar-chomping prop man in the wings. A solid minute of silence crept over the place. Then the director had shouted from the center of the auditorium, "We've got no place for you, chum. Go back to Winnipeg."

Oliver had come to Sullivan's pool hall knowing there was a fifty-fifty chance Necky would be there waiting for his money, but in order to get the money, he had to play the marks, and the marks played at Sullivan's because it sat right there on the corner of Randolph and Wells, where every rube passing through Chicago found himself on a rainy Thursday, looking around for City Hall. He could work, sure, if he could find a job. But the only thing he had experience in was acting, and after the morning's train wreck onstage, he felt he'd received a sign from on high that it was all over. Winnipeg? He didn't even know where the hell Winnipeg was.

Only the last year of the war had felt like a break. Everywhere he went, a girl called out to him, lonely and in need of love, certain to find the dimple in his chin irresistible, his canned jokes funnier than anything she'd heard before, his prick a miracle. He saw many a framed picture turned to the wall in those days. And nobody stateside cared about his twisted left foot. But then Truman brought the boys home, and with all their shouting and elbows and swagger, they filled every bedroom in America, leaving him to his, up a crummy narrow stairwell smelling of dead cabbage. He spent his free time at Sullivan's pool hall after that, putting on his best act of losing so that he could come back and win double or nothing, chalking it all up to a fluke, your regular con.

And on this day of all days, in the middle of oiling up a real dope from out of Oklahoma City, of all places, in walks Necky, stripped to his undershirt, half shaved, a little swipe of blood on that long neck of his. Oliver's first thought was that Necky had come for him. He'd showed up to collect his two hundred dollars, and knowing he wouldn't have anything to collect, he'd come to put a hole in him. But then the hubbub of greetings at the front of Sullivan's turned to gasps and shouts, and Necky reached up with both hands and grabbed his own throat and then fell out of view, just like that, and before Oliver could even shuffle forward for a look, someone had already said in a disbelieving voice, "He's dead. They killed him."

Well. Eventful day for sure. Oliver left the rube where he was, twisting his pool cue in both hands, looking pale and sick as an old fish, and made for the back door, the alley, three blocks over, and up to the fourth floor to the room he was renting, where he left the light off and sat by the window, allowing the terror to strike him. They'd killed Necky, opened him up along that famous throat of his. And Oliver had seen the blood like it meant nothing at first and then spurting between his fingers. He'd never witnessed anything like it. Most sickening, though, was the knowledge that his first thought hadn't been for Necky or Necky's wife or Necky's kids. No, none of those things. Necky stretched dead on the floor in Sullivan's meant Oliver was off the hook. He'd never have to pay that two hundred back. It was looking at that rube from Oklahoma City, so clearly frightened, that the miserable part occurred to him: he'd put a lousy price of two hundred on a perfectly swell guy like Necky, who'd done so much for so many, who had half a dozen kids or something like that, who could tell a filthy joke better than anybody he knew. It was as if he'd handed the killer a knife.

So he took it as another sign, a second sign. He was washed up as an actor, for one, and he needed to get his life in order, for two. When, after a couple hours, he followed his stomach to the automat cafeteria down the street, he wasn't planning on getting any more of them. He was only planning to go to church or find a clean union job or settle down and marry the first librarian he ran across—really, whatever it took to become a useful member of society—and wasn't at all expecting to slide into an empty booth with his chicken salad sandwich and coffee and apple pie and see that story, the one that would change everything, about the navy pilot flying over the Cascade Range a week prior who said he saw lights flying in the night sky. Nine shiny objects that reminded him of tea saucers, and how nobody, but nobody, could explain them.

He read the story at least three times. Then he carefully ripped it from its surrounding page. Back in his one-room apartment four flights up, he stared through the open window trying to make out the stars from all the city light, feeling a familiar buzz, even hearing it, behind his ears. Once when he was onstage at an audition for *The Front Page*, this same buzzing overtook him and it was like the whole theater had filled with insects fluttering in the unnatural light. Words had spilled out of him then in a sort of ecstasy, but when he turned to the wings, another actor was wagging his head and laughing out loud. This time, though, Oliver didn't feel any shame, and when he read the first lines of the news story again, he felt the buzzing coming on with even greater force like a drug.

The next morning he was out of Chicago on the highway, thumbing his way west with anyone who would take him. He started with twenty-eight dollars to his name, and by the time he reached Boise, Idaho, where he was stuck for two days before finding a ride for the final leg of the trip, he was down to nineteen. Turns out a hitchhiker with any money at all is expected to pick up the lunch tab. He'd bought food for a salesman and two truckers and coffee for a pair of women who looked white as anything but could hardly speak a word that wasn't Spanish, but the colored family with their trunk over-packed with everything they owned and three kids stuffed into the back seat with his long legs and arms in their way wouldn't hear of it. They insisted on covering his dinner and a sandwich to pack for his next leg. The Stuarts. Jim and Tandy and the kids. They played a game of rhyming funny words and laughing that he never caught on to but which warmed him inside. When he parted with them, in Boise, yes, in Boise, they were settling for a job, likely the only black family anyone in that city had ever seen, and without him asking they offered to let him sleep curled up and cramped in the back seat of their car, outside their rental house, under a tall fir tree.

The following day, standing along a narrow state highway with a clear view of rolling blue mountains on the horizon, he was struck by the thought that one of the first things those people in the flying saucers—and he never had any doubt there were people—would think about the human race was what a bunch of narrow-minded cowards we were, running off to our little corners, pointing hateful glares at anyone who looked or sounded or acted any different. They'd probably laugh. People from the skies. From distant planets. He thought of them dressed in clothes made of shiny tinfoil, outfitted with transistor radios, their lives a lackadaisical glide between stars, full of spare time, talking philosophy and poetry with their feet propped up on thick down pillows. Yes, they'd laugh at our foolishness. And if they meant well—and surely, why doubt it, they meant well—they'd swing down out of the air and set-tle our troubles for us, get everything in line, have everyone shaking hands with everyone else. He could see it, America in another ten years: the whole melting pot getting along, focused on tomorrow, a gleaming technological utopia of television communicators and robot cafeterias and trains zipping along at a thousand miles an hour. Even out here, deep in the old frontier country, there would be magnetic rails to ride in cars that took you around without having to steer, and nobody with any real jobs, just living life, anything of want a distant memory.

Nineteen fifty-seven. The numbers seemed to hang out before him in the thin mountain air. Yes, ten years on, in '57, all this would look different and everything would have changed. Hell, ten years earlier, when he was only twenty, there was no European war and no Pearl Harbor and it was just the long legs of the Depression stretching ahead of them. Things could change fast. Look at him now, even. A couple days before, he'd been in Sullivan's, watching Necky collapse out of view, and now here he was in some place he'd never dreamed, the sort of place you expect the cavalry to ride through, a landscape made for Randolph Scott or Gary Cooper, delivered here by a saintly colored family who didn't ask him for a dime. And him a stinking pool hustler, a would-be actor. If he could set off like this in no time flat, meet people like the Stuarts, already feel like he'd walked out of an old skin, there's no reason to think a whole nation couldn't make a change, couldn't turn a corner, if the right thing was presented under that nation's collective noses.

Well, maybe his thinking was getting out ahead of himself. Or maybe it already had been. Really, these thoughts had been bubbling in his head in all the silent stretches as he rode with one stranger after another, never getting around to telling any of them the truth of the invariable question "What sends you west?" His story to them had been a sick aunt, his last living relative, in need of him now, a message by telegram, all malarkey. In truth he had three sisters, one of them still at home with his parents in Fort Wayne, and even both grandparents still alive on his mother's side. He'd never spilled the beans on those nine shiny objects, on the people inside them, and instead his mind had raced forward, dreaming its dream.

All his thoughts out on the highway that morning became a jumble. If he could just put them down in some kind of order. He'd brought nothing to write with, and as long as he stood by the road with his thumb out to every passing car, the best he got in return were a few honks. With the sun nearing noontime, he was beginning to lose the thread, starting to dissipate. His mood soured, and with it, the people in their saucer-shaped airplanes soured a little as well. Maybe they wouldn't take pity on the people of Earth. Maybe they'd look down on us once, sigh, and move on. Or worse, maybe they'd figure the best way to respond to our kind was complete annihilation, a rolling blue gas passing over every city and town, all life on this forsaken rock stumbling and gasping and then, whammo, out like a light.

Oh, boy. What he needed to do right now was get out of the sun awhile. Eat that sandwich. Maybe get some coffee in his system. And write his middle sister, Eileen, to tell her everything he'd been thinking the last two days. She'd understand. Eileen was a girl of big dreams, after all, a heavy reader married to a scholar of Shakespeare only two years her senior, a world traveler, really, having gone to London just last summer to survey the damage from all that bombing. He and Eileen had always been closest, she just a year under him, with Dolly and Mercedes so much older and younger, respectively. As kids they'd been best friends, and even when it was said by everyone that they'd grow apart for the natural reasons brothers and sisters do, that stage had never come. Surprising to think that only now a letter to her would come to mind. If he hadn't been in such a hurry, so alive with the inspiration of all this saucer business, he would have sat down and written her before leaving his apartment back in Chicago—which now, one realization tumbling over the other, seemed like a city he might never see again.

He ate the sandwich walking back into Boise proper and found a little stationery store that sold books and magazines on Bannock Street, where he asked the girl behind the desk, who had been reading the newspaper until he sauntered up with his goods, whether she'd heard anything new about the glowing objects seen by that navy pilot over the Cascades. "Glowing whats?" she said flatly, as if it weren't a question. When he leaned on the desk with one elbow, all of a sudden happy to share the story with an interested party, she stopped him halfway through to say, "No, sir, I don't think anybody around here's heard of that." And by the way her eyes wouldn't look at his anymore, he knew he was finished talking.

But then he found a little diner where men in suits raced in and out, apparently with connections to the state capitol and its goings-on, and with a cup of coffee steaming next to him, he set down to writing Eileen, telling her everything. He started with how he hadn't landed a part in the last year, how he'd lied—yes, lied to dear Eileen of all people—about the role in that production of *Frankie and Johnny*, which really he'd

never even read for, how everything otherwise had been sliding downhill and his only living—how could he have lied to
her about it?—had been at Sullivan's pool hall, where he'd
seen a pal of his—oh, let's be honest; Necky was a loan shark,
is what he was—fall dead just two nights ago, but that guess
what, just guess what, he'd made a big decision in life, he was
going to change everything, go in a new direction. He'd read
about something really spectacular, something that made his
heart race, something about a guy in a plane seeing these glowing lights, visitors from possibly another solar system when you
think about it, and so he'd headed west, in Boise now—pretty
view, Boise, wish you were here to see it—and in another day
or so he'd be in Washington State, at Mount Rainier in fact,
where the lights had been seen. Had she heard about them?
The pilot said they looked like saucers. Get that? Glowing tea
saucers in the sky. Well, anyway, he was going; he'd see what he
could see, follow the direction life took him. Maybe he'd end
up a lumberjack or a fisherman or whatever people did with
themselves in that part of the country, but maybe—and here,
really, Eileen, just think about it—maybe he'd see the saucers
himself, or even the people inside them.

He was going to tell her then about what he thought would
happen next, with the people inside ringing in a new age, an
endless jubilee year where everything shined and hummed,
but realized he'd already filled so many pages that these hopeful visions were going to be hard to fit into the envelope. So he
signed it right there: *Send you another letter once I'm settled, Ollie.*

Envelope licked and sealed, tucked away for when he found
a post office, he set back out to the highway with his thumb.
Afternoon was dropping into evening. More cars were on the

road. After half an hour of being ignored, he chased down a farm truck that slowed to a stop just ahead of him. The door popped open as he neared. Inside sat a wiry man with two days' beard and clothes so sun-faded and threadbare Oliver felt guilty even asking him the favor of a ride. "It's no trouble at all," said the man. And once Oliver was up in the truck with the door slammed closed, he added, "I'm only going a couple miles outta town 'til tomorrow."

"Tomorrow?" Oliver said, and suddenly wanted back out of the truck. "What's tomorrow?"

The man eased the rattly truck back onto the highway and cleared his throat. "Headed off for Tacoma. Brother's getting married."

"Tacoma, Washington?"

The little gray farmhouse really was only a couple miles out of town, in the jagged hills skirting the mountains. It was a tiny Sears house, with only two horses grazing in the wide scraggled field between it and the narrow winding dirt road they'd taken from the highway. The man eventually introduced himself as Saul Penrod and, without really speaking on the subject, made it clear that he'd be putting Oliver up for the night. And while this was more than a little strange, certainly, the thought of sleeping in something other than a moving vehicle was a pleasing one, and more important, the promise of a ride all the way to Tacoma—virtually his exact destination, as if this fellow had set off on a matched journey—felt like yet a fourth sign that a new path had been lit before him, that he had little choice as to continuing on or turning back.

He'd never been to a farmhouse before, never had any reason to be on a farm. Of course Saul was as reticent as a door-
stop, saying only that he had "an acreage" when Oliver had
asked what he did for a living, and the rising and falling tilled
brown field behind the house, stretching off into the fenced
distance, looked like a combed wasteland, its potential life a
blank. When one of the horses whinnied as Oliver followed
his host across the ragged lawn, he nearly jumped out of his
shoes. The beast had loped toward them like an escaped zoo
animal, its long globby-eyed face and pointed ears towering
above him. "Christ," he said reflexively, and by the way the
farmer's shoulders spiked up, he could tell that sort of language wasn't going to fly around here. "My apologies," he
stammered. "But can you get that thing off?"

"Oh, Dipsy?" Saul said, barely sparing a glance back at him.
"He doesn't see many strangers. But he's nothing to fear."

The horse had stopped in place, its tail whisking the air, its
wet lips parting inquisitively, its teeth a row of overturned
dominoes—not in the mood for trampling. Still, Oliver was
shaken, his nerves jangled, and the lonesome landscape
around them unexpectedly troubled him. Back in Fort Wayne
he'd been a town boy, living in a great house, his father a
banker, Eileen always at his side. They and everyone they
knew had automobiles and paved driveways and closed ga-
rages from as early as he could remember. This place, these
animals, the land: he was surprised to see they meant nothing
happy to him. He'd held no longing for the outdoors. And as
Saul creaked over the slat-board porch and reached for the
door, Oliver saw the choice to come here as a mistake. He felt
afraid.

"Come on in," said Saul. "The missus has dinner on the stove."

The missus, looking for the life of her just as winnowed and sun-cooked as her husband, wore a blue cotton dress without a hint of decoration. Martha, she was called, and it didn't take much imagination to see that she made her own clothes. Next to the front window in the waning light stood a great foot-powered sewing machine, though it was clear they were other-wise wired for electricity. A single bulb already glowed in the kitchen where she stirred a pot of lamb stew, unmoved by the idea of making table for a total stranger. Still, she set out a fifth plate.

The old man hung his hat on an ice pick at the back door and then stepped outside, where he put his fingers into his mouth and whistled. After a few minutes of dusty silence, this brought two young men through the doorway, thin as sticks and feral about their mouths, dressed in scuffed brown work clothes. Their hands were as dirty and craggy as tree roots. They eyed Oliver with a glare that notched a few hairs above suspicion and just below violence, so he simply nodded at them, his mouth gummed up in silence. He'd been a talker all his life, something Eileen warned him would one day get him into trouble. Around these folk, he could see it was best to have nothing to say.

The boys pulled out chairs without introductions, and so he went along, trying his best not to look at them. They were all Bible people, clearly, eating only after Saul had finished a prayer, the evening's entertainment a muttered discussion among the family on the story of Job. Luckily as a kid Oliver had been to church. He didn't have any great insight, but at least he was half-familiar with the story. The man got a bad shake from God, he wanted to say, but clearly the real message was something else. The two sons appeared to interpret the fella's trials in a way that got the old man's back up, and in the end the mother put her hand on his arm and whispered soothing words. In no time at all the boys screeched their chairs out, leaving their dirty plates, and disappeared down the hall. Oliver listened to the creak and shuffle of their boots, and after a pinched quiet, leaned sideways in his chair to be sure they were actually gone and not standing in the hall loading pistols. Nothing was said about whatever had just happened, and all the better, as far as he was concerned. After another silence, a patchwork blanket was produced from a wooden cabinet. Martha gestured at the sofa. Lights were shut off.

With the woman washing dishes in the next room, he lay staring at the dark ceiling, sure that he was a fool, that he would never sleep, and then fell into a dream of the highway, of seasons and years passing with his thumb turned at the sky, of lights whizzing through the air that he couldn't catch, of Eileen sitting cross-legged in their playroom back in Fort Wayne, unfolding a piece of paper, trying to show him something. He woke with a shudder, the morning sun breaking in at the window, an absurd rooster stabbing the quiet like murder.

He'd left his bag at the foot of the sofa. Inside, the letter to Eileen was unsealed. Either the glue had gone bad or one of these strange people had opened it, very carefully, and then slipped it back in his sleep. He had a distinct feeling it was the latter, but knew he wouldn't bring it up. Let them read his letters. Let them think what they want of him. He just wanted a ride west.

Breakfast was served, eggs and coffee, and he was surprised to see that Martha had dressed and packed a little leather case at the door. Apparently she would come along. The boys, however, were still nowhere to be seen. He silently worried about the possibility that they would be outside glaring at him, spitting on the ground, their terrible stick arms folded up tight.

Within half an hour the three of them were in the truck, Martha in the center, the two horses staring through a fence at Oliver as they munched from a bale of hay. "I can't thank you enough," he said. "You've both been so kind."

"Do unto others," said Martha.

Saul said nothing, started the engine, and lurched them forward out of a craggy rut. Then came the highway, the winding mountain highway, a silence between them so long and definite that Oliver familiarized himself with the subtle whirs and growls of the engine as a man familiarizes himself with the notes of a song he is trying to learn. Later, as they descended into a grassy valley bright under the morning sun, his head felt as if it were floating a little above him, and he could hear something like the buzzing of bees all around, just as he had the night he read that newspaper. Then he discovered too late that he was speaking. "A few nights ago a man, a jet pilot, a man in the navy, he was flying over the mountains up in Washington State. Lights appeared in the dark, up there with him, right alongside. By the radio he called down to his base. Surely they must know what these lights belonged to, what type of aircraft was up here with him. But they didn't. And when he looked again, he saw the lights were speeding up. They weren't lights at all. They were silver disks catching moonlight. He counted nine of them flying smoothly in the sky, above the clouds, and then all at once they turned away, shrunk into the distance, no different from the stars."

He waited for one of them to say something. Another farmhouse passed by and a narrow river gleamed snakelike ahead of them. "We know," said Saul. "I never had any brother to visit. You were a sign."

In any other circumstance like this he would have laughed, but here he couldn't. He'd been seeing signs of his own. "A sign of what?"

As if Martha were having a conversation with someone else, she said, "We'll leave Paul and Jack with the farm." And then, tapping her husband lovingly on the arm, "They're good boys. We raised them."

"That's right," said the old man, his wild white hair catching in the open window breeze.

He could see, could understand, that these two meant to follow him, to leave the two young men, their sons, behind. To what? For what? The buzzing sound intensified and they were rocking on a sea of golden bees shimmering in the light like coins and he knew something with certainty that he couldn't put into words and as he looked around he knew as well that these weren't bees but something else, something more timeless than the world, and it seemed to Oliver that the truck accelerated into the gilded pulse, launching into the frontier like his wildly beating heart. "Let me tell you," he was saying. "We're only here to make a better place—"

THE BEACH CONVERT

CLAUDETTE DONEN—1952

She met Eileen first out of all of them, so she called it Eileen's church. Plus, everyone from the place deferred to Eileen when they came to the restaurant, and Eileen was the first to talk to Claudette, to borrow nothing but a canister of salt, which she promised to pay back tomorrow, though Phil in the kitchen under his framed photograph of General Eisenhower said to her, to Claudette, that they weren't in the loan business, and Claudette said it was nothing, that she'd pay for it if the woman didn't come back, and *the woman*—because she wasn't yet Eileen to her—smiled so prettily that Claudette would have given her anything.

On the second day, when Eileen returned with a store-bought canister of salt, she said that her very own brother was a kind of preacher, and later that night after her shift, Claudette had stood in the gravel parking lot with the ocean lapping quietly at the beach and the moon glowing on the waves and watched the old warehouse, empty only a few short months ago, listening to the sounds of a cheery song raised up by fifty or more voices. Eileen's church, then: a warehouse halfway downhill to the beach from Phil's Roadside Café, itself an any-place sort of place with wide glass windows and hash browns and a parking lot big enough for a government office.

On the third day, when all Eileen did was come in and drink coffee with an older couple, Phil stood there with his ham-pink face and his hairy arms crossed and his chest besmirched with every food a person could eat, and he announced after Eileen left that the woman wasn't a member of any church at all and whatever they were doing in that old warehouse was likely illegal, and anyway, he was certain they didn't have the permission of its owner. But on her day off, Claudette walked to the restaurant anyway and then walked around the rusted square building there on the slope between the train tracks and the beach and found a group of children playing in the sand all dressed in the same clothing, the youngest wearing things no more complicated than bags, the school-age kids in shirts and short pants, all that pale glue color of cotton nobody had bothered dyeing. Among them stood a single older gentleman in a robe like a biblical shepherd, his white hair jutting up out of his head from the breeze like a gale-swept John the Baptist, the very man she'd seen the day before drinking coffee with Eileen, the man she called Saul. Claudette had heard the woman's name by then, too, she'd heard the name Eileen, though she hadn't screwed up the courage to talk to her about anything other than the menu and whether she wanted more coffee, and so when the older gentleman turned to her and the wind caught his shock of gray hair and put it in a different shape, she said, "Is Eileen here?"

"You're from the restaurant," he said, and made his thin lips into something like a smile. "You can call me Saul."

"I'm Claudette," she said, and then, gesturing at the children, "Beautiful kids."

"They're all the mothers'," he said. He turned toward them with pride. "Every single one a miracle. All of them born since the holy vision."

His words struck her as something like a traveling preacher's, and she knew then she would tell Phil that yes, it was a church, and he could forget calling the police on their singing. For now she asked again if Eileen was there, and when he turned back to her with that same half-smile, she said, "It's nothing. I was just around and thought I'd say—"

"If you can keep an eye on the children," he said, and then he said nothing more, but turned in his flowing robe with his wind-caught hair and walked barefoot to the warehouse door and went inside, leaving her in the grass-clumped sand looking frantically over the children, worried already that one of them may have wandered off. But they were nearly immobile, the younger ones sitting splay-legged, digging little holes with their fists, the older ones shaping piles or vague castles with careful hands in groups of two or three. Quiet children, apparently, and entirely disinterested in her presence. To tell the truth, they sort of gave her the creeps. One of them in particular, a little blond with the same abruptly scissored haircut as the rest, stared at her as he dug a hole near her feet.

Claudette had never really thought about having a child. Still, like anyone, she tickled a baby's chin when she saw one, talked in all grins to those old enough to sit in their own chair at the restaurant. She'd never found them disturbing or unnatural in any way, and yet here she was, taking a cautious step back and then another, feeling an awkward danger in their presence, when all of a sudden came the old man's voice from the door: "Come in, children. It's time for your reading." And, waving to her as the children dutifully started toward him, "She'll be right out, ma'am."

It was funny. Not until they narrowed into a line on their way up toward the warehouse did she note they weren't all white children, not at all, but a mix from every race, in their innocence and matched clothes and the bright afternoon sun somehow tricking the eye, or making that difference unimportant. Something like a scatter of salt and pepper on a diner table, the grains identical unless you went looking. But in all honesty, not the sort of thing she was used to seeing, not even in the movies. With the children disappeared inside, she was still thinking on this subject when out came Eileen, looking slim and jaunty and dressed like Bette Davis in a gray pantsuit with wide white collars and a big white sun hat and dark glasses. The sight of her holding down her hat in the breeze and waving made Claudette's chest leap, the way she imagined it would had Bette Davis herself appeared here on the Del Mar beach and waved at her like she knew her, and Claudette did everything short of running away to control herself. And then before they walked the beach for the first time, chatting about small and forgettable things, Eileen said the words Claudette would always think of when she imagined her later. She said, "It's so wonderful of you to come visit me."

As if she'd been hoping Claudette would drop in all her life.

After that, they walked together on Claudette's days off, and otherwise Eileen came to the restaurant for coffee or a little something to eat during the late-afternoon lull in her shifts.

They made fast friends, and when, sometime in those first weeks of their friendship, Eileen said that she'd left her husband to come to California with her brother, Oliver, and their friends, Claudette couldn't help but ask, "Did you remarry?"

Eileen laughed, seated alone in the tiny booth at the window, the afternoon sun slatted in on her like a comb of light, and said, "I'll never remarry. Oh, no! Once living with a man that way was enough."

"I've never been married," Claudette said, feeling her ears go hot. "I mean, it just hasn't happened."

Eileen leaned back with her wide brown eyes and said, "You, dear? Some lucky man is going to snatch you right up."

"That's not what I meant," Claudette said, speaking too quickly, rushing it again.

A look of concern troubled Eileen's face. The restaurant was mostly empty and Phil was shaking the transistor radio again and the fan was going and the coffee urn in Claudette's hand felt heavy and a pair of colored women from Eileen's church came through the parking lot in earnest conversation and the man two tables down pushed his empty plate out to the edge and cleared his throat and Eileen said, "I understand, dear. It's nothing to worry about."

That night in bed she thought about their conversation and a dozen quips she could have used to make light of the situation, terrified she'd said something she had always wanted not to say, or by not saying it, she'd said to Eileen just the opposite. Whether it was one or the other, she couldn't tell, couldn't discover in herself the proper angle, the entry point, the set of words she would need to clear it all up. She told herself she couldn't be too careful. Once last autumn a pair of women sat in the corner booth with books they talked over, animatedly, for an hour after finishing their meal. She'd liked their comfortable way with each other, their confident voices. She'd liked the way they took turns making each other laugh. And she'd *known*, of course she'd *known*, but even then she could never say, and what business would it have been of theirs— really, what business at all? Rolling around, unsleeping and wild, the only thing she could hold to was that she was positive Eileen felt something, too, a silent secret between them, even if she would never in a million years do anything about it. She knew from their walks and her laughter and her eyes and the way Eileen touched her on the back of the arm for no reason but affection, knew from the interest she had taken in her, this waitress beached in a little town halfway to Los Angeles, no longer speaking to her parents, her apartment behind old lady Markel's house, her car a dented Buick so old she worried the city might tow it away as junk when she wasn't looking.

But the next day, as she tied on her apron, just before the lunch crowd began sauntering in, Eileen entered, her hair done up in a little yellow bonnet to match her dress, a pink shawl over her shoulders. She waved and took her usual seat, hours early, and Phil grabbed Claudette by the elbow and said, his breath like a cigarette rolled in old bacon, "Your friend there's gone off her rocker. This ain't the damn fireman's ball."

"She just likes to look nice," she said.

He hadn't let go of her elbow. "I don't want you talking to her so much."

"What's it to you?" she said, and tried pulling her elbow loose. But he was strong and he had a grip on her and his eyes told her to stop pulling and who was in charge and she hated him, hated him something awful. "She'll want her coffee," she said. "She's a paying customer."

"Just remember who's paying *you*," he said, and let go of her arm. As she walked away, her arm throbbed, and lifting the coffee urn was actually a strain. She turned back, hoping he would have gone on about his business, but he hadn't, and was instead looking down appreciatively at her legs. That was Phil for you. A regular creep.

The tension in her smile must have been evident, must have been, because as Claudette walked the tile floors toward the back corner booth and Eileen took off her glasses, her magnificent eyes narrowed, and when she said, "My dear, how are you?" a disturbance rang in her voice like the botched note from a piano.

She assured her it was nothing, she was just tired, and that's when it happened. That's when Eileen asked her if she was free for dinner after her shift, around eight o'clock. Her *yes* streamed out ahead of her thoughts.

She had come from San Diego, her father a dentist who in his spare time and with her mother's sensible eye for accounting had invested in real estate up the coast, making gobs of money and losing little of it during the Depression, having never gone in for stocks, so that by the time Claudette was born in '32, the family would have seemed to a lot of people to be rolling in crinkly hundred-dollar bills. When she was old enough for school, this had put a chip on every other child's shoulder: the rich girl from the house on the hill, with all the pretty clothes and a driver and a mother who was pictured nearly every week in the newspaper at this or that ribbon cutting or as the patron of some museum or university, and a perfect snob, the children were all sure, a terrible and perfect snob who deserved to have her face mushed in the dirt. And they did mush her face in the dirt, kick her shins, pass dirty notes about her father falling in love with all his patients. Her only friend in those early years had been Cleo Fontaine, nearly her opposite in every way save how the others reviled them both. Cleo showed up at school with a black eye, picked at the scabs on her knuckles, relished the disdain thrown on her by the girls in their class. She had come in the second grade, the new student, and after the first month of classes, the two were inseparable, banded together, their own line of defense. Together they would sit in the narrow field next to the schoolhouse picking blades of grass from the dry earth, talking about the movies and radio, talking like girls, just talking. When she told Cleo that her mother had named her after the film star Claudette Colbert, her new friend rolled on the grass laughing, then made a joke of pulling up her skirt to show a little leg, just the way Colbert had done in a movie neither of them had seen. Even if the gesture was something they only knew secondhand, it became theirs, and anytime they were already in hysterics, one or the other would send them both into gasping laughter by pulling the move. Then, like a rain that falls overnight when no one is looking, at the beginning of the next school year, Cleo was gone.

By the time the war was over, when Claudette was thirteen, none of those early troubles mattered. She had shown herself to have a talent with writing, a knack for history, and declared that she would one day be a world traveler just like Mrs. Garfield, who taught geography, spent her summers abroad, and though well into her gray hair without a child of her own, said without a lick of unhappiness that her students were her children. Claudette was no longer alone then, or dependent on a single friend. She had a whole group of girlfriends—Sally Munce, Dorothy Wethers, Nan Williams, Margie Nelson—whom she spent all her time with, studying in the afternoons, going to movies on the weekends, and volunteering now and again for the rubber or steel drives. They had sung together as a quintet, with Nan on piano of course, at the school talent show. And so when Father told her she would be sent to a private residential preparatory school north of the city beginning the following year, she rebelled. She said, in fact, that she hated him, that if he'd wanted to send her to private school he should have done so years ago rather than making her endure everything she'd endured, not now, not now that things were what they were. "Endured?" he said, combing at his mustache with his finger, lingering at the bottom of the stairs as she wept. "What on earth have you endured, darling?"

She didn't explain, not then or in the months after, and didn't complain again even when her crate was packed and her goodbyes goodbyed. At St. Anne's, she wore her black and white uniform, she attended classes and mass, she did what was asked of her. Among the other girls she disappeared, unnoticed and unremarked. Only graceful blond Philippa gave her any sense there could be hope for her here. But she knew every morning when she awoke to Sister Madeleine ringing her triangle bell in the hall that she would take the first opportunity she got to leave the place, to dash out its thick wood gate and into the world, into freedom, into a life she would make all of her own.

That the day of her escape didn't come for more than two years, just a month shy of her seventeenth birthday, would seem comical to her only after she'd started work at the restaurant in Del Mar, and long after the day the vegetable truck pulled up outside the school's cafeteria and the pudgy-faced young deliveryman met eyes with her from fifty yards away. She'd let him reach under her blouse as they sped northward a few miles from the school, only to run away from his shouting voice as he pumped gas along a speeding state highway half an hour later. Long after all that, she could finally laugh at herself for eyeing the gate every morning and afternoon and evening, could laugh at the girl she'd been in those days, could laugh at her fear of being found out by her mother and father and dragged all the way back to St. Anne's—or worse now, back to San Diego.

Not that she'd gotten so far. But twenty miles proved a great distance indeed once she'd added a sympathetic old lady who didn't mind waiting on her first week's rent and a HELP WANTED sign at Phil's Roadside Café and a haircut and dark eye shadow and a waitress's white uniform. Far from Philippa, sure, far from the world of her parents, who to this day hadn't shown up. Occasionally she worried about them, how she'd hurt them, but really they were strangers, people too busy to even know her, and so at other times she figured her disappearance must have come as a relief. Last year she'd gone to the horse races and there, scanning the crowd with rented binoculars, she thought while holding her breath she might see them.

But she'd never once, no, not once, been troubled by the fact that they hadn't come around looking for her, that her name and their desperation to find her hadn't filled the air-waves and headlines all over Southern California.

No, she told Eileen that night, when she told her all the rest. No, that didn't trouble her at all.

They'd had dinner at a seafood restaurant on Camino Del Mar, and really Claudette just couldn't hold back anything. She'd just kept talking. Talking through dinner so that Eileen was finished long before she was, talking as they walked back toward Ocean Avenue, talking as they took off their shoes and walked onto the beach in front of Eileen's church just as the last orange glow of sunset faded into the blue night. Then, sitting together with the pads of their feet in the damp sand, feeling close to her and more open and honest than she'd ever been with anyone, she said, "You never talk about your church."

Eileen tilted her head just so, and though Claudette didn't turn to look, she knew that she'd nearly rested it on her shoulder. She could feel her fine hair, the loose and straggling outer halo, brush against her neck. They had touched. "My church?" she said. "I never thought to call it that."

Claudette had expected her to talk about it, though she had never stopped to think how strange it was that Eileen hadn't. Now as the waves murmured and fizzed in the dark before them, the subject seemed hush-hush, clandestine. The idea troubled her. "I didn't want to ask," she said quickly, defensively. "It's a person's private business."

With her knees up in front of her under her long skirt, Eileen arched forward and hugged her shins. Her eyes appeared to focus on a little rift of wet sand between their feet. "Not at all," she said. "We want everyone to understand the vision. It's just—"

A single wave crashed, propelling a line of foam toward them, nearly reaching their bare feet.

"It's just that you may not agree with our way of thinking. People often don't."

Claudette didn't really have a way of thinking, at least not about religion. Her parents had taken her to church only sparsely as a child, and even then it seemed like a social function, a necessary part of being upright citizens whose name now and again showed up in the paper. At St. Anne's she'd gone to mass as an obligation, finding it dreary, the pews uncomfortable, the priest's messages lacking epiphany. The closest she'd come to religious ecstasy there was looking at prints of the famous Renaissance paintings in the library. Sometimes, though, now, the sounds she heard from inside Eileen's church, or whatever it was, filled her chest with an expectant sort of lightness. Their songs and the exhortation of a man's voice, maybe even Eileen's brother's, followed her home at night like whispers just behind her ears. It occurred to her she'd never even seen this brother. "Ever since you came to town I wanted to know," she said. And then, recalling the older man in his beige robe with the children, said, "What's the vision? I've heard that."

The Vision, Eileen explained, spelled with a capital *V*, came to humankind at the foot of Mount Shasta, and not to her brother, but to their former leader, a woman by the name of Sophie Rhodes. "We were following Sophie before we came here," she said. "Oliver met her years ago in Washington State, before I joined him, back when I was in New York and still married. She was very charming, very unconventional. She had the Vision, and we revered her for it, revered her so much that she could live like a hermit among us. From the beginning my brother spoke for her, because, you see, he'd had his own vision, his own ideas before meeting her, when he first headed west after the sighting—the original vision you might say—and last year when she led us back to Mount Shasta, back to the site of the Vision itself, promising that there we would be taken up, that a new dawn would come, well, when that didn't happen, when we all stood in the rain hungry and in need of a bathroom for two days, when all the name-calling began, it was Oliver everyone chose to follow. Sophie Rhodes left us. But when she left, the Vision transferred to him. And now he is the One. He's what we call the Tzadi Sophit."

Clearly she was being told a flat joke, and so she laughed, kicking a little sand with her toes. "And what kind of name is that?"

Eileen's eyes had been focused out to sea as if she could see a great distance in the dark, out past the moon-reflecting waves and the faint curve of the horizon. Stars were out now, glimmering, watchful, and Claudette was more confused than before. In fact, again, she felt a little scared. "The name isn't important," said Eileen. "What's so funny?"

"Nothing," she said. And then, trying to turn a corner, "What about the Vision? What is it?"

"Do you think we're alone in this solar system?"

"Us?"

"Humankind. All of humankind. Do you believe we're actually alone?"

Claudette thought of the millions of people all over the

planet and the millions more mammals and birds and insects, the worms and fungi and bacteria, the trees. "No," she said. "Of course not."

"What if I told you there were people like us from elsewhere? From other worlds?"

It seemed to Claudette that the evening was bending toward a tepid joke. "I've seen about that in magazines," she said. "Martians and all. I don't go in for it, personally."

Now Eileen dropped her legs to one side and turned to face her, leaning back on one arm, her chin raised slightly, her wide eyes intense. "But it's true," she said. "I happen to know that it's true. And they have a message for all of us. That's the Vision, Claudette. Their message is the Vision. One day we'll build a home for all of us, for everyone, and the Vision will be made real on Earth."

The precipitous sinking in Claudette's chest felt like her heart had stopped beating, and perhaps it had. She would have believed then that a person's heart could stop beating because a few words had broken it, just as, an instant later, when it thudded back to life and her ears burned with its over-heated flow, she would have believed that her heart had shut down in order to stanch her embarrassment. Claudette could feel the muscles in her body already moving steps ahead of her, leaping up to her feet, walking away. But she remained on the sand, seated, as Eileen kept telling her about the Vision and the people from another world who traveled in gleaming spacecrafts and the perfect society they would create here on Earth thanks to the message, or Message, that woman named Sophie Rhodes had received nearly five years ago, around the same time her brother got his own message as well. It was all so confusing, really confusing, and to top it off, Eileen told her that all the hubbub around flying saucers was because they were coming from their distant planet to change our lives. One day they would land and speak to us. Or by magnetic force take us into the sky with them. Who were they? That part didn't seem to matter. Just saucer people, like anyone else but from another part of the Milky Way.

Oh, how foolish of her to believe that Eileen would be the one, how stupid to spend all that time dreaming of the two of them together, fingers intertwined, facing life inseparable, how outlandishly dumb of her to think of Eileen in her bed, to think of her body, the warmth of her there on a chilly night. Because now all she wanted was to be away from this strange woman, away from her intense eyes and the words falling from her ill mouth. "You're pulling my leg," she said, interrupting.

Eileen's chin tucked toward a shoulder. "Not at all."

"Maybe you could tell me more about this tomorrow," she said. She was so embarrassed at her own words, felt so rude for not taking Eileen seriously. But she needed to get away. "I'm just so tired, it's not making sense."

"I've upset you," said Eileen.

"No, I'm not upset. I'm only tired." And then, seeing that Eileen didn't believe this at all, she added, "I'm sorry. It's been a long day. Tell me more about it tomorrow, will you?"

At home half an hour later with all the lightbulbs on and the radio playing Rosemary Clooney's "Half as Much," she realized there might be no tomorrow, at least as far as Eileen was concerned. Over the last month, she'd let herself imagine

Eileen as a sort of savior, a romantic dream brought here by unseen forces to change her life forever, to deliver to her that partner she'd thought she'd never find. She had never dared, had convinced herself she wouldn't dare. And then these weeks had shown her she could. She'd grown comfortable with her, making small talk at the restaurant and walking along the beach on Tuesday afternoons. Her very presence in Del Mar felt to Claudette like a breathless escape from some other person's story, some plan outlined by a stranger. She'd let herself believe her days as a waitress at Phil's Roadside Café were numbered. They would live together, she'd imagined; they would sit on a sofa before a big picture window with Beethoven playing on the hi-fi, their legs folded on the cushions, knees pointed at each other, the world aglow. Together without anyone paying them any mind, just like the women she'd seen last autumn. But then Eileen had told her about this Vision nonsense, and it was like she'd been sitting there on the beach making up a story meant to wreck everything, a gag set to make a mockery of their future.

And what future? *Really,* she thought, pacing as the radio announcer began the night's sign-off, the national anthem playing faintly behind him, *what future?* She had no idea if Eileen felt anything of what she felt for her. Hair brushing against her neck? A few smiles? Her eyes lingering? That sense of heat in the air when she was around? The woman could be like this with everyone. She could, being mad for some UFO gibberish, simply be walking around in a constant euphoric state, practically foaming at the mouth. And Claudette, knowing nothing about romance, never having acted on what she'd always felt to be true, had misread a madwoman's attention as an extended, slow-moving pickup.

She'd made something of the same mistake before, with Philippa, in another life. To Claudette's eyes, she was the only beautiful girl at St. Anne's, with her Parmigianino neck and her long white face, her wide eyes and pointed chin, her broad shoulders and slim form. It was a wonder to Claudette that Philippa could be so incredibly smart as well. She was always at the head of the class, always getting the sisters' attention, always saying just the right thing when a question sailed through the room. And such grace. Compared to Claudette's short, uncurved frame, to her flat-footed walk, Philippa moved about like a ballet dancer skittering over a canvas of pure silk. How painfully her heart lurched when Philippa's eyes fell on her own. How terrified were her unstill hands. In the cramped dark library with its single window she had appeared in the dust-glistened beam of sunlight with her eyes ablaze, looking back at Claudette as if she were measuring her up. After a year of her looks and all the dreams she'd dreamed alone and awake of Philippa touching her, now she did, now her hand reached out and grazed her cheek. A thunderstorm might as well have struck over their heads. But then she said, "Your face. It looks just like a boy's. Like my brother's." And she'd never spoken to her again.

This old rejection, not even rejection, this old embarrassment, this old wound, surfaced like a fish in opaque water. She hadn't seen it coming until the light of her mind struck its glistening flesh, and its sudden presence emptied her out cold. She threw herself onto her bed and sighed, yes, sighed, like a foolish girl in the movies, because that's what she was now, a foolish girl, and there was no denying—

Except that another idea surfaced just as quickly and sent her upright, and then all the way onto her feet. She didn't have to be a foolish girl. She could go to her. If she loved Eileen, which in truth she'd known now since the beginning, known the way one knows an oven is hot to the touch, then she didn't have to stay herself, she didn't have to have doubts, she didn't have to hold on to all her notions about what can and can't be true. If she loved Eileen, then this message, or Vision, was all secondary. Wasn't it? Don't people sacrifice things, after all, don't they sacrifice all they have, when it comes to this unmistakable need, this desperation? Isn't that love? Isn't that the idea? She'd seen it a hundred times in the movies. It had to be.

But wait. Hold on. So she would throw out Claudette? All of the old Claudette? And be who? She pictured herself as St. Bartholomew holding his old skin in Michelangelo's painting, something she'd seen in one of those books in the library at St. Anne's. Yes, who would she be? Could she simply fake it, tell Eileen she believed in the Vision, if it meant being near her? Could she live with herself? And would anyone buy it? She wasn't, after all, a very good actress. Even for being named after one. But that didn't matter, no, it didn't matter at all anymore, because she was already wrapping a shawl over her shoulders and grabbing her purse. She was already out the door.

Walking down Ocean Avenue past midnight, without a soul around, in the dark with only streetlamps and the moon and the stars and that endless hush-hush of water from down at the beach, she felt prickly and goosefleshed, chillier than she should, and as the muffled sound of voices neared, as the outline of Phil's Roadside Café took form and color and then was upon her, next to her, nearly behind her, it became clear that a song had been raised in Eileen's church, a plaintive, rhythmic song, a dirge. From the high windows of the metal building, once some plank of war manufacturing, light sprayed out like the beams of a dozen lighthouses. How had she not seen such a glow? It seemed to her impossible that this could happen, that something could be made manifest before your eyes as if you weren't already looking where it would have been. But there it was. Light shining out onto the street and the slope and then the beach, light on the gray-seeming water. Light, nearer, on the form of a man standing on the slope between the restaurant and Eileen's church, a stout and tall man with his arms crossed, a man she thought at first was facing the church but who in fact was glaring right at her and suddenly near, though he couldn't have moved a foot. "Phil," she said, almost without breath in her throat. "What are you doing out so late?"

He gave her a flat, unbelieving smile. "I could ask you the same."

His car had been parked in front of the restaurant. Of course. His car. She had seen it, hadn't she, a black-coal lump in the corner of the lot. And why hadn't she driven? Why had she walked here? "I needed some fresh air."

"It's one o'clock," he said. Then, tilting his head back with a jerk, "Can you believe these stooges? Singing to beat the band in there in the middle of the night."

"It's—" she said, looking over his shoulder, wishing for anything that he hadn't shown up in her way. "It's strange."

Finally he turned back toward the church and let out a long noisy breath from his substantial nose. It was a signal of his that he was fed up with something. "I couldn't sleep," he said. "I laid down next to Harriet and I knew that instant I couldn't sleep."

"So you came here?"

"It happens sometimes. I'll do a little prep work. Drink some coffee. Have a slice of pie." He did the noisy breath thing again. "Sometimes I sleep in a booth. Other times I just stay awake. Lately I've been listening to these stooges, like I said."

"It's pretty music," she said.

He looked over his shoulder at her with his eyebrows tilted. "Sounds like somebody's grandmother died."

"Did you say you had coffee?"

"Not yet," he said. "You want any?"

He led her the short walk back up the hill and unlocked the front door with a big set of keys. Inside, the place looked strange and blue with none of the lights on. "Don't bother," he said when she reached for the switch. "If you turn on the lights, we'll get customers. Take it from me."

Then he turned the lock again behind them.

"I'll start coffee," she said, but what she really wanted to do now was leave. Instinctually, without being able to see his face all that clearly, she knew that something was wrong about all this. Coming in here had been a mistake. Her heart had started pounding out the message, and her nerves made her talk. "So you say you do this all the time? And what's Harriet do? Doesn't she worry? Do you leave her a note or something?"

He was moving toward her, slow, a mass, a silhouette. "Harriet? She snores through anything."

"But in the morning doesn't she wonder?" she said.

"Claudette, you sound scared," he said. "You want me to do that? You're fumbling. Look at yourself."

She was fumbling. She'd dropped the measuring spoon on the counter with a whole scoop of grounds spread black like a burst star. She thought again of those children on the beach, of all the undifferentiated grains if you look just right. "It's nothing," she said. "I'll just—"

And then he was there, just behind her, breathing down her neck, his over-big hands touching the backs of her arms. "Claudette," he said, "I always thought we could give it a try, you know?"

She moved and he didn't grab her and for a second she thought it was over, just Phil being Phil, nothing special, but as she stepped away and rounded the counter, he moved for her again, her eyes now adjusted to the light, his face coming through with detail. It was a look she'd never wanted to see on anyone's face, a look of disgust, a look of hate. In his upturned hand, her pink shawl draped like a wet rag. "Phil," she said, her voice cracked into a million pieces. "Stop it, Phil, this isn't funny."

"Why'd you come down here?" he said. "Don't bullshit with me."

"Phil," she said again, though it may have come out as a scream. She could hear nothing but the shuffle of blood in her ears.

A pair of headlights swung through the café. The bite of gravel on rubber. A car had turned around, bending their shadows into frightening abstractions along the ceiling.

Then he lurched at her again and this time she screamed

and could hear it, but his fingers wrapped all the way around her arm like a hand wrapped around the stick of a broom and she screamed again. "Shut up!" he said. "Jesus Christ, woman."

He was pushing her now, but not toward a booth, not toward the kitchen. He was pushing her toward the door. In his free hand jangled that big set of keys. "Phil, what are you doing?" she shouted, though her voice sounded to her ears like it was bottled. "Please."

"I'm throwing you out," he said. "Go home."

She couldn't breathe for the terror, couldn't make sense of what he was saying. Surely he wasn't actually letting her out the door, but then he really was, he really had, and standing on the gravel lot, she said, "Phil, what are you doing?"

And again he said, looking at her with that hate in his face, flinging her shawl onto the checker-patterned floor, "Go home."

She backed away as he relocked the door and disappeared into the shadows behind the counter, his form only a faint cloud now, near the percolators, making coffee. It took her a moment to gather her senses, to move from the terror of what Phil had just done, the immediacy of it, the miserable certainty that had hit her stomach in there like a boxer's punch. And only then did she register the lights off at Eileen's church, the singing halted. It was as if they had witnessed all of it and with a sudden mortification toward all humanity had shut down their exaltations, their prayers, their mournings. She stood in the gravel lot with her legs shaking under her and felt a betrayal and fear she couldn't string into thoughts. She felt empty, a container spilled into the tide, an outline of chalk on a blackboard. A burning foolishness overtook her. She had brought this on. She must have.

But no. She'd done nothing wrong. She'd dropped her shawl and the old wet rag lay in a puddle on the diner floor, haloed in streetlamp light. She'd never been attached to it, just a thing to put over her shoulders at night, yet now it glowed with meaning. Like St. Bartholomew's skin from the Michelangelo painting, like the old Claudette. She didn't know what she was now. Didn't know yet what she would become. But she was filled to the outer edges with another Claudette, who turned homeward, north on Ocean Avenue, her legs bounding like a gazelle, every shadow a reaching white hand to avoid.

In the morning, after only a brief nap, she washed her face in cold water and packed all she could in the small suitcase she'd bought last summer when she thought she was going to save for a trip to Los Angeles. Even the framed photographs of her mother and father she'd taken with her to St. Anne's she now tucked between blouses, sure she would settle elsewhere, if not at Eileen's church, then somewhere, anywhere else. She would travel the world, she thought, checking her makeup in the mirror. She would see all the seven wonders, just like Mrs. Garfield.

That had been her plan. That's what she'd come up with overnight, wrapped in her bed with all her clothes still on, sweating from the warmth but unable to marshal the strength to throw off the covers. She would go to Eileen's church, she would rap at the door, she would ask to be let inside. They all lived together in there. She knew that. It's why Phil had said more than once they were communists. Surely they would take her in. She would live among them and learn their rituals and she would find a way to believe in enough of their ideas to make it okay. She had to do it, not only so that another day could begin and she could walk away from the restaurant for good, but so she could be with Eileen, so she and Eileen would stand a chance, so they could be together. She would be the new Claudette. She would mash down the lid of her suitcase and latch it shut and set it on the passenger seat next to her. She would start the car. The engine would lurch and wheeze and cough to life. Then she would drive the six blocks and never look back.

She did these things.

When she cut the engine at the edge of the slope leading down to the beach, loose sheets of paper were blowing around in the sand. At first she thought the children were out playing with them, chasing them along the edge of the water. But no one was out there. Only the loose sheets of paper fluttering and rising and racing about like gulls drunk to madness. And there, on the shadowed side of the building, the door where the older gentleman had called to the children, the door from which Eileen sailed toward her that first day she visited, hung open in the breeze, keeping offbeat time for the dance of all that paper.

Her feet fell ahead of her down the slope. The bright morning light made everything unbearable, unreal. She shielded her eyes with a hand, but it helped little, and though the sound of cars on Ocean Avenue and the surf splashing filled her ears, it still felt like silence. At the door she gripped its handle and peered inside. She'd never seen inside, and now it only looked like darkness. Nobody home. She stepped up into the old warehouse, her heels clicking against the slick concrete floor.

"Hello?" she said, and nothing answered.

After a moment, objects took shape. The windows up above dropped light onto a pile of cots seemingly thrown together in the far corner, and opposite this hunkered a wide desk. Nearer by, a single long table and a modern kitchenette stood like unmatched members of a misplaced apartment, neither part of the original place. Aside from this was only the high ceiling, the vast emptiness of stale air between. Altogether the space reminded her of a gymnasium, with the same old human energy left behind with the lights out, the same faint scent of bodies recently at work. A vague memory of girlhood, of sneakers and gym shorts and Sister Edith blowing her whistle. Of Philippa turning her wide eyes on her.

They were gone, clearly, all of them. Eileen had left without another word, like a customer out the door when her back was turned. Claudette had been cool to that Vision talk and that coolness had been enough to put all this nothing in here. Or no. It had been Phil, shouldering and harrumphing in the shadows of the kitchen last night as she stood outside in terror, reaching up for the phone, holding it to the dark shape of his head, finally calling the police, a man determined to crush something in the world, and so he did.

Her stomach turned with the certainty of it, the clear image of his shadowed bulk, just as clear as the CLOSED sign on the door of the Roadside Café uphill, and the dark quiet here, where Claudette strolled through the place, looking over everything, telling herself that she would want to remember what was left, that later on it might be important to know what parts of Eileen's church survived. It was surprisingly close to nothing. Under one of the cots she found a single jack and the stub of a cigarette. In the wide parts-factory bathroom where they had hung a sheet to divide boys from girls, she found a finely sharpened pencil. On the seat of a chair she found a dried maple leaf, perhaps come here from far away, an immigrant in this sandy climate.

In the bottom drawer of a desk she found the only thing with human markings, the only thing with even a note of personal quality, a rolled blueprint held together by a thick skin-toned rubber band. She took this to the open door and unrolled its drawing to the bright day. Here was a small town of ideal little houses, a grid of streets, a perfect neighborhood of matched squares fronted by circles, each labeled with the word *tree*. At the top left corner in a rectangle not part of the plan were the words *Eden Gardens*. And beneath this, the phrase *A Revealed Vision of the Message, Del Mar, CA, 1952*.

And even below this, in smaller lettering, *Eileen Cuttredge (Danville)*.

A place as dull as anywhere, from what she could tell, but with a name you could search for all your life. She didn't know what it was supposed to mean or why it remained, but still she rolled it tight and bound it with the rubber band, seeing it as her only memento of Eileen, the only thing she'd left behind, maybe a way to find her. After another pass along the sheet-metal walls, she stepped out into the sand and bright morning. The hushing comb of the foam-lipped water muttered its endless message. She was at the edge of the world here, as they all were, but she wouldn't stay. She stood for a time letting the water soak her shoes, thinking of where Eden Gardens would be and how far, and then left.

ON ICE

MARLENE RANAGAN—1957

He **was definitely balding, all** right. That forehead of his, inching back, practically sounding a retreat from the battlefield of his wrinkled—

Such a stupid metaphor.

—his wrinkled, freckle-splotched brow. And those eyes of his, looking more and more like her father's, pinched at the edges and always bloodshot, like any minute he could burst into tears. To look at him now, shakily sipping at a whiskey and orange juice—

Who in god's name drinks such a thing?

—at 2:17 on a Saturday afternoon, gazing at the television screen like this old cowboy-and-Indian movie held the secret to his existence. Or like a squirrel, the way a squirrel stares into the middle distance, certain something is coming for him now, no, now, no, now. Out the window behind him the white carpet of snow and more snow coming down, all of Long Island a gusting arctic nightmare. He'd been up early at the Halfords' trying to sell a shelter in this weather, everyone involved hungover from last night's party at the Sumners'. Another tonight with most of the same faces at Ira's and for god's sake she wasn't looking forward to it and was he talking? Right now? Was he actually saying something to her? Was she expected to understand his mumblings over the terrible racket of all those rifles and hooves and war whoops?

"—then I'll just take a little nap, you know, to straighten out my head before—"

Yes, that definitely was worth listening to. Absolutely necessary. Couldn't conceive of finishing this potato salad without first hearing Charlie's plans for wasting all of Saturday afternoon stoned drunk or asleep, so that when they both appeared at her brother's doorstep that evening she would be the one to have to carry all the conversation, though what she really wanted to do, all she wanted to do, was sit in a warm bath listening to that record Jeff Linwood bought her of the *Brandenburg Concertos,* and then to maybe eat a slice of pie—yes, pie, warm berry pie.

She'd have to send this lunkhead back out to the store if she were going to make it, the pie, yes, and finally a little television, something silly and rather stupid, in her robe and pajamas, her legs folded onto the couch, the furnace purring away downstairs like an escaped leopard. But no, she couldn't send him out, not after all his hard work and on a Saturday, no less. No, the afternoon was for booze and cowboys and sleeping it off, certainly not running out to the grocery in the snow, and even more certainly not fixing that damned leak under the bathroom faucet.

They'd been happy once, some time ago. Charlie a charming goof, full of big ideas he'd regale her with into the night, she enamored with him. He had listened to her then, too, wanted to know what she'd done this day or that, where she wanted life to take them. But his last big idea had been this house, this town, and in the years since its realization she had faded for him into the wallpaper, his eyes squinting at her like a stranger's when he came in the door.

"Could you turn that down?" she said, without realizing the words had started to leave her mouth.

And Charlie, bless his dumb face, said, pointing, "This?"

"Yes," she said. "The thing making all the noise."

He reached forward from his chair, too lazy to stand up until the distance proved again, for perhaps the hundredth time, unspannable by the grunting stretch of a short, tubby, balding—

"They're about to save the girl here any minute," he said.

"I'm sure they are."

And only then did he stand up, take the two steps forward required of him, and turn down the volume. "I'm going to make one more of these," he said, shaking his ice. "You want one?"

"We haven't even had lunch."

To which he huffed, grimaced, and dropped back into his chair, defeated, checked. "Look," he said, and pointed with his glass.

On the little screen, a white-hatted hero rounded a tepee, his pistol at the ready. The cowboy's arched eyebrow, apparently meant to look brave, reminded Marlene of Bela Lugosi.

Then Charlie said, like there had ever been any doubt, "He's got 'em."

She didn't stick around to see the grand denouement, the tearing back of the tepee's flap, the knife to the girl's throat, the ace shot that would somehow only wound the chief's arm, freeing the girl and leaving the evildoer sprawled and moaning, the orchestra whipping up a little sentiment, the closing image of an eagle taking wing over the name of the production company. That's how they all ended, every Saturday, the only difference being that this time Charlie was actually dressed by noon in his salesman's clothes but for the loose tie, having returned an hour earlier with snow in a ring on his hat and piled up on his shoulders, chattering about finding a black man downhill wandering in the new addition, of delivering him for unexplained reasons to Ira, of what a saint he was for helping out a colored stranger. He'd come in animated, rambling to her about how this same stranger got stuck in the snow downhill at Eden Gardens looking for a friend of his from the Korean conflict, some guy with a Spanish name, who, Charlie wanted her to know, had joined up with a group of people devoted to flying saucers. Or at least that's what the stranger had told him. No explanation for why he'd be looking in Eden Gardens, that town that wasn't even a town yet, built in a fit that autumn by a shady company no one on Long Island had heard of, the field of Cape Cods left empty ever since, no word on when they would be sold.

And why to Ira's, she'd wanted to know. Because he had the extra bedroom, Charlie had said. Because he wanted to show him off to everyone at tonight's party, her own head had corrected. Because he was Ira, president of the Ridge Landing Human Relations and Equality Association, and having him there would prove a point of some kind.

Oh, she didn't care about any of this. Did she care? She didn't care. Of course not. What she cared about was dicing the green pepper and celery small enough so her brother wouldn't complain, though she knew he would complain because he lived in the Stone Age, when potato salad, according to him, was only potato and mayonnaise, with maybe a pinch of salt and pepper, none of this fancy vegetable stuff. Ira was a complainer. To her, at least. To everyone else, he was Ira. Tall, happy-go-lucky Ira. With her, he was their father all over again, bossing and complaining, needing everything just so. And Hellmann's doesn't know from potato salad? she thought of asking him. Because right here on the advertisement it says otherwise.

She'd bring it with her, wrinkled, torn from *Redbook*, in fiesta colors, the announcement at the top in fun letters exhorting her: *It takes REAL Mayonnaise to make REAL POTATO SALAD*. But that wasn't all. Look, Ira, look.

Things, she thought, are getting out of hand today. Well out of hand. And nothing about these green peppers was bringing it back together.

She needed her Miltown pill, had thought today she could do without, had been thinking for a week now that she simply didn't need it. Another of Linwood's ideas, of course. He'd laughed when she'd admitted to him that she took the pills, had said there was nothing wrong with her at all, only the need for a little adventure, a little distraction. He'd said this with his blue eyes and his combed hair and that well-tanned skin of his, over drinks at Perry's Steakhouse on Main Street, his tie loosened at the neck, his orange-brown suit a marvel. She had been there with him—oh—her most daring act. To be there right in town with a married man, herself married, and in the afternoon of a Tuesday three weeks back, sipping cocktails, neither of them mentioning their spouses. It was a scandal. Except nobody noticed. He'd told her she didn't need any Miltown and she'd laughed, too, but the thought wedged in between her ears and finally she decided she didn't want to take it, that if she didn't take it, maybe he would really want her, and that last thought had put the gasp in her, and another week had gone by while she wondered what to do. Then last night at the Sumners', tipsy and dancing, he'd looked at her from across the room, his eyes piercing, something sad and broken there, and she'd known like a slap to the face that she wouldn't take her pill the next morning, or the one after, that she'd do whatever she had to do in order to fall into his arms and feel the rocklike surface of his body and yes, of course, go to bed with him, yes, she thought that, little Marlene Feldberg, the good girl, had thought exactly that, right there in Nancy Sumner's living room as a Duke Ellington record played and Angela Quinn rambled at her shoulder about some movie she'd seen at the drive-in and the teenagers kissing one car over and didn't she think Doris Day was just a little too happy for her own good, and now, with a splitting headache and her mind racing and her hands jittery as two fish, she regretted it. Regretted thinking that thought about Linwood, regretted not taking her pill, regretted the unreachable distance between her and Charlie and even marrying him in the first place and then nearly every day in between and, oh, wow, yeah, now she's crying, actually sniffling over these stupid green peppers and so she leaves them, leaves them and walks down the hall—

Charlie still sitting in front of the television, another Western just getting started.

—to the bathroom and opens the medicine cabinet and pops the top off the brown bottle and drops a pill into her hand and throws it back and cups a palm under the faucet and drinks. And just this action, this decision, gives her a feeling of stability. She isn't falling to pieces. Christ. Nobody was falling to pieces in the first place. In the mirror, still looking young, though her hair seemed a bit messy and she'd brought with her down the hall the knife she'd been using, Marlene gazed back at herself with a reassuring smile and took a deep, cooling breath. She was fine. Everything was fine. Everything but the *tap, tap* drip under the bathroom sink.

She would make the potato salad and they would go to her brother's and everything was fine but that *tap, tap.*

He really had taken a nap and grumbled from down the hall, still in bed, for her to make him some coffee, near sunset, long after the snow had melted a bit and then frozen again so that the view out the picture window glistened with the dropping orange light of a fattened sun. Marlene had been sitting there, perched on the arm of the sofa, dressed in her silver-blue party dress, looking out the window for some time. The Miltown made her this way, but Dr. Robertson said it was good for her, that it evened her out. After a few mechanical actions—the coffee, the hall, the bedroom to pick out his clothes—they were out the door, her heels a danger all their own on the slick uneven drive, crunching out into the street, Charlie still waking up, yawning, opening and closing his eyes, sighing.

"Please, Charlie," she said as they turned down Ira's street.

"What?"

"With the theatrics," she said. "It's enough."

He drove a block before sighing again. "I'm tired. What do you want?"

"For you to act civilized, after all."

"After all," he said with a distant vagueness that bespoke irritation. "Anyway, your brother expects us to smooth everything over about this Negro, so you'd better prepare yourself for that."

"Smooth over what about 'this Negro'?" she said. "For crying out loud, Charlie."

He released his hands from the wheel like they weren't already sliding between ruts of compacted ice and waved his fingers around, his unevenly cut fingernails and knobby knuckles the tails of two peacocks. "You know everyone is going to be up in arms."

"About what?"

"A Negro at Ira's party," he said. "Staying overnight."

She scratched the top of her neck where her hair strained up into its pins and clips. "Charlie, with every day that goes by, you sound more like a bigot."

He stopped, slammed the brakes, slid to the curb. Three blocks from Ira's.

Her heart choked. "What are you doing?"

"You've been after me," he shouted, his face dark, his finger wagging. "Just lay off. All right? Can you lay off?"

He was acting more like her father, that demanding, bossy man, and she didn't like the association. In their early years she never would have imagined him raising his voice, never would have pictured him losing control. Father had been like that, a walking mousetrap ready to snap your finger at the slightest wrong step, able to switch personalities with a single jerk of his handsome lips. Charlie was changing, going ape. And she was beginning to think Halford and his Civil Defense toadies were rubbing off on him, uglying up his thinking. "Don't try this with me tonight, Charlie," she said.

"Then lay off."

She hated him: fat, balding, and now this. "Okay," she said. "Can we just go?"

He turned the key and the engine died. "We'll walk from here."

Out in the cold, brisk and cutting, she clutched the neck of her coat. He was sure now that he'd shown her what for, that he'd come out on top. She'd seen him like this before, marching around like he'd just won the Battle of Midway. "You're being a monster, Charlie," she said. "It's embarrassing."

But he went on, stalking, stooped, his feet shuffling forward like skis, oblivious to what an ass he was being, to the ten-car pileup their marriage had become to her.

Then it was inside, not only with Ira but also with Rose, always better than her in every way, the perfect housewife to her half-Catholic no-child household, all that Mother had wanted compared to all that Mother hadn't. Rose, with her hair done professionally, somehow in this snow, just for the party. Had she called someone in? Do hairdressers do house calls now? No. But here she was, Rose, proof that they must. Kissing at the air next to Marlene's cheeks like a society woman out of the movies, she said, "It's so good to see you. Can you believe this weather? An absolute mess, isn't it?"

Marlene shrugged out of her coat. "Charlie here insisted on walking the last three blocks," she said, and there he was, looking at the carpet, his lips smushed, as Rose did the same kissing routine on either side of his face. "I think he's trying to give us pneumonia."

Rose was only half listening or she thought it was funny to say, "You're not feeling well?"

And either way, she was dressed in blue jeans and an over-size Hawaiian shirt, practically a tent, too big even for Ira. She dipped into a cardboard box near the door and came out with two leis, pink and blue, and told them to put them on. "I completely forgot," Marlene said. "I would have dressed in something Hawaiian."

"You don't have anything Hawaiian," said Charlie, smiling. He never knew when he was being mean or stupid. You almost felt sorry for him. "In fact, I don't have anything Hawaiian."

Rose hooked the blue lei over Charlie's head. "Now you do," she said. "Come on in."

Little Deborah slumped down the stairs, holding her place in a book with a finger. She had tied her curly black hair back with a bright-red lei. Otherwise she was dressed like Dennis the Menace in baggy denim overalls and a T-shirt. "Hiya, Aunt Marlene," she said. "Hiya, Uncle Charlie."

"Hey, sweetie," she said. "Where's your brother?"

"Oh, Maxie?" interrupted Rose. "He's upstairs putting the finishing touches on his volcano."

"Volcano?"

Back in the kitchen Ira shook a rocket-shaped cocktail mixer, *uh-huh*ing along with the story a handsome young black man with a tuft of hair under his lip told about once meeting the mayor of New York in the kitchen of a Harlem restaurant. "So I said to him," the young man said after glancing at Marlene and Charlie, "if this is a stickup, just leave me out of it, man. I got enough trouble."

Charlie laughed in that stilted way of his even though they'd joined the story late, stepping all over whatever could have made it funny in the first place. Ira and the black fellow both just looked at them, frozen a moment, before her brother said, "I want to introduce you to Marlene Ranagan, née Feldberg, my little sis, Charlie's wife."

"A pleasure," Marlene said.

"Stanley West," the young man said. When he took her hand, his was dry against her skin, and the strangeness of what was happening couldn't be missed. She'd never touched a black man's hand. As impossible as it sounded, after all the Ridge Landing Human Relations meetings she'd attended at her brother's house on bringing peace between black and white, after all the letters she'd written to lawmakers about racial integration, after all the good she'd said about that southern preacher on the television, she'd never touched a black man's hand except to exchange money or take a light bag of groceries, feeling good that she wasn't making him take it all the way to her car, and suddenly this felt like a crime she'd been committing for years without her knowledge. Stanley was looking into her eyes, smiling, talking. "Your brother says you went to art school?"

"Oh, I started painting," she said, a little taken aback. "Then we moved out here and I'm so busy with the housework and everything and—"

"Stanley's uncle's a professor," Ira interrupted. "City College. Stan here's a regular college intellectual."

To this Stanley seemed clearly embarrassed. And for a moment, a flash in his eyes, Marlene felt a kinship with him, both of them dealing with Ira's forced joviality, both of them all too often in uncomfortable situations. She imagined the two of them seated and speaking openly, old friends, talking about these men, these loud white men, and all they demand from them each and every day. How fine it would be to let their hair down, as it were, to see each other eye to eye.

But then, her ears hot like lit matches, she saw that this was ridiculous, laughable. They didn't know each other. A gulf separated their skin. No matter how many Human Relations meetings she'd attended at Ira's house, she was only herself, someone's wife, and he was a stranger and walking in a life so different from hers that to presume otherwise was downright silly. Why, only a moment ago she'd surprised herself by touching his hand.

And so she did it. She really laughed, a good old-fashioned guffaw, leaning at the waist, nearly toppling forward.

Of course a person shouldn't laugh right after that person's brother remarks on another person's intelligence, especially when that other person is under the needling eyes of the whole neighborhood for already looking different. She caught her breath in a gasp of horror, nearly choked, as Stanley's face turned hard at the floor.

He cleared his throat, tapped his feet, waited for something else to happen. Ira, for his part, tried to work something thoughtful out of his mouth. Instead all that came was "Well—"

"I'm sorry," she said. "I was thinking of something else."

But really the situation was beyond repair, and as Charlie launched into a pointless tale of how he'd sold a shelter to a professor who knew a thing or two about the Soviet threat, their small group had moved on. Even Marlene had blankly taken a drink when her brother offered it, had held it ladylike at the neck between thumb and forefinger, had downed it nervously, had—

My god, he wouldn't even look at her.

—proffered the empty glass to Ira with a tight smile and held her second aloft as she glided back out of the kitchen to the dining room, where Rose arranged the snacks and dips on a console table beneath the big starburst clock they'd purchased from a catalogue, choosing the exact one Marlene had shown her in the photograph, the one she'd wanted herself. "You moved the dining table?" she asked, as if the answer weren't evident by the empty floor. "It makes so much more room."

"Ira says there'll be dancing," Rose said, spinning around, her chubby little face gleaming a red-lipped smile. From a narrow space between the console table and the wall, Deborah peered out, pushed back her glasses, and disappeared again. Rose didn't seem to notice. "He's got all this *island* music. Had the shop special-order a few things if you can believe it."

"Oh, I believe it," Marlene said. "He'll stop at nothing." She looked around them, conscious others could hear. "Listen, what do you know about this new friend of yours? He seems, um, quite interesting, quite intelligent."

Ugh. Was she putting on the flirting act?

Her sister-in-law didn't miss it. "Why, sweetheart," she said, and then, as if it meant everything, "My goodness."

Something clicked. A literal sound behind her ears. She threw back her head even, as if she could shake it off her neck. "Rose, you are intolerable."

And so she was off to yet another room, the living room, where the grainy screen of their television showed a man onstage with a German shepherd, the dog doing backflips, one after another, its tail flailing as it rose and tucking under as it dropped, the man smiling maniacally, an invisible crowd cheering. She looked at this, decided she was a fool, and dropped onto the sofa.

A couple of hours later she'd already had more to drink than she should have, and while nearly everyone invited had shown up and Ira's ridiculous island music played and yes, people were actually dancing in the carpeted dining room, Linwood still hadn't appeared. Linwood, whom everyone called Linwood even if his first name was Jeff, the way people called Truman Truman, as if he were already a noted figure of historic significance, Linwood and his wife, Alice, with her expressionless face, her not talking, her wide tube of a body stuffed into some dress or another. Oh, damn. Damn, damn. She was worked up. Even with the Miltown, she was a wreck tonight. There was nothing wrong with Alice Linwood. A sweetheart. A model citizen. A perfect mother. Of course the only even slightly meaningful conversation she'd had with Alice had been about reincarnation, which apparently the woman took seriously, and about which she didn't appreciate Marlene's jokes.

I met a man once I could have sworn was a horse's ass, if that's what you mean.

Do you think Ike used to be a wet blanket?

If I was anything before this, I'd wager I was a fish. You know, for the drinking?

Well, in hindsight they hadn't been all that funny, but for crying out loud, the woman seemed near to tears trying to make Marlene take the concept seriously. "I have visions," she'd said at the Linwoods' dining table months ago. "You can believe in them or not. But I see myself in a wood shack in Ireland, my hair red, a mysterious man coming toward me, offering to buy my family's property."

"It's the plot to *The Quiet Man*," Marlene had told her. "John Wayne? Maureen O'Hara?"

And Alice Linwood had jerked up to her feet and huffed. "I've had those visions since I was a child. There's no reason to insult my intelligence."

"Insult your—"

That had been about the closest they'd gotten to knowing each other, at least in person, and the rest she'd heard from Linwood—her dullness, her disinterest in change, her chill in the bedroom. With both of them late or skipping out, her mood darkened. In fact she began feeling betrayed. She hovered and flitted about the house, moving from room to room, even stepping out onto the shoveled back patio with its glistening view of the snowy lawn, always trying to avoid Charlie and Ira and Rose and of course this fellow Stanley, who twice met her eyes and looked again embarrassedly to the floor, so that eventually she felt chased this way and that, keeping her distance from everyone, a loner, her mind focused more and more and then even more on the absence of Linwood, who'd told her he'd be there, whom she needed tonight of all nights to see.

And then in the midst of all this the front door opened and Rob Halford was there, followed behind by four others, even that creep Penrod with his skull face, those sharp cheeks and sunken eyes, that whole starved look of death about him, though he wasn't any older than she was. Penrod, who had arrived only last summer, when work on Eden Gardens began. He was the worst of them. The nosiest, his slight frame around those bigger men made up for by a purse-lipped meanness. All of them in sports coats, all of them members of Halford's ridiculous Civil Defense League, with the same matching Halford flattop and shouldering through the living room like they were looking for someone.

Oddly, she'd thought for an instant they were here looking for Charlie. After all, he'd been over to Halford's that morning, and besides, only Charlie straddled the tall and spiked fence between Halford's miserable group and her family and friends, that political divide that naturally should not be straddled. Only the possibility of money, of a paycheck, could make these vile men stomachable to her husband. Or were they stomachable? Or did he have a stomach, did he have any guts at all?

It didn't matter long. At some distance she followed their oversize shoulders into the dining room and saw that Halford, his lip twitching just under that horseshoe-shaped scar of his, was looking directly at Stanley West, and that his pals, these copies from a carbon sheet, were doing the same. Paul Penrod muttered something ugly, something she didn't want to hear, and she gasped.

But the strangest thing, for a moment or two, was that no one else seemed to notice. Only little old Marlene. Standing there, having rounded the other side of Ira's—

Or Rose's?

—open plan kitchen, her heart for some reason racing, her right hand quite literally clutching her pearls—

Well, fake pearls.

—she practically shouted to the assembled guests and non-guests, "What's going on here?"

And then everyone turned her way, and Rob Halford, his face gone slack, his eyes and lips pinching into a smile, said, "Hello, Marlene. How's life?"

A chill of terror passed over her. She was making a fool of herself. "Good," she said, and though just about everyone was looking at her like she had started speaking in a different language, she went on. "How about yourself?"

That somehow broke the spell. The room appeared at once to take the full measurement of Halford's arrival, along with his friends, and those uninvited guests turned pained smiles on Ira, who—

Always being Ira.

—stepped forward with his hand extended, claiming he was glad they stopped in, offering them drinks, shouting to Rose to get their newest guests leis. "There are still a few on the coatrack," he said. And then, to Halford, "It's a Hawaiian party, see."

After that she had a drink, and then another, and eventually she danced, too, even with Rob Halford, who jutted his elbows out at his sides like a short-winged bird, and at some point later she looked around and saw that she was sitting on the brick ledge of her brother's custom-built fireplace, engaged in conversation on the subject of Frank Sinatra's love life with an overweight woman named Sandy she'd met only once before, and then immediately after, there was Charlie, pulling at her shoulder, telling her they should go home. "I don't want to," she said. "Go yourself."

He seemed to bite down on something hard in his mouth. "I really think we ought to go," he said.

"Then go. What do I care?"

And then Sandy was gone and the fire was too hot and Charlie had wandered off and a tribal rhythm shuffled from the record player and she saw beaches and palm trees and black porous stones and girls in grass skirts and across the room, the only still thing in her line of sight was Stanley West, gazing back at her, looking for the life of him like he was worried only about her, a dear friend, and so she smiled, waved her fingers one at a time, and he was gone. When she looked around she saw that little Deborah in her overalls had taken a seat on the sofa across the room, a book open on her knees, *Jane Eyre*. She tried to ask her what the book was about, but the girl only raised her palm as if halting traffic, and then went on reading. A moment later, absurdly, Max came down the stairs holding a science-fair volcano. She watched him carry this into the dining room, watched the others put on their coats, watched the whole party filter onto the back patio. Then someone shouted.

It was Charlie.

The first phone call came, not from someone concerned about her husband's well-being, but from Elizabeth Huston, who wanted to again assert her demand that they pay for the damage to her new fur-lined coat from Bergdorf's, which had been a Christmas present, after all, and only worn one time before. "Bring me the receipt," Marlene said, still waiting on the water to boil for coffee. "I told you last night to take it to the cleaner's and bring me the receipt."

"Well, it's just unheard of," said Elizabeth Huston in that mincing voice of hers. "To start a battle royal in your brother's backyard like that."

"I understand," Marlene said. "Nobody's happy about it."

"All that lava," Elizabeth complained on. "I couldn't believe what a mess it made."

"Liz," she said. "Can I let you go? I've got coffee to make here. I'm sorry."

"Well," said Elizabeth, and clicked off.

But then a few minutes later, after Marlene was seated alone at the dining table with her cup of coffee, the phone rang again. It was Joan Halford. "I likely don't need to tell you this," she said. "But Rob told me I should make it clear."

"Joan," she said, "I don't know what got into him."

"Please," she said, but by the intonation in her voice what she meant was not to bother explaining. "Rob wants Charlie to know not to come to tonight's Civil Defense meeting. He wants him to know he's out of the League."

Marlene had expected something like this, but for what it would mean to Charlie's career, she had hoped cooler heads would prevail. "I understand," she said. "I'll tell him."

"And, Marlene?" Joan said. "I'd rather you didn't come to Thursday's Tupperware party."

Not that she'd remembered such a thing on the schedule. She hadn't gone to one of Joan Halford's Tupperware parties since last summer. Now it seemed she should be there, that not going would be like a steel gate crashing down in front of her, and the realization—

The terror.

—that followed, namely that everyone would be talking about her and her husband, the mauler, and that this talk would compound a public sense of them likely already spreading through the snow-covered town. Soon nobody would speak to them. Soon they would get the evil eye everywhere they went. They would be considered radicals, so tied to their belief in colored rights that they were willing to attack a fine upstanding patriot like Rob Halford, the actual president of the Citizens Civil Defense League, and soon enough, as well, this view would be projected onto Ira and Rose, and anyone who dared to show up at Human Relations meetings. Soon it would spread to Jeff and Alice Linwood.

And where had he been last night? He who could have kept Charlie in line?

"Joan?" she said. "Are you still there?"

But she was speaking to the dial tone.

By the time Ira called half an hour later, she was down the hall pinning back her hair for the shower. In fact she had the blue rubber shower cap in her hand when she picked up the phone. "Sis?" he said. "The old man feeling any better?"

"I wouldn't know," she said. "Last I checked he was still snoring."

"A black eye?"

"*Two* black eyes, a split lip, a torn sports coat," she said. "And the whole town gathered outside with stones."

"It's not that bad."

"Isn't it?"

Her brother, sounding more forlorn than she would have expected, took a long breath on the line. "This isn't *The Scarlet Letter*, Mar. It was a fight. He was drunk. It'll pass."

"Rob Halford's a pig," she said. And, surprised at her own defense of Charlie, she added, "That slob deserved worse for what he said."

"I don't know that I disagree," said Ira. "I probably don't."

Really, she was feeling like a wife now, a partner, ready to stick her neck out for Charlie in spite of all his—

Uh, myriad.

—faults. And so she said, "Then why are you calling on a Sunday morning?"

"To check on the old man," Ira said, exasperated all of a sudden. "He looked like hell when we dragged him out to the car. Why you two parked so far away I'll never understand."

"Okay, okay," she said. "I'll wake him up. I'll call you later. How's that sound?"

"It sounds like you're getting with the program," he said. He'd always been like this. Hadn't he? Doing whatever it took to seem like the one with more self-control, more of a level-headed outlook on life? So it was little surprise when he segued to "How about you? Doing okay?"

"I just told you how I'm doing and you said it's not that bad," she said. "What else do you want?"

He seemed to converse with someone off the line for a second. Rose. "I'm going to need Charlie's help later. Getting Stanley's car out of the snow?"

Stanley. Stanley West. She'd nearly forgotten. The whole source of the problem, really, though that wasn't fair to him. The reason, she amended in her brain, that Charlie felt so compelled to tackle Rob Halford and wreck everyone's evening was more complicated than a single person's being there. It was Rob Halford, after all, who was really to blame. Halford who had virtually begged Charlie to punch him in his fat mouth.

Then came an odd feeling: she was proud.

Proud of Charlie.

A funny feeling, really.

"What time do you need us?" she said.

"Us?" Ira said. And then, "About noon would be good."

It was eleven-fifteen. "We'll be over in a minute," she said, and hung up without a goodbye.

He looked like he'd been run over by a truck. Seated on the edge of the bed in his boxers and undershirt, rocking a little back and forth, his feet not quite reaching the carpet, his hair sticking up on one side and flattened on the other, he appeared to her a little crazy as well. A little, well, loony. And his face. Fatter than usual, blotchy, with a scar on his lower lip and, yes, two big round black eyes, really purple, turned toward her now in full sad sack.

Like an owl.

A sad, fat owl.

"You look awful," she said. "Did you even use those frozen peas?"

He didn't answer with words, but instead pointed to the rug next to his side of the bed, where the bag of Birds Eye green peas waited for her to retrieve it and, she thought, throw it away.

"Ira called. He needs our help getting Stanley's car out of the snow?"

Charlie raised a hand to the side of his head with a jerk, like someone had just slapped him there. "Who's Stanley?"

"Your new friend," she said. "From Harlem?"

"Ugh," said Charlie. And then, still rubbing at the side of his head as if against a new sore, "He's from Mississippi, isn't he?"

"By way of Harlem," she said. "Anyway they're headed down to Eden Gardens to pull the car out. I said I'd go."

He went on rocking back and forth as she dressed and brushed out her hair and put on her makeup. At several points in this process she thought to say something, but couldn't figure what that would be, so instead she just went about her business. Only when she was finished did he say, "I don't think I'll make it."

She met his eyes in the dressing mirror. Bloodshot as hell. "I was beginning to think not."

"I can't show my face," he said.

"Well, you do look hideous."

He smiled, but clearly this caused pain in that fat bottom lip, and so his hand moved from the side of his head to his mouth. He mumbled through his fingertips, "That's not what I meant."

"I know," she said. "But you did what's right."

He was looking down at the carpet, or at his naked foot making circles in the carpet. "You really think so?"

"Yes," she said, and then wondered if she meant it. "I think so."

"You only wish I hadn't punched him."

"Well, he punched you, too."

"That was after I punched first."

"Who's counting?" she said, standing from the dressing table. "He deserved to have somebody punch him."

His eyes popped open wide. "I just remembered the Civil Defense meeting."

She went to him then, leaned her hip against his shoulder, scratched lightly at the thin hair on the back of his head. "That's who else called," she said. "They don't want you coming tonight."

He didn't speak then for a long while and she went on leaning and scratching, trying her best to comfort him the way she used to do, back when they were closer. And finally when it seemed he had nothing more to say, she told him that she had to leave, that Ira would be expecting her, that coffee was made on the stove. "He said this town was too inclusive already, even without any blacks," Charlie said as she stepped away. "He said things would be easier if it was just good old Americans."

She stopped at the doorway. "What in god's name is that supposed to mean?"

"He was talking about Ira," he said. "He was talking about you."

Out the front door, their town seemed to her now changed. Sure, more of the snow had melted, and deep dirty ruts cut through what had last night been the pristine white of the roadway. But the sharp feeling in the air, that sense of—

Look, look. Mary Tillerson glancing through the blinds across the street.

—being watched, or worse, of someone lying in wait for her, somewhere in the short cold space between the patio and the car, that feeling was a product of discovering—

Quite late in the game, really.

—that at least one, if not many, of her neighbors had it out for her because her family were Jews, because she didn't come from their stock, because they held a secret loathing for her in their hearts. Somehow, though it now seemed far outside the realm of rationality, she'd believed all that was over. After all, they were homeowners. Citizens. Here in the suburbs. But what a child she'd been! What a little girl. Clearly she'd thought they were living in a fantasy world on the parkway, far from the fault lines of humanity.

Well. Let's not go that far.

She'd always known Rob Halford was a bore and a bigot, and, well, just a little touchy when it came to anything and everything to do with property and capitalism and the ongoing threat of a communist invasion. He'd paid out of his very own pocket to have a theater owner from Hicksville bring a projector and canisters of films to put on a showing of *My Son John* in the junior high cafeteria/gym, half the town in folding chairs under the basketball goals and facing the wall above the kitchen. The sight of all those pots and pans had made Marlene hungry. Nobody had thought of popcorn. Anyway the picture had been a Grade A bag of horse hooey, something about finding out your very own teenage son could become a commie if you didn't wave a flag in his face every three minutes and chant the Boy Scout Oath in his ear as he slept. It was terrible, so terrible she and Charlie had stayed up all night talking about it, reciting its dumbest lines, pretending they had a little communist hiding in the bedroom down the hall—

The, uh, nursery.

—and getting so ridiculously drunk that they actually, for once in a long, long while, had fun together. Mind you, that had been two years ago. The movie was already old by then, its time already passed, Senator McCarthy long gone from the national scene. But Rob Halford had taken it seriously. He'd taken a lot of things seriously. When it came to the bus boycott down in Atlanta, she'd heard word through Elizabeth Huston that he'd been trying to put together a posse of men from Ridge Landing to make the long drive down to Georgia—

And do what?

—though he'd set the plan aside when his letter to the sheriff's department there gave him no response. He'd even asked Bill Huston, who had turned down the offer politely, saying he couldn't miss work. "They're from Alabama," Marlene had told Elizabeth Huston. "Is it any wonder, the way those people behave down there?"

Though the answer, so obvious to anyone who knew Rob Halford's inclinations, was conveyed by Elizabeth with only a shrug.

Yes, she was putting some hard thinking toward the Halfords this morning, and in the car she still felt a tense need to keep looking over her shoulder. Her concentration wavered enough from the purpose of her trip that she turned down Oak Street, realizing her mistake only when her eyes drifted up the snowy lawns to the Linwoods' house, where neither of the cars were parked and no ruts were in the drive. Strange. There'd been no talk of leaving town. But they must have left, indeed. And early yesterday morning, given that wheels hadn't troubled the snow in their drive. She couldn't square that in her mind.

Stopped in the center of the road, riffling through her mind for an explanation, Marlene became aware that someone really was watching her, a woman in a pink bathrobe, a woman she didn't recognize, standing cross-armed in the picture window of the house next door. Who lived there? Who was that? It didn't matter. Did it? The main thing was to get moving. She eased off the brake. She looked forward. And as she passed the neighboring house she resisted the temptation to look back at the woman. But she was shaken.

A quick circling of the block put her on her brother's street, and within a minute she was parked outside. Or rather, she was sliding a bit in the refrozen snow and then coming to an uneasy stop, one wheel clearly up on the lawn. She didn't bother correcting or backing out, just cut the engine and pulled the emergency brake. She'd read an article in *Life* about a woman in San Francisco who didn't set her brake when she went in for her dry cleaning. The car ping-ponged down a steep hill, hitting cars on both sides of the street, before sailing through an intersection full of pedestrians. Six counts of manslaughter. And besides, all that on her conscience. Marlene could barely handle the guilt of having kicked the family cat once when she was in sixth grade, not for any reason at all but that she felt like it. A month after, he escaped into the world through an open window and was perhaps taken in by some other home. She'd never know. Sometimes in the night she'd wake and remember him, Fuzzy, and know right then and there that she was up for the morning, haunted by a crime more than twenty years old. So she pulled the brake.

When she was halfway across the lawn—

Funny, Max hadn't made a snowman. When did Max stop making snowmen?

They were all getting so very old.

—the door opened and out came the stooped men in their coats, the men and the boy, Ira and Stanley and Max, all looking shocked by the cold, huddled together close as they stepped down from the little salted porch. Apparently they'd been watching for the Buick awhile.

"Where's Charlie?" Ira said, turning his head to get a look at the empty car. Her brother was so tall, so big-eared, that the blue stocking cap he wore now turned him into a sort of cartoon. And where had he gotten that too-small sheepskin coat? His bare wrists stuck out like obscenities. "Mar," he said now that they were gathered in front of her on the lawn. "You hear me? Where's Charlie?"

"He's staying home," she said. Then she met eyes again with Stanley, who this time didn't look away. Her breath caught in the cold. "I'll help out all I can."

"Thanks," Ira said. "And about last night—"

"Ugh," said Max, opening the car door.

"Forget it," said Ira. But she could tell by the pained look on his face—

Like that time Nicky Sicorelli called him a lousy Jew bastard for asking his sister out to the movies.

—that he felt as unsettled as she did, as jittery, as betrayed. Still he spoke in that gregarious voice of his, patting Stanley on the shoulder. "Let's see about getting your car out of the snow."

The car was stuck in place, up to its headlights, and no sooner did they get there than Ira said, "We're going to need Al's tow truck. Mar, you want to go get him while we dig out the tires?"

It wasn't as if there was a choice. In fact, it wasn't exactly clear why they'd come down the hill. All that was down here except for the snow was Eden Gardens, its houses having sat finished for months without a single FOR SALE sign in sight. Its very existence and the rumors it would break the old racial covenant Ridge Landing had been settled on were the fuel that kept Halford, Penrod, and the whole Civil Defense League perpetually aflame. Really, they should have called a tow truck before any of them left the house, but here she was, Ira's little sister, shrugging. "Yeah?"

"I'll go," said Stanley unexpectedly. Then, catching her eye, catching the surprised look she was certain she hadn't hidden, "You don't mind, right?"

She pointed at the car. "Not at all."

Seated inside, straightening the lay of his coat, he said, "Appreciate the help, ma'am."

"It's nothing," she said. Then came the backing up and turning and pulling forward and backing up and turning again and pulling forward and then one more backup and with a turn they were on their way uphill again, back toward the puffing rooftops of civilization and she could barely handle the strangeness, the unexpected tension, of having him there in the car next to her. She was huddled up on the wheel like an old lady. Cresting into Ridge Landing proper, she could take no more of the snow-crunching quiet. "That was a long time coming with Halford," she said. "The man's a perfect imbecile."

Stanley seemed to consider his response a moment, his mouth open, almost smiling. She noticed then the speckled scars on his ear and down his neck. "He's a familiar type," he said. "Wish I could say I was surprised."

"We're not all like him," she said, rushing a little.

"Oh, no."

"I mean in town here. We're not all like Halford."

"It's cool," he said. "I follow you."

"Some of us may just hate this place, if you want to know the truth."

He laughed. "Like Max?"

Somehow they had traversed only a single block. There was Elm Street, rutted, kids out playing, parents scraping windshields, others pushing shovels. "He seems to like you," she said. "You guys were really yucking it up in the back."

"Oh, that," he said. "The kid's big on music. I was telling him about seeing Fats Domino on the A train last summer. Reading *The Wall Street Journal,* if you can believe that."

She had a vague sense of the man from television, hunched gleefully at a piano, a rock 'n' roll singer. Still, his reading the paper meant little to her. So she smiled in a noncommittal way and after a moment asked, "Charlie said you're here looking for your friend?"

"That's right," he said. "Tommy Vasquez. You know him?"

She'd never heard the name. In fact, she had doubts anyone named Vasquez had ever set eyes on Ridge Landing. "But you were looking down there. In the new addition. In Eden Gardens."

He turned in his seat and without looking at him she could see that he was watching her closely. "I've been looking for it awhile."

"Eden Gardens?" she said. "Nobody lives there. Some developer put all those houses in and left them empty. Creepy, if you ask me. Sort of a sore spot in town here."

"I heard," he said. "Hey, where we headed?"

It was as if the street had reappeared from a cloud—

Thonk.

—and clunked her right in the forehead. They were on Oak Street. Linwood's street. A strain radiated from her chest and made her arms feel heavy at the elbows. She touched the brake. "I needed to stop here," she said, and then did just that, crunching the wheels into the compressed snow at the curb. "I'll only be a minute."

But when she started up the walkway, when she saw her reflection in the broad picture window where no curtains hung, she could see as well the form of Stanley West, rounding the car, following her up to the Linwoods' door.

They were gone. Linwood and everyone. Just gone. That's what she breathlessly told Charlie, looking through the crack in the shower curtain at his grubworm body, the fat folds under his arms and above where his belt looped, cowered there against the tile wall with the spray hitting his hairy flesh, a veil of steam between. "They've moved away or something," she said. "I can't believe it."

And shit, shit. She really couldn't believe it.

"I let myself in," she said. "The door was unlocked."

"What took you so long?" he said.

And she said, for no reason at all, "What?"

"I said, what took you so long?"

She knew that tone in his voice. Anger. Over what? About what? An icicle of fear settled on her neck, the thought that he knew something about Linwood, something about how she felt about him. "I had to look around," she said finally. "I had to take a look, you know? None of it made any sense."

He literally had his forehead against the tile. She hadn't noticed that until he swiveled his two black eyes at her and said, "I was worried."

"About what?"

He stared at her in a mean way, or maybe it was just the black eyes, and then said, "You were gone awhile. Ira just called. Said you left an hour ago and Max is missing."

She'd told him about going into the house, where everything was gone but a couple of cigarette butts and some loose change and a single wire hanger. She'd even told him how Stanley West had come in with her, asking what they were doing in an empty house. But she hadn't told him about how Stanley West had put his arms around her when she started sniffling—

Started crying, really, in embarrassed heaves.

—or how he'd stroked her hair and told her everything would be all right and that really, Mrs. Ranagan, there's probably a simple explanation, or even that she'd blubbered about how close the Linwoods were and how none of this made any sense and she felt the world was falling down around her ears. She hadn't told Charlie about any of that, and she hadn't told him about how she'd returned after leaving Stanley West with the tow truck, how she'd walked from room to room alone as if it were her house, as if she were looking for some trivial little thing she'd left behind. The Linwoods had lived here only a year, had rushed into town like visiting celebrities, befriending anyone and everyone, their outlook on life totally cosmopolitan. Sure, Alice seemed a little flaky, a little Greenwich Village, but Jeff Linwood was like Adlai Stevenson dressed up in Peter

Lawford's good looks. And now this, something that made no sense to her at all, something she'd had to talk past until she couldn't.

"Hold on. What do you mean?" she said. "How can Max be missing?"

"He's gone," Charlie said. "They can't find him."

"He's probably out playing," she said.

The other thing she hadn't told him was how when she stood alone in the Linwoods' dining room staring out the window at the bright white glow of their backyard, she'd known once and for all that this life with Charlie wasn't going to work out, that all they were doing now was watching the clock. This infatuation with Linwood, the electric feeling that ran through her in Stanley's arms, all that was wrong and off-track in their lives: it was clear to her now that none of this would settle into place and be okay again. In a rush she saw it clear as glass. She wasn't in love with Charlie. Whoever was at fault, that's where things stood.

He was leaning now, his forehead against the shower wall, the water spraying against that thin patch of hair between his shoulders, running down his pale and rolling back, down his tucked-in buttocks, down his hairy legs. "An hour's a long time," he said.

"I was trying to find out what happened to Jeff and Alice. Our friends? Did I mention they're gone? And now you tell me this thing with Max." She let the shower curtain fall. She was getting nowhere with him, with his suspicions, with his endless hangover. "I'm calling Ira."

• • •

She did, but nobody answered. Out looking for Max. Or maybe Max had returned, had come in scuffing snow off his boots, had sipped hot chocolate at the table, his nose still red from cold. And then, the family whole, they'd ventured outside for a walk or braved it on the roads to the movie theater in Hicksville. Sure. He was home and fine.

How funny now that years ago she'd thought he would be hers. Back in the war when Ira's first wife had taken ill, when the baby Max came to stay with them those months in '44, first to get the poor kid off the first wife's hands and then, as things grew worse, as de facto parents, godparents, Myrtle—that was her name, Myrtle—off to the hospital one night and just as quickly gone, dead, lost to the past, and Ira showing up on leave, dark-eyed and befuddled, unable to comprehend what had happened to this girl he'd left behind in love, his whole life a sudden wreck, and after one long glare at the baby he'd once put all his hopes in, saying he didn't want to have anything to do with it, it was hers. *It's a he,* she'd told him. *And he's yours, not mine.* But no, Ira didn't want him. She should keep him and he didn't want to hear anything about it again. Better the kid never know anything about him or Myrtle. *Take him, take him, I don't want him.* He'd stormed out, still dressed in the pressed green uniform, Charlie and Marlene hangdog in that tiny white-walled apartment in Queens, unable to speak, the baby wriggling in a blanket between them, the radio ludicrously playing, both of them thinking, *Hell, it looks like we've got a kid here of our own.* A little earlier than expected, but so. So? It was crazy, that's what's so. Like they were Bible characters, taking in any old kid in a basket. She tried calling at Ira's old building, where Myrtle had been living only days before, tried everything to catch him and put a stop to this madness, and he was gone. Long gone. He'd begged, in fact, to be put back into action. Had told the army he had no kid and didn't know the girl who'd died all that well and just send him to the front one direction or the other. But they didn't send him to the front. Ira was a radioman, an engineer by education, and while he'd seen action in the Pacific, the position Uncle Sam wanted him in after Myrtle's death was an oversight one: checking in on the distribution and quality of communication equipment from an office made for him at Fort Jackson in South Carolina. Soon enough he was visiting by train at every opportunity, still hounded by depression, but more and more interested in the fate of his only son, and during one of these visits he'd crossed paths with Rose, a friend of Charlie's sister, there that day to help out with the housecleaning, and by war's end they were married, Max gone, that year and a half erased, their apartment empty of life, and the boy who'd been theirs, who'd called them Mama and Dada, began a second life, learning all over again who was who, soon to have a baby sister, all of it forgotten like the shapes of raindrops after they've been absorbed into a puddle, at least to him, at least to Max.

Now she was tearing up. Oh, for chrissake, with the tearing up. Crying, really. Sobbing into a kitchen towel. Charlie—

Of course.

—watching television in the other room with the sound turned up high enough to drown out her sniffling. But crying again for all of it. The afternoon dragging by, the phone still not answered, the miserable wrestling match her husband had started last night, and Max, her boy in that short dream, that eternity, and all the years since without luck, without a child, their lives this time under a roof together and what else.

Okay.

Keep it together, already. Just a rough night and this day. So what? Nothing to go ripping your life up over. What she was really upset about was Linwood. All the nonsense she'd churned up in her imagination, like he was Clark Gable on horseback, riding into town to rescue her from her boredom and pills, a soufflé she'd whipped up and now could see right before her eyes deflating. That wheezing sound. Or was that Charlie softly snoring? She peeked in. No. That would be too good, wouldn't it? The wheezing sound of her dreams really just Charlie snoozing.

No, no. There he was, wide awake, smiling like a madman, one of those Sunday-night comedy programs on. Milton Berle knock-off. Not nearly as funny and looking like someone out of middle management. The only good thing about this show was the woman with that high-pitched voice and big eyes. Her name a total loss. As for that sound, she said, "What's that?"

And Charlie looked up at her expectantly. "What's what?"

"The noise." He cocked his head to one side and then, without getting up, reached to part the curtain. "It's a truck. A snowplow. They're parked outside."

This seemed obtrusive to her in her weakened state, as if the truck had shown up unannounced for dinner. "Whatever for?" she said. "Tell them to move along."

Charlie laughed. "Tell them to move along? Mar, you're rich."

So she went to the door. She opened it. Two men sat in the

cab of the big truck, huddled over steaming cups of coffee. One of them raised a mittened hand. They were stopped in the road taking a break. Really none of her business. Night had fallen fast. And it was cold. Freezing. She waved back.

With the door closed, she said, "I'm getting ready for bed."

"It's six o'clock," he said.

On television, the middle management type was wearing a fake mustache and the pickle-shaped hat of a fortune-teller. For some reason he was strolling in what appeared to be a pet store. Charlie watched this intently, drunk again. "I know that," she said. "I'm tired."

When she woke in the night, she thought the tapping at the window was one of those men from the snowplow truck, stalled out or lost, in need of some kind of help. This didn't really make her leap out of bed. She turned on her back and stared a moment at the bluish ceiling. Beside her, Charlie was asleep, apparently having come to bed sometime after she'd drifted off. The tapping came again. It was quiet and at the window nearest her. So she pulled back the covers, surprised at how she felt unafraid, and slipped her feet into her house shoes. From the back of her dressing chair she took her robe, and with it tied fast against her waist, she went to the window. Behind the curtain, through the haze of the frosty glass, stood Jeff Linwood.

Of course it couldn't be. This man in a checker-print coat and red stocking cap, hands stuffed in pockets, eyes scanning the street, simply had to be someone else. She used her hand to wipe the glass. But the haze was on the other side. Still, her movement or the noise it made turned his attention back to her, and it really was Linwood, looking shorter only because he was outside, a foot lower than usual, his eyes—

Blue and shimmering light.

—looking up at her slightly, as if he'd ducked down, as if he were reaching down to lift her up onto the—

"Marlene," he said, whispering like a stage villain. Then he gestured toward the kitchen. "Come outside."

She made her way down the hall, thinking she must still be asleep, so odd were the circumstances, so alien were her actions. Still, in the living room she found the mud boots she'd worn out that morning, and though they were cold on her naked feet, she stood into them, stuffing the silk legs of her pajama bottoms inside. Then she put her coat on over her robe. Certainly she looked ridiculous. Laughable. And when she turned to see Linwood standing there on the patio just on the other side of the sliding glass door, in better light than she because of all the glowing snow, she thought for an instant that he would laugh at her. He didn't. Rather, he waved her toward him, looking a little frantic, a little shaken.

When she slid open the door and stepped out, the cold was almost unbearable, her pajama pants like thin sheets of ice. "Linwood," she whispered. "What in god's name are you—"

"Shhh," he said, and with a lunge reached behind her to push the door closed. He'd brushed against her roughly, and did so again when he lurched back to his full height, his face in the strange light somewhat unfamiliar, a little—

Well . . .

—violent. That's what it was. Something perfectly frightening in his eyes, his lips tense, his teeth shining. And yes, that was his hand on her arm rather tightly gripping her, pulling her, forcing her over the patio and into the thick snow of the yard. "Come with me," he said, though she was already coming, they were already off into the Johnsons' yard, and his hand hadn't left her arm. And just where were they going anyway and why had he shown up in the night and for chrissake, why did it have to be so damned cold out here and—

She yanked her arm free. "Linwood."

In the empty backyards her voice rang out like someone else's, like a distant woman shouting for her life. Linwood stopped a few paces away, his arm still extended, and shook his head. "Come on," he said. "I can't stay."

Then he marched into the blowing wind.

The snow had crusted into ice along the top so that when she started after him, she tripped on the hardened edge and stumbled forward, catching herself on one knee, her hand plunged into the cold. "Wait!" she shouted. "Hold on."

He didn't.

She had to run across three back lawns and got to him only as he loped down into the relative flat of Rosemary Avenue, where the quiet night emptiness was like the landscape of a Jack London novel, all of it a glistening and frigid death. She asked him what they were doing, and when he didn't respond, when he crossed Rosemary and climbed up into the yards of the next block, she kept asking him questions, one after another, all of them ignored. Why was their house empty? Where was he going? What on earth was happening?

They crossed diagonally, cutting between two houses and through the front lawns and across another street and between other houses, all in the thick bed of snow, their tracks wandering back in the direction of her warm bed and sleep. It came as a surprise when Linwood stopped and she saw that they'd reached the crest of the hill overlooking the new development of Eden Gardens. A pretty view: the houses glistening in white under the naked moon. Like a Christmas card. But something had changed.

My god, she was freezing.

"Look," he said, and raised an arm at the scene as if he were offering to shake its hand. "See?"

She did see. At the center of all those empty houses, somehow unnoticed before he spoke, a single chimney leaked a stream of grayish smoke that rose in a thin line, windless, before dissipating into nothing. A moving truck hunkered in the street. The cold had gotten to her. She trembled, a miserable uncanny feeling in her throat. "Someone's there," she said. "Someone's moved in."

Then, as if her eyes hadn't yet focused before, she saw the rest. Other chimneys, other moving trucks, lights on in windows. A complete impossibility. Eden Gardens had been settled in the night. The place had been empty so long that it was frightening to see life here now, frightening to imagine all these people showing up without warning, and at this hour—

Linwood grabbed her by the shoulders and pulled her to him and it was just like Burt Lancaster manhandling her, raising her by force to plant a passionate kiss, except Linwood didn't kiss her. He shook her, shook Marlene like a child who'd gotten out of control, and with his eyes hard, he said, "We'll be down there. All of us. You have a home."

She looked away from that frightening face, a face that couldn't be Linwood's, and saw over his shoulder that a car had pulled to a stop on the road facing the long slope toward Eden Gardens. She could scream. She wasn't alone. Her lungs filled sharply with air. "You're not feeling well," she said. "Something's wrong."

And then just like that he shoved her backward on her ass into the snow and marched away. Marched toward the street. Toward the car.

She struggled to speak. She tried to push herself upright.

The passenger window rolled down and there was Alice Linwood behind the wheel, her gloved hand waving at Marlene, her kids sitting in the back, Anna and Mike, all of them watching Dad approach, good old Dad, good old Linny, as if he hadn't just shoved a woman—

Marlene! In her pajamas, for crying out loud.

—into the snow right in front of them. They watched him, watched him open the door and get in, and then all together, as a family, they disappeared, a pair of red lights, down the hill toward the new addition and out of her view.

Leaving Marlene in the snow, her whole body frigid, her heart racing, her mind oatmeal. What on earth had just happened? Why had he dragged her out here to shove her in the snow and leave her in some stranger's backyard? And why all these people moving in on a Sunday night? What in the hell had he been talking about? She stood, brushed the snow off her behind, shivered, and cursed. Then cursed again. Her eyes fell back on the first house she'd seen with a smoking chimney, on the door—

No.

Was it?

—yes on the door opening, first just a crack and then all the way, a black darkness there, a rectangle of dark where the lights should have been on, and then after what seemed like an eternity a single form, too far away to be distinct—

A tall bald man, dressed in a glimmering robe, a character out of the *Flash Gordon* comics.

—stepped out onto the little front porch, waved at the approaching car, and crossed the lawn, seeming even from this long distance to be relieved to see the Linwoods' arrival. She didn't wait to see them park, or wait to see if they went inside. Instead she ran. Ran and ran. Her feet crashing through into the powdery under-snow, her legs always unstable beneath her, her chest a fire of heaving expectation. What was this incommensurable terror? She could not bring herself to look back, though she was certain someone must be just behind her. And why, long after she'd gone back inside and sneaked into the bedroom and pulled the covers tightly around her, listening to the *drip-drip* of the bathroom faucet down the hall—why did she still feel so cold, did she know that this cold would never leave her? She curled onto her side toward Charlie, toward his unshaven face and open mouth, toward the quiet mass of him, and closed her eyes as tight as she could.

THE NEPHEW'S INHERITANCE

STANLEY WEST—1962

Because he'd come in late. Because he was tired and a little tipsy, and he'd only just opened again *Ulysses*. Because stately plump Buck Mulligan. Because the night before they'd had it out over the direction of his life and so he'd snuck in, nabbing the saltines in the kitchen on the way, eyeing the dark line under his uncle's door, tiptoeing it like a cat burglar all the way back to his little hovel of a room with no window, hardly a closet, just this narrow mattress on the floor and that picture of Theda in her fine blue hat and all his books stacked against the wall. Because Wozniak had talked his ear off that evening even after close and it had been dark by the time he'd hit the streets and he'd come in late off the train in Harlem and nearly missed Billy Washington's sextet blowing at Frank's Place, had really heard only two songs and a little goof at the end where they faked Beethoven's Fifth, *buh-buh-buh-baah,* and because of that he'd been mashed up at the corner of the bar with Frank himself pouring him whiskey he'd had no plan of drinking, and because when the crowd started to thin and a couple of white ladies holding hands started dancing to the radio music and everyone was clapping and laughing, Billy Washington sidled up and said, "What'd you think, man?" and Stanley dissembled, he outright lied, said every tune knocked his socks off, pointed at his shoes and said his feet were ice cold because they'd knocked off his socks, and Billy had laughed and put a hand on his shoulder and the look in his eyes said he knew he'd shown up only at the end and missed nearly everything but it was okay because look here at all these people now rushing around to congratulate him, he'd really put it together with this band, they'd get a contract for sure, be household names even, but without losing their edge, without losing their standing in the neighborhood. Because his eyes had said that and Stanley felt himself sliding away from his oldest friend around here, pals since college days laughing at *Mad* magazine when they should have been studying, sliding into the fog of the also-ran, he'd had more of that whiskey and traipsed along behind the band and half a dozen others to the Lucky Spot, where he had two more drinks before his feet really were cold and actually he'd gone cold all over, his mouth heavy and mum, and then he'd been out the door alone and home up the stairs feeling like a sucker. Because the noise in the other room, in his uncle's room, sounded just enough like snoring that he could choose to ignore it, and because it wasn't until the whole apartment took on an eerie silence and stillness that he hopped up out of bed, shaky all over with a premonition of doom, and barefoot in his pajamas went to his uncle's door and twisted the knob without knocking.

Because of all this, he'd thrown on the light and found his uncle in bed, the sheets on the floor and the pillow across the room, the glass of water toppled but unbroken, the great man's grand belly exposed to the bare bulb above like a balloon. A pink tongue on his chin. Eyes wide on the wall they shared. He, Stanley, could have choked out some word or another, could have shouted Uncle Frederick's name and fired curses up at the ceiling, but nothing came. Nothing forced its way up from his chest. He sailed forth and knelt on the creaking floor and held his uncle's face in both hands, rough and flabby and brown, the dark patches under his eyes, the preposterous hairiness of his ample nostrils, the deep lines of his forehead rising to a beach of soft gray halfway back, nearly aligned with his jug ears. This man who'd been so damned handsome Mother said he was sent out of Mississippi at fourteen for his own safety, first to Chicago with Great-Aunt Charlene and then to college at Howard and graduate study at Temple and a year in Haiti and later New Orleans before settling here, in Harlem, a professor of literature at City College, a mammoth figure not only physically but intellectually, a wearer of ascots and striped pants, the only man around who had met Jean Toomer and Zora Neale Hurston but also argued on television with a southern congressman about segregation and in the very same week shaken hands with none other than Pablo Picasso—this man, this impossibility, was dead.

His head had gone clean sober like lightning, but back in the front room with all the lights on, his feet remained drunk. He tripped on the rug, on the coffee table, on the leg of the tall iron lamp next to his uncle's reading chair. Still he walked a rapid circle around the furniture, unable to suss out his responsibilities here, especially in the middle of the night. To make calls? To whom? And to say what? To ask for what?

He went to the phone, lifted it, and set it down. In the kitchen he started coffee, then returned to the phone, then set it down again. An hour later he'd finished a second cup of coffee and looked in at his uncle's body, finally pulled the sheet up over him, and returned to the phone for the third time. The Hattiesburg operator rang him through to his parents' house, but no one answered. It was only four in the morning. He asked her to try again.

When his mother's voice came over the line, wary and half-asleep, he told her Uncle Frederick was dead. "Stan?" she said. "Stanley, is that you?"

"I just found him," he said. "In his bedroom."

"Son, what are you calling here for in the middle of the night?"

He looked at the phone. Was she hearing on her end? "I said Uncle Frederick is dead. In his sleep. A heart attack or something."

"Frederick?" she said. And then he heard other voices, and Mother's voice half whispering, and the deep bellowing shout of his father saying something he couldn't understand. When she was back on the line, her voice was shaky and thin. "Son, we'll be on the morning train. You at the hospital now?"

"I didn't go to any hospital," he said. "I'm right here in the front room in Uncle Frederick's chair."

She let out a little squeak. "Darling, you've got to call a doctor."

"I wasn't sure what to—"

Again he heard his father's voice booming. Then Mother said, "Promise me now you'll get right off the phone and call an ambulance. Boy, you don't live in the sticks."

Then came the long morning and the ride to the hospital with that pair of suspicious-seeming white men, both as well shaved along the chin as a pair of eggs. Squatted over his blanketed uncle, leaning this way and that, taking corners by holding the metal handle of the old man's gurney, Stanley felt like a light-bulb browning out on a summer night. The idea of his parents' coming up from Mississippi was too much. He wanted more than anything to avoid it.

Here were these two: one a housemaid, the other a me-chanic. Smart, sure, readers. Instilled in him all the gumption he'd needed to come here and start college after Korea, and—whether they liked the outcome or not—to quit college and take a job down on Fourth at Wozniak's Used & Rare Books, and worse, to declare himself a poet. Still, country folk barely hanging on to life in town. They'd first want church and tears and embracing, but then Father would be on to giving him hell, reminding him that such a trip wasn't what they could afford, implying he was somehow responsible, and Mother, Jesus, Mother would be begging him to return to Hattiesburg, that swampy green tub drain of a place, that nightmare of white sweaty faces telling you with their eyes who you could and couldn't be. He would never go back. They were the ones in need of a move. *Get out of there,* he'd told his mother over the phone a dozen times. Go to Ohio. Pennsylvania. For ever-loving God, get in the car and drive to Colorado. But they never listened. They had watched every one of their siblings leave Mississippi, nearly all their childhood friends, too. But they had stayed.

He was rattled, hungover, and jangly as a ring of keys. His heart clattered just imagining.

Then were the open doors and the faint dawn and those suspicious white men dragging Uncle Frederick out again, or not really Uncle Frederick but the gurney and the blanket and some weight in between, the man himself not even an after-thought. They went inside without telling him what to do, and when he followed them to a pair of double doors, a nurse came up and asked him to have a seat. Nothing and nothing and still nothing but waiting. When he asked, when he approached the nurse who'd stopped him, she said to wait a little longer. The man who came out of the double doors later, a light-skinned fellow with a cool ease to his gait, was an orderly. "Coronary embolism," he said. "Died in an instant. You got a place to send him?"

There was a church, a pastor he didn't know all that well. The moment he thought of him it all seemed so simple. Arrangements were made. The pastor, over the phone, sounded queasy, like a man who had just finished eating a great deal of food that disagreed with him. Stanley was thankful when he rang off. Cradling the phone at the nurse's station, however, he realized he was back to not knowing what to do. At first he returned to his seat. But no one would be coming for him. So he put back on his coat and left.

Outside, the sun shone blinding down the cross streets, the city come alive for morning work. In the chill wind he popped up his collar and huddled forward, back toward home, his mind finally beginning to settle, his ideas gelling into complete thoughts. He'd been undeniably close to his uncle. The man had done everything for him. When he'd returned from Korea with nothing more than a pressed suit and a temporary lack of humor, it had been Uncle Frederick who had written a letter to his mother with the offer to move up here, to New York, and attend City College on the G.I. Bill, no strings attached, just an old-fashioned leg up on life of the sort that had been given to him by Stanley's grandfather, a Pullman porter, who had brought back from his long weeks on the tracks all the leather-bound classics, the *Odyssey* and Keats and Shakespeare and St. Augustine. The boy needed somewhere to go, he'd written, a place to turn around from. And Stanley really had turned around. In Harlem all his life was made, from reading, sure, from intellectual discussion, yeah, from the long meditations on Beethoven and Monet, of course, but more than that or at least equal to it were the streets themselves, the life and energy, the sheer flood of black folks going this way and that, living out their lives, doing America like people who wouldn't be told they didn't deserve a chance to do it their own way. He discovered jazz, really discovered it. In clubs after class and sometimes before he made friends of the type he'd never had back in Mississippi or even in the army, confident black men and independent women, people just like himself ready to talk about anything, sure of some future without the curling worm of disappointment completely taking over their guts, folks like Billy, who made reaching up seem as natural as anything. School itself had been a brain wave. Reading Plato and using beakers and studying maps of South America and Asia, surrounded by people who saw him as a goddamn human being, capable of anything, even if at first his country accent made girls smile at him like a little brother and men give him this look like their brows had just fallen to sleep.

It had been in those days, those heady college days when it seemed the whole world opened up to him at once, that his mother sent along letters they had received in Hattiesburg from Tommy Vasquez, his good buddy Tommy, who had seen with him one night in Korea that funny light swimming in the night sky. Tommy and his wife and kid had gone in for some UFO fan club, from what he could tell, and were living in the desert with people who called themselves the Seekers, running what sounded like a scam to build their own town. He'd apparently sunk all the money he had from selling their house in the venture and was working, happily, he wrote, at a small-parts factory, signing over his checks to the guy preaching to a congregation of flying-saucer nuts. In fact that's about how Tommy had described it. Well, not as nuts, but as a "shared community," everyone believing in this so-called preacher feeling compelled on his own to sell his belongings and fork over all his cash into a communal pool for some big plan, someplace they'd all live together.

It was worrisome, for sure. But at the same time his old army pal seemed to have found a place for himself, a kind of peace and hopefulness that got Stanley thinking. He wanted to know more, to meet these people Tommy thought so highly of, to see their operation for himself. Being of two minds, he wanted to burst the bubble of what looked fishy, to spring Tommy from a wackier communist trap than he'd ever heard about, but he also wanted it to be true: folks living together, trying a new kind of social experiment, maybe even finding meaning in it. He worried about that, after all. Meaning. Purpose. Worried some sleepless nights that he was on a boat by himself without a paddle. So he wanted to see it. But when he wrote back to the address on the envelopes, he got no response. All he had to go on was the name Eden Gardens, what Tommy said they planned to call their new town. He looked, he called around, and a year later in the cold dead of a blizzard he caught wind of it. A town called Ridge Landing out on Long Island was fighting to keep its covenant after a mystery developer called Seeker Industries had built a hundred new homes on its southern border and word had come that buyers were on the way. Just an hour or so on the parkway. So close he could hardly believe it.

He'd gone there, yes, and a week later with the runaway Max he'd returned, and that's when it happened. That's when he'd seen the dark far edge. The mob of them pounding down that hill. The blood in their eyes. The spittle. The little black-haired girl bleeding in the snow, so much blood he didn't think it was possible, and when he went to her, when he knelt there, his head struck, the silence, the night.

After Ridge Landing, after waking to misery and broken bones, when Stanley's view on humanity was something closer to a black cloud than the bright blue sky his uncle imagined, he'd quit school with a sort of vengeance, halfway into his sophomore year, his decision made and announced right there in some Long Island hospital room, broken arms and rib and concussion and all, when he told Uncle Frederick he didn't want anything of the straitlaced world, that he'd decided if he was going to be anything, it would be a poet or a painter or a bum on the streets, certainly nothing like the future his uncle had planned for him—trying for integration but by whose definition, not anybody he knew, just some average American middle-class pointlessness, a poisoning in the blood, the product of a white sickness the rest of the world had managed to avoid. "Like the damn blankets those settlers gave the Indians," he had said. "Sick to the core. I won't stand another minute of it."

Uncle Frederick, dressed in a tuxedo, rushed from a gala for none other than Ralph Ellison, stood in Stanley's hospital room with his shoulders slumped, eyeing the casts and the heart monitor, anything but Stanley himself. Then he said, "You're only disillusioned. That's probably the worst of the damage."

"Disillusioned? I'm lucky I'm alive."

His uncle came over to him, put a hand on his arm. "I mean your anger," he said. "This feeling you have inside."

"I'm not going back to school," Stanley said. "There's no point to it. I'll live in a coffeehouse downtown. I'll go to Paris."

"I understand," Uncle Frederick said, shushing him with a hand. It was clear that Stanley had hurt him somehow, disappointed him. Still, he went on. "But I don't want you going anywhere. You've got a roof. You can write. Paint. Whatever you want. But you've got a place here and I don't want you out of my sight."

Stanley had grumbled. What he wanted if he wanted anything was to explode into a million parts and be scattered to every corner of the earth like a scentless mist. "Forget it," he said. "Just forget it."

"You'll feel better." But then his uncle changed the subject, swatting the air with his gloves. "Of course you'll need work. A job. A man has to feed himself."

He found work at Wozniak's, first shelving books and then as the main clerk and finally as what Wozniak called the assistant manager, though aside from a modest raise this meant no more than carrying his own key and having to pay out of his pocket when books went missing on his shift. He read ravenously from that day forward, and began in a series of legal notepads to scratch out a few lines of what he felt could be poetry, scribbling over and tearing out most of it, finding ways to busy himself around the neighborhood when he couldn't think of anything to write. If anyone asked, he would tell them he was working on "this thing," tilting his chin a little like he was letting them in on something, but as the steam cooled from his blowup with Uncle Frederick, he hardly wrote at all.

Mostly, he could see now as he looked back at that time, he was moving through a stage of dress-up, telling himself he was a poet and acting the way he thought poets should act. He went to readings and dropped names, got into heated arguments at nightclubs about things he knew very little about. Around strangers he pretended to know this or that writer, and the next day would dive his nose into their pages at Wozniak's, reading like a bearded holy man in the wilderness. It was an image he liked, and his clothes and general upkeep took on a looseness, a carelessness that drove Uncle Frederick up the wall. But this had been part of the reaction, the turning against, and at the back of his mind the hopeful order of Eden Gardens lay like an ashy smudge.

Soon enough he met Theda, for whom he played up his poetic gifts, and who took his current self as the only self that had ever been, buying his bohemian act as much or more than he bought it himself. In her eyes, he was a real somebody, a regular Tennyson, a strutting moody genius unimpressed with even Langston Hughes, friend to jazz musicians like Billy Washington, who he liked to point out had been offered a spot with Monk around that time and chosen to start his own trio instead, on Stanley's advice no less. Ah, she'd loved him, loved the pose he was putting on, and after a couple of years had even thought he'd get his act together enough to go with her, away from New York, to Chicago, where she had been accepted into law school. His first reaction to this news hadn't been to congratulate her achievement but rather to state unequivocally, right there in Wozniak's, that under no circumstances would he leave New York. This was home, he said, the greatest city on earth, and it would take more than law school to drag him kicking and screaming into the Midwest. She'd stared at the floor as he gave this boyish speech, and when her eyes rose again to meet his, his mind seared the moment into his memory like a brand. "I'll just have to go alone," she said. And then, standing, her shoulders back and proud in an unexpected way, "I'd thought you were someone else, Stanley. I really thought you were someone else."

Oh, Theda.

He *had* been someone else, really. Couldn't she see, as he could so clearly see now, that everything he did at that time was part of the act, part of the show meant to signify that he was his own man, a creator, an artist? What had started as a pose to convince his uncle and himself had gotten out of hand, and it was inconceivable that Theda, always smarter than he was, couldn't tell that he was only bluffing, doing what he thought was expected of him. Instead she'd left, promising to meet up again later that night at Frank's Place to talk about it a little more, and so he'd spent the afternoon making up his mind. He'd apologize, he'd grovel if he had to, he'd tell her how excited he was for her, he'd beg to go with her. By evening he felt confident in this plan, sure that he could play off his earlier stance as a joke fallen flat—looking forward, even, to a new life in another city. He could find a job there. He could write. He pictured the two of them working across a small round table in a noisy little apartment, piles of paper between them, she studying case law, he finishing the poem that would announce him to the world with the undeniability of "Howl" or "The Waste Land," his great work, his *Guernica*. These fantasies spun off into bizarre directions. Returned to the city, Theda would be dressed in a gray suit and skirt, her feet arched in glossy heels, in court winning a major case before a spellbound jury, all as he sat on one of the back benches, scribbling genius into a fine leather journal. At Frank's he didn't see her, but took their usual table without thinking that she might not show. But an hour later he knew. Round at her place, her roommate Maddie answered the door. Packed and left, she said, on a train by three in the afternoon. No forwarding address. Just a month's rent and a note saying she'd gone to Chicago and her toothbrush forgotten in the bathroom. He suppressed the demand to see that toothbrush, to hold it, but felt no more foolish for slumping off down the hall and down the stairs and down the street again to Frank's, where another couple had taken their table already. He glared at them from the bar until the man met eyes with him and flashed an animal sneer when the woman wasn't looking. Stupid numbnuts Stanley! Dragging his heels all the way home that night, knowing he didn't have the Shakespearean courage to trek madly westward in pursuit of love. He could see she was through with him.

And he, too, was through with him. That Stanley, that pose of hip genius, more talk than labor, he'd parted ways with him somewhere on Lexington Avenue, returning to his uncle's that very night dressed in the same clothes he'd left in but somehow another man. In the months after he was more solitary, jotting down notes at work, humming the rhythms of his words on the train uptown, plugging away in the back bedroom deep into the night on the disjointed poem he knew would make his name, a jazz-style ramble through every uncollated memory that had made him this particular young man, confused and broken, too smart for his own dumb good. He sparingly did anything that wasn't writing and rewriting, or reading whatever book or newspaper or magazine was at hand. Soon enough, his only conversations were with Uncle Frederick and Wozniak, two bookish old men who could just as well stare out a window as talk to another human being, and when they did talk, it was of poets and musicians and grand historical figures like Caravaggio and Napoleon and Disraeli. Stanley found their society stimulating, if a little moldy around the edges, and soon realized he was spending a great deal of time sipping tea and coffee, murmuring little assenting sounds in response to statements that would have six months ago bored him to tears. He was, he realized one night when he tried forcing himself out for a good time at Frank's Place, turning into a dusty old bookworm.

It had been that night when Theda left, two years ago now, walking sullenly home before midnight alone, when he'd crossed paths with the skinny white man in the brown suit who said he knew him. "From Ridge Landing," he had said, turning alongside him to follow. "You remember?"

Stanley had looked down into the man's faded blue eyes. He was middle-aged, but meatless enough for his face to resemble a skull, and with a danger in his gaze and pointed teeth that filled Stanley with dread. Altogether he looked like something you'd see on Halloween. "I don't know you," he said, walking a little faster, his mind too focused on Theda's leaving to deal with whatever this was meant to be. "Go on, man. I got somewhere to be."

The man gripped his arm. He had no trouble keeping up. "No, I know you. I've watched you. I know all of you."

"You're crazy," he said, but when he looked again at those eyes, he knew better. This man *did* recognize him. He *was* from Ridge Landing.

"Let's talk," said the man. "Where's a good place?"

"Off me," Stanley said, pulling free his arm. "You got the wrong guy."

Then the skinny man smiled up at him and they both stopped there on the sidewalk, the street mostly abandoned to lamps and night. "Boy," he said, like they weren't in Harlem at all. "I know one colored son of a bitch from another."

Stanley didn't know what else to do, so with both arms he shoved him, shoved him down to the ground, and then he ran on home, too cold and shaken to look back. He remembered that man, all right. Penrod. Not easy to forget. Saw him now with an overwhelming clarity. It hadn't been the fellow who wrestled Charlie Ranagan in the snow, toppling that mock volcano, wrecking that dumb Hawaii party, where Stanley had been on display like a pinned butterfly, pushed into the role of emissary for some civil-rights-minded white folks, but the little man next to him. His toady. The one who'd pointed across the kitchen that night and mouthed, or even just said out loud so quiet only Stanley would hear, *There's your nigger.* And that there had been the start of it that first night. Gone wrong, as he could have expected. Voices raised. The bigger man shouting some accusation at Ira Feldberg, something about a black family moving into town, something about who could and couldn't live there. And then Charlie Ranagan, stately plump Ranagan, with an outright sucker punch to the big one's right jaw. Then it was all tumult, screams and scuffles, little near fights on the perimeter worked up and calmed back down. The two bloody-faced principles embraced and spinning as they flew out onto the back patio where everyone had gathered to watch the kid Max set off his papier-mâché volcano.

When the woman's coat was ruined and everyone gasped and the gladiators were cleaved apart, Stanley had looked back inside to the kitchen, where that man, the skeleton-faced man with the faded blue eyes, stood there smiling like he'd just sold a car that wouldn't make it around the block.

And to think all that was still a week before what happened downhill.

Penrod had stopped him in the street two years ago, and Ridge Landing happened three years before that. Still, these experiences rippled like a chill breeze against his skin, and by the time he reached the stoop of his uncle's building, his mind had wandered so far from the events of the past night that he wasn't prepared for the loneliness upstairs. He climbed the two flights like a man being filled from the top with sand, each step a little heavier. Inside, in the whorling silence, speckles of dust turned uneasily in a shaft of yellow morning coming from his uncle's room. He went there and looked at the bed, stripped to the mattress, the sheets and cover preposterously folded and set in a corner, two pillows balanced on top. None of the books had been moved. But oddly, and perhaps necessarily, the Aaron Douglas hung askew.

It had been his uncle's prized possession, one of those layered pastel silhouettes, here a scene of old-time slaves gathered to sing around a fire. In the background, highlighted by a reverberating star pattern, stood a futuristic city, toward which a single musician pointed, his other hand engaged with holding a flute to his lips. Always and forever it had hung on the wall behind the headboard. The frame must have been bumped overnight. Someone had to have climbed up on the bed to lift the top of the great man's heavy body. He thought of Billy Washington's sextet, leading them all forward, his saxophone pointing the way. And he thought of losing the city, the apartment he couldn't afford, the life he'd been creating.

Then, with a lurching gash through the morning, the phone rang.

Mother was on the line. "Did you go to the hospital?"

"Yeah," he said. "I mean yes, ma'am."

"And what did they say?" she said. "Is he all right?"

"All right? He's dead. Something with his heart, like I said."

"Did they even try helping him?"

He glared at the wall a moment, or rather another of his uncle's paintings, this one some English hunting number with a spotted dog pointing at a hunched rabbit. "He was cold when they got here," he said, sure he sounded monstrous. "I already told you he was dead."

A silence and then a murmuring. He imagined their house, out behind the Covingtons', a little crackerbox with only three windows and a toilet outside even though it was set up with water. Mother had been cleaning for the Covingtons now six years. In that house they paid rent. How that life wasn't slave life was a matter of nuance. At least his father held a job in the shop of a car dealership downtown. "We're still coming up," she said. "Going to have to take the noon train. Just your father and me. Your sister's staying."

"What for?"

"Why's she staying? Because she's got her studies."

"What for are *you* coming?"

Another silence, this one shorter. "Young man, that is my brother you're talking about. I'd cross the river Jordan to—"

"Okay, okay," he said. "I'm sorry. Come up here."

Still she was bothered. "To think I raised a boy who doesn't want to see his mother."

"That's not what I said," he said. "What time are you getting in?"

Murmuring. "We'll have to look again," she said. "We'll have to see the schedule."

He shaved, his eye wandering again and again from the mirror in search of his uncle, who was sure to appear in the bathroom doorway to deliver an unprompted lecture on the tragic arc of Charles V's life or the deeper implications of the Fourteenth Amendment, and after rinsing and drying his face, he stepped back out again to look at that blank mattress, that wonky picture. In the shower he turned up the hot water, scalding this side of his body and that, stepping out to a cloud of white steam he could nearly drown in. Soon enough he was dressed, his nerves shaky, sipping coffee in the front room. Beethoven playing. The *Pastoral* Symphony. A reprinted

Brueghel behind glass on the wall. A book of Edna St. Vincent Millay's poetry at his elbow.

> *Where dark Persephone the winter round,*
> *Uncomforted for home, uncomforted*

Uncomforted for home, indeed. The feeling sinking through his intestines was like a carousel gone off its track, shunting one wall of those curled tubes and then another, the children holding to their poles by fingertips, everyone screaming, the music sped up to comedy. Who would save them? He rubbed at his eyes and stood. If his parents were coming, if it wasn't a bluff, he should make up his uncle's bed. He should straighten the Douglas. How could he have not done so earlier? With a nudge the work would be done. But then he sat on the stripped mattress. Sat and then fell back. He stared up at the white ceiling, at the yellowish bulb, at the blinding miracle arc inside. Maybe he'd never felt so heavy in his life. Maybe if he just relaxed. He pictured his mother in that favorite yellow dress of hers, the one she wore when he was a child, the one she made again with new fabric, patterning and cutting from the original, to wear the day he left for basic training. How it made her skin glow at the arms and neck, a beauty, the shining sunlight of a summer morning. Behind her, Father, short-sleeved, sweat rivering down his muscled arms, that old crushed hat tilted back on his head. They would be cold here. They'd be freezing. First thing they'd need would be coats—

Stanley, Stanley. In the bathroom he looked at himself, his hair no longer conked as it had been when he was in school, but cut trim with a narrow part shaved on the left side, his eyes only a little sleepier than they'd been when he first left for Korea. His freckles showed, though usually he could see them only in the summer, a pair of frowned crescents spotted along the ridge of his cheeks. Cherokee blood, his mother had told him once, something she'd heard from her grandfather. But his father had laughed at the prospect. Indians didn't have freckles, he'd said. You ever see freckles on Indians in the movies? He splashed cold water in his face and brushed his teeth. Peed a stream he didn't think would end, though he hadn't felt the need just before. In the kitchen assembling coffee, he wondered how he could get through a single day without Uncle Frederick around. Maybe he couldn't.

This man Penrod troubled him, this ghost. He hadn't been the ringleader of what happened at Eden Gardens, not necessarily. He'd been something worse. And now he'd come to mind first thing after leaving his uncle back at the hospital. He could see him clear as a photograph, clear as if he stood in the room next to him. That white man with his skull face was surely a sign of bad things to come, a prefiguration of where everything was headed, excavated and elbowing his way back into Stanley's life that night two years ago when Theda went her way. He pictured Penrod standing alone under a naked tree, all silhouette, the dying light behind him, like the subject of an old fairy tale, a lesson to keep kids out of trouble. And something began to form in his mind, an idea, the start of a poem.

But it was almost noon, time for him to be at work, and he needed out of this damned apartment. He phoned Wozniak and told him he was running late, but not about his uncle. "It's nothing," Wozniak said. "The place is just a wreck, is all. You'll see."

When he got to the dust-scented shop, Wozniak parted the mustache of his beard in that habitual way of his, brushing the gray-and-black hairs with thumb and forefinger, and launched into a harangue on the topic of teenage delinquency. "Are there no parents in the world?" he wanted to know. "Are people dumping these kids in New York like unwanted dogs?"

Stanley hung his jacket over the back of a chair. "What is it this time?"

"What is it this time, you ask." Wozniak pointed at the front window. "Go back outside and ask me that question."

He didn't have to go outside to see the problem. Someone, apparently a roving gang of teenagers, had wrecked the front window display. Books were knocked over and splayed open on the floor. The little writing desk was toppled, its globe cracked. The mannequin who studied Cervantes in the window had been stripped of his pants and smoking jacket. The clothes were now a pile in the sill.

Wozniak stood at his elbow. "Why are you laughing?" he said. And then without pause, "Are you crying, Stan?"

So Stanley told him. Arms crossed, the two of them stood at the front door, with only a stoop-shouldered NYU professor sniffling and leafing through books on the back aisle, and he told him the whole thing: Uncle Frederick, his parents on the way, the bastard two years ago who now seemed bent on returning, at least in his head. "I think I should leave town," he said. "Maybe track down that girl I used to see? Remember Theda?"

"Misery," Wozniak said, his eyes wet. "The miserable misery of it all. Sheesh, Stan. What am I to do?"

He hadn't really thought out a plan, but now a good enough one came to him. "I've got nothing here without my uncle. Just give me a week to go to Chicago."

"Who will I hire in the meantime?" Wozniak said, unperturbed by Stanley's weeping and blubbering. He pointed at the overturned mannequin. "One of these numbnuts?"

"Lean him up at the register," Stanley said. "He won't give you any trouble."

At that Wozniak laughed, and reaching up to clasp his shoulder, said, "Stanley, I'll need you to clean up this mess. And to lock up. Can you lock up tonight before you go?"

He felt a warmth and humor with this cranky old man that he already missed. "I'm not leaving yet," he said.

Walking away, gesturing madly at the air, Wozniak said, "I couldn't have a conversation with a mannequin, even if it would save me money."

In the window ten minutes later, sweating under the bare bulbs, his sleeves rolled up to his elbows, he saw her, a complete impossibility: a woman at the glass, brushing loose hairs from her forehead, testing the shape of her lips in the reflection.

He knew her in an instant, though he couldn't believe she would appear here today of all days, right after his uncle's death. It didn't matter that she had changed, that she now wore her hair longer, the tight curls splayed out like a broom past her shoulders. She wore a shabby men's overcoat, her narrow calves in panty hose sticking down like legs under a tablecloth, her feet in black shoes without heels. She was far from where he'd last seen her, clearly living another life entirely.

It was Marlene, Mrs. Ranagan, and the last he'd seen of her had been the day after that suburban horde careened down the hill from Ridge Landing with bats and lead pipes and more than one gun, when she came to visit him in the hospital, his eyes nearly closed from the bruising, his arm in a clean white cast. Uncle Frederick had been there in that tuxedo, seated next to him, reading to him from a magazine he'd found in the waiting room. Then suddenly this white lady wearing all black, bearing flowers of all things, murmuring about how Charlie couldn't make it, he was home nursing his wounds, but he doesn't look as bad as you. *Oh, I'm sorry, that's not what I meant at all. Not at all.* And extending her hand to Uncle Frederick and introducing herself as the wife of the man who had first seen Stanley, or seen him downhill in the snow—oh, never mind, that's not what's important.

Marlene, all right, here in this spot, holding a heavy bag of groceries, its serrated top presenting a crown of celery stalks and Wonder Bread. He was standing not ten feet from her, holding the mannequin's smoking jacket in one hand and the copy of *Don Quixote* in the other. For an instant he hoped both that she would recognize him and that she wouldn't. But then her eyes turned up toward him. A green he'd thought was reserved for natural stone. He recalled seeing them that first time, at the Feldbergs', the night he'd seen her in that tight kitchen in a blue dress, her shoulders bare, her short hair held back, her hands a little busy, and yes, he remembered now, though he hadn't thought on the subject in years, she was the host's sister, Ira Feldberg's sister. Of course.

Her eyes brightened with recognition. In an instant she swung inside and stood before him, the grocery bag leveraged against her hip like a child, her voice familiar like the line of an old song. "Is it you?" she said. "Stanley, are you real?"

"Me?" he said, though he didn't want to let on that it was she who seemed unreal.

She swooped in with her free arm and embraced him intimately, hugged him, tightened her breasts against him, her throat letting out a satisfied sort of hum. "I can't believe it," she said. "I just can't believe it at all."

"Mrs. Ranagan," he said, careful to keep his hands free of her.

"Not *Mrs.* anymore," she said. "Not for years."

She released him and took a step back. Her bread was smushed. He couldn't think of a word to confront those green eyes, so he said, "Then just Marlene?"

"Just Marlene," she said, and laughed. Then looking over her shoulder in the vague direction of Wozniak, "Marly, actually. Marly Feldberg. So you've been working here?"

"That's right," he said. "And you? What's your story?"

"Painting," she said, and then described a studio just around the corner, a series of what she called abstract canvases, a life on her own in Greenwich Village.

Behind them, Wozniak cleared his throat. "Well," Stanley said, "I'd better—"

"I'll come back," she said. "I mean, if you don't have any plans."

He didn't, unless you counted getting on the evening train

away from this place forever. But her forwardness had surprised him. He stumbled over his words. "At six," he finally got
out. "I'm off at six."

She had been an acquaintance, a fellow witness to what happened out on Long Island that freezing winter. The person
he'd gone to with Max, against the kid's will, after finding him
stowed away in the trunk. At Uncle Frederick's insistence, Max
had lived with them for four whole days. Or had it been five?
The point is, Max had run away from home and used Stanley
as his ticket out of town without even asking.

And what matters, what really counts, was that he'd driven
back out there with Max on the worst day possible, and on top
of that, he couldn't take him straight to his parents. The kid
was a hot item, his disappearance reported on the radio and in
the paper. A black man they'd known only one night and part
of a morning showing up on their doorstep with their missing
teenage son would send the whole town into hysterics. It had
been his uncle's idea to put the old raincoat over him, and the
hat. All Stanley added was the sunglasses. "And this," he'd
said, still idling at the curb outside the Ranagan house. "Flip
up this collar." Max grumbled, of course. He'd been a royal
pain in the behind since the moment Stanley recognized his
voice in the trunk, surrounded as it was that Monday morning
by just about everyone in the neighborhood. He'd wanted to
send him packing that very minute. Only Uncle Frederick
was sure the boy was in some kind of trouble. Suffer unto me
and all that. Instead, it had turned out to be a sort of school
field trip into the mysterious world of black folk. Shadowed

around everywhere by this shrimp of a white kid asking him, *You any good at music? Why're your palms pink? What's soul food mean anyway?* And asking him how to walk and talk and what a woman meant when she said "Where you off to, honey?" even when you've never seen her before in your life. Just thinking on it had given him a headache. "Listen," he told Max that day. "Don't you fuck this up. I ran into you downtown and you asked me for a ride home, right?" The kid nodded. "And you ran away on your own. Without my help. Without breaking into my car?"

"Your uncle's car," Max corrected. He was a mean snot through-and-through.

They were on the concrete path in front of Marlene's home when he realized, subconsciously or not quite subconsciously, that he was taking Max to his aunt not only to defuse the situation but because he wanted to see her again. She'd given him this longing look at the party last weekend, and the next day spoken to him in a way that old friends do, like there were no walls between them. He'd thought of her. He'd given her thought. Of course nothing could come of it. But there she was in his memory, her eyes. And so, he realized, he was here with his bag of excuses and Max dressed like some B-movie detective, or rather the B-movie detective's first suspect, the one that turns up dead ten minutes later. On the walk and then the porch and then knocking at the door and her face giving him that look of alarm he'd expected.

"I'm sorry," he'd said. "I'm sorry to bother you."

"Stanley," she'd said, as if just discovering the name from the air. "Is that right?"

"You got it. And this here is Max. I found him down on Third Avenue."

She turned her chin at the kid like a bird taking note of some miserable new terror. "What?"

"I ran into him yesterday," he said, gesturing, keeping up the whole routine they'd practiced driving out here. "He said he's been gone a week—"

She had him by the lapel, pulling him inside. "Get in here," she said. And with him stumbling about next to her, she reached for Max as well. "Get the hell in here before they see you."

In her living room, as Max stripped his costume away in a pile on the sofa, she told them what had happened. All of Eden Gardens had been settled in a day, the new homeowners moved en masse with a fleet of trucks. At the same time the disappeared—yes, disappeared—Linwoods had been replaced by a young black family Max's parents appeared to know— moved in, apparently, on the urging of the Human Relations group. These changes lined up with all the worst fears of Rob Halford and his Civil Defense League, leaving the town on a knife's edge for nearly a week, everyone on all sides gnashing their teeth and wringing their hands.

"And those people downhill—" she said.

"The Seekers," he said, relieved to know what was going on. "They're the people I was looking for when my car got stuck."

"No, this is something else. Like nothing around. All kinds of people living next door to one another. Colored, white, Mexican, Chinese? Every kind, I tell you. Word is two men are living together on South Elm. Not just as roommates either."

"Then yeah," he said. "That's the Seekers."

Marlene pointed vaguely at a wall. "These wing nuts? I thought you were looking for an old army buddy?"

"He's . . . uh," he said, trying to find his words. "He's one of the wing nuts, I think."

She paced a little, wrenching her hands together, embarrassed or confused or both. "It's fine. Really, it's all fine to me. If you ask me, that's how America would look every day. Don't get me wrong."

"I'm not getting you wrong."

"But it's Rob Halford and the rest of them. They're already burning torches outside the Linwoods' old place. Somebody hung a Confederate flag."

It occurred to him that he'd noticed a shaky orange haze down one of the streets not far from here. Night was just falling. "Torches?" he said. "You serious?"

Now the kid, like a know-it-all teenager right off the television, flopped onto the sofa with his arms crossed behind his head. He aimed his face at the ceiling and said, "This place is hell, I tell you."

"Max," she gasped. "Language."

Stanley went to the window and parted the curtain. Aside from, yes, an orangy glow in the distance, all was quiet. A suburb at night. There, catching only a glint of the disturbance in its side mirror, sat his uncle's car. Most of the snow had melted since last week to reveal dark patches of wet-seeming grass to the starry sky. "Just who are these people with torches?"

"Those Civil Defense League goons and a few others. Some of them not even from here. Just 'concerned citizens' or whatever."

"That man Charlie had a fight with?"

At this, the kid snickered.

This drew her attention back to her nephew, and she stood beside him, tousling his hair. "That's Rob. Rob Halford. He and Penrod are the worst of them. The whole town is a time bomb."

The kid tried shrugging her off his head. "Why don't you just call the police?" he said. "This is nuts."

She brushed at his hair again. "Shh," she said. "Everything has been so terrible and here you are and your parents are going to be so relieved."

"If it was up to me," said the kid, "I wouldn't be here. I mean, do you want to be here? For this?"

Stanley couldn't tell if he was asking him or his aunt, but still he answered, "Can't say that I do."

After that had come Charlie, still sporting two black eyes, baffled at Stanley's presence and even more so at the kid's. He had a harried look to him, like a man waiting for the electric chair. "What are you two doing here? Max, what's all this?" But before either of them could say anything he rambled on, "Ira's downhill in Eden Gardens. Everybody's down there. There's a man in charge with a long robe and everyone knows something's about to happen and they've got a shelter built into that old dirt pile and they're going to round everyone up to be safe." He was, strangely, changing his socks. "We need to go now. All of us. Right now."

And what could he remember after that? The short skinny man in the brown suit watching them from across the road. Marlene saying, *It's Penrod,* and his looking vaguely familiar. The name now resonated down his memories, a distant bell.

And he remembered everyone piling in his uncle's car and the man in the brown suit running off, back toward the orange glow, as they sailed downhill to all those people shivering outside and Tommy, yes, there was finally Tommy Vasquez with his wife and daughter, but Stanley didn't have a minute to say hello or explain he'd been looking for him just days before. And there were four or five dozen other adults and children and the man in the burgundy robe with the shaved head and arched eyebrows and the others in robes too, just a few of them, everyone to a face absolutely terrified. There was some order the people in the robes were trying to make, some kind of plan, shouting for everyone to go to the shelter, reinforced with steel, shouting for someone to call in the police. But nothing came together. It was only an instant, after all. A sense of chaos and dread and the desperation for that order. The man in the burgundy robe shouted over all of them to stay calm. And then a child screamed, a little girl, her hand pointing uphill, where from the back lawns above them came the horde and its torches and the shouting and the melee and none of it making a lick of sense, just an impossible nightmare in the too-bright snow.

But that little white girl. Max's sister. Inquisitive, bright-eyed, in a yellow dress like his own mother's the last time he'd seen her, carrying with her both days a copy of *Jane Eyre,* which she'd told Stanley to his face only days before at the party that it was about the best book she'd ever read, better than *Black Beauty* and everything.

Deborah Feldberg was her name.

He could see her now as clear as ever. Her black hair against the snow, her face sound asleep, blood sprayed out and pooled and so red his heart had stopped. Going to her, falling to his knees, some words escaping his mouth before the whistle of movement toward his head. Then the hospital and Uncle Frederick and Marlene visiting with flowers. The girl dead.

And he hadn't seen this woman again for five years, until today, after everything else. The shock of her presence made Stanley feel like someone watching his life through a telescope. It all seemed that far away.

"And now she's single," Wozniak said half an hour after she left, giving him this look that meant something naughty was in the air. "And she's come into my bookstore to brush up against my clerk? I'm appalled. Look at me," he said, fanning his face with a hairy hand. "Absolutely appalled."

Wozniak was putting on a theatrical character Stanley hadn't seen before, a half-attempted Blanche DuBois, fluttering lashes and all. The man claimed that he'd done loose Shakespeare in Washington Square during the Depression, so these little impressions weren't wholly out of character. Yet it didn't seem the time or place for joking around. "Okay, okay," Stanley told him. "I said I was going to meet her, didn't I?"

"I declare," said Wozniak, slurping now from a bowl of cold chop suey. "I don't even give a damn."

"You're getting your southerners confused," Stanley said.

Wozniak pushed the bowl away and wiped at his beard with a hand. "Listen," he said. "You need something to clear your head after all this, and here's this attractive woman. I don't see the problem."

• • •

But he knew there were problems. For one thing, his parents had said they would be arriving tonight by train, and whether he believed this to be so or not, he would need to check in. For another, the more space he put between himself and that crummy trip to the hospital, the more despair took over his mood. He was tired. His uncle was dead. A whole man gone from the world. With his head increasingly on balance, he realized that what he needed to do was to contact his uncle's friends and former colleagues at City College. They needed to know. Everyone needed to know. *The New York Times* needed word of it, for crying out loud. *Giant Among Men: Negro Intellectual Dead at 68*. Sure, that's what they'd say. Not just in the obituaries but on the front page, in letters as big as those telling you who won the presidency. He ran on this steam, moving about the store with a new sense of determination, until he was shelving novels in the late afternoon and ran across a leather-bound copy of *Jane Eyre* that looked just like the one Deborah had been carrying around with her, just like the one in the snow an arm's length away from her still body.

After that he was cold all over again, and tired. He sat at the desk waiting for customers to come in and out, to bring their books to the register, to finally go away. He was counting up the register and finishing paperwork when Marlene appeared at the locked door, still in her men's overcoat, waving a dirty-gloved hand.

He put on the best face he could, laughing as she told him on the sidewalk about her life these last years, about leaving behind Long Island and an unhappy marriage, about rediscovering her love for painting and taking the risk of showing her work in a competition just a couple of years ago. "That changed everything," she said, leading him toward an open door between two restaurants, really just a public staircase. "I got written up in the *Voice*, if you can believe it, and a week later had a dealer. That summer was my first show."

"Incredible," he said, though he could hardly concentrate on her story. "You know, I'd forgotten you painted."

She was squeaking up the stairs ahead of him. "Oh, always," she said. "Even back then. But how could you know? Anyway, my first show was with three other women painters. 'A theme,' my dealer said, though we couldn't have been more unalike."

At the top of the stairs she shook her keys from her bag. Someone had scrawled a stick-figure woman with wild hair into her door, the jagged word WITCH scraped beneath. He pointed. "Looks like you've got an admirer."

"That's from the second Charlie. Remember Charlie? My ex-husband? There was another Charlie. A Greek. Karolos, really." She swept open the door to reveal a deep room with a bed and big windows and sunlight and no kitchen at all. "Karolos Gianopoulos? The sculptor?"

He laughed. "I'm afraid my knowledge is limited," he said. "At least when it comes to Greek sculpture."

She said seriously, "Oh, he's American. I only mean his family."

He walked inside, just past her, the unmade bed already at his shins. Most of the room was a studio: canvases stacked against one wall, three different easels going, paint tubes and brushes everywhere. Next to the washroom door stood a table, displaying nothing but a bottle of red wine and a single baguette. Though evening was already slanting the daylight out of the streets, these wide back windows fed a bright orange into the place. "Nice spot," he said. And then, trying his best to remain upbeat, "So you're pretty successful with the painting?"

Rather than answer, she smiled in an impatient way and set her bag on the bed. "I guess Karolos isn't a household name," she continued. "But he's known around here. A real character. Came at me with a knife the day I told him I wouldn't marry him. He still drops in now and again to threaten me."

She said this last bit as if she were remarking on a nearby store where she'd found good produce. "He sounds charming," Stanley said. "Can't wait to meet him."

"Oh, he's in London right now," she said. And then, touching his arm, "Come here. Drink. Eat."

He looked at her paintings. They were surprisingly good. He didn't know all that much about modern art, only what he'd learned from his uncle, but he liked them. They were what she called abstract realism: heavy scabs of paint that looked like landscapes and still lifes and portraits but also looked like nothing at all. One, said to be a seaport at dusk, looked more like a rusted graveyard fence caught in a pair of headlights. Another appeared to be a row of skyscrapers modeled after blades of grass. Behind that one, a hillside dropped to a field of pointy-roofed houses. Beside them, a red puddle glared out like an angry eye. It was, he knew, Eden Gardens. He didn't need to ask.

"Do you like Mondrian?" she said. "Do you like de Kooning?"

"Sure," he said. Then, trying to shake off the image of that cursed place, he asked her about how she got here, how long she'd been living two blocks away from where he worked. "I mean, how is it I haven't seen you? It's so strange."

"In this apartment?" she said. "Just over a year. You can see I hardly have room for books. And I mostly read the poets anyway. Elizabeth Bishop? Wallace Stevens? Sometimes I read Eliot, but all the references bore me."

He took a breath that seemed to inflate his lungs more than they needed. "I love Stevens," he said. "And Bishop."

"Oh, brilliant," she said, and raised her glass as if to toast him from across the little room.

"And Eliot, for that matter. 'A pair of ragged claws' and all that?"

"Yes, he's quite good, but who ever knows what he's saying?"

He laughed. "You won't believe this, but I'm a poet. I mean, I'm a nobody. Not a published word. But I try."

She gave him a puckered smile, like someone holding back a grand expression. Then she said, "I'm not surprised at all. You always struck me—"

When she didn't say anything more, he pointed at the paintings stacked against the wall. He sipped again at his wine. Now it was his hand shaking. A quiet settled over the room. Somehow they were finished talking. "They're beautiful paintings," he said. "I really like them."

"Take one," she said. Then she set her glass of wine down on the floor. It was time for him to go. "They've been selling very nicely, but I absolutely want you to have one."

"I couldn't," he said. And then, embarrassed, "Not tonight. You see, I've got to get back uptown. I'm expecting family. My uncle's died."

"Oh, dear," she said, her hand on her chest. "I'm so sorry to hear that. Can I see you— Can we— Maybe next week or something?"

He stood. "That would be good," he said. And when he thought of going to Chicago for Theda, the idea seemed like an impossibility, like a journey out of Marco Polo. "Let's plan on that. Come by the shop, will you?"

On the stairway again, standing above him, brushing back her hair, she said, "You always struck me as the poetic type. That's what I wanted to say. But *always* seemed like such a silly word given the circumstances."

He leaned against the stairwell wall, halfway down. "Can I ask you something?" he said. "Do you remember that fellow Penrod? From Ridge Landing? You ever see him around?"

Her face clenched. She looked down at her shoes. "Not long after I moved downtown, I waited tables at the White Horse a couple of months. He came in once, and when I got to his table, he grabbed me by the wrist. I don't remember what he said. My boss passed by just in time and threw him out."

"Well," he said, "we'll have to talk about him again, too."

She shook her head derisively. "That man," she said. "He isn't even a man. He's like something out of Dr. Moreau's island. A dog on two legs."

Half-dead on his feet, Stanley could barely hold his eyes open on the uptown train. Everything on earth had hit him today and all he wanted was to rest. When a seat opened, he dropped into it like a wet sack. He thought of that Ornette Coleman record his uncle hated like the devil, with its overlapped tones, the trumpet and sax walking together off step, their play of connection and chaos. If he tried, if he just leaned back his head a little, he could hear them.

Upstairs in his uncle's bedroom he found the mattress leaned against the wall, the steel frame exposed. A cigar box rested in the grayish dust. He knelt, sat back on his haunches, and lifted the box, filthy and worn. With a single finger he flipped the top. Inside were a pad of envelopes. He pinched a few of them out. Splaying them like a hand of poker cards, he saw what he'd least expected. They were all addressed to him. And from Chicago, too. All of them from Theda. One, two, three, four, five, six of them. So then he sat cross-legged, his mind cleared out like an empty room.

He tried reading them silently to himself, but instead they came through in her high musical voice, singing an abstract song about a new job and friends and the cold wind of some distant winter and the bright blue of Lake Michigan another summer. She had met a man at some point and later he was gone. She asked if Stanley was ever going to visit, if he was ever going to write. She'd received her degree in record time. There had been a job offer. A promotion. A new apartment. She had taken an airline flight to San Francisco and back. She'd started volunteering her Saturdays to a civil rights group, her Sundays feeding the homeless. Her mother had grown sick and passed away. She, Theda, was going to be in New York soon, she would be here now, couldn't he meet her outside?

On the street downstairs Harlem had disappeared. In its place stood the familiar dank of Hattiesburg at night, in summer, with no one around, the familiar electric fear of the place constricting his throat, prickling the back of his arms. He stood on the sidewalk in a state of panic, and when he turned back to the door, his uncle's building had become the glass-front Talbert Leigh Pontiac dealership where his father worked. Surely if he could find his father, all this could be sorted out. But around the corner where the service bays should be, where the men worked with their sleeves rolled up and their eyes pinched against the smoke from their lipped cigarettes, the wide display windows repeated themselves. Like a slow-motion movie, nearly one frame at a time, a single car glistened under the lights. A salesman in square glasses gestured at its curving form, stepping closer here, closer. Then around the next corner was the same, but here the salesman approached a woman who looked just like Theda, holding out to her a contract and a pen.

How could this be? He reached to tap the glass, to get her attention, and found that he wasn't outside Talbert Leigh Pontiac at all, but just outside the barbershop on St. Nicholas, his heart still racing. The streets were shadowy, blue and chilled in an early-evening sort of way, the sun setting earlier now that autumn had swept its leaves into the city. He leaned against the window with one foot on the glass, knowing that if the owner had been still there, he'd be out the door shouting that the storefront wasn't Stanley's personal footstool. From somewhere, music played. An open window two floors up. The muted voice of one of those lovebird white-boy singers:

When I touch your lips
The world is golden
You look in my eyes
And I'm emboldened

Ugh. Folks actually listened to this stuff without turning their stomachs inside out. And apparently whoever was upstairs needed to listen to it louder and louder and louder. Strings built to an intense crescendo that kept rising and rising. He craned his neck toward the window, was about to shout something, and then it all stopped.

The street and beeps of horns and muttering voices. "Stanley?"

Standing before him in a trim cream-colored coat was Theda. "Where?" he said. "How did—"

She pointed across the street and then jaywalked right into it, careless of traffic. "Right over here," she said. "Hurry."

Cars honked all around them. A cabbie waved a hairy arm out his window and shouted something he couldn't understand. "This isn't safe," Stanley told her. "What are you doing?"

She glanced back at him again just as they reached the sidewalk. "Have a little courage, Stan. Isn't that what you always needed? A little courage?"

The line felt canned, and for a moment he stopped at the curb, looking at her. There she was, lit from above, his dear Theda, looking for the life of her like Dorothy Dandridge, her eyes catlike now as she gazed back at him. He loved her, miserably, and this time he wouldn't lose her. Besides, she must only be kidding about courage. She knew all about his time in Korea, those three nights behind enemy lines separated from his platoon, with only Tommy Vasquez and that poor Mark Willoughby, the night they'd seen the glowing forms in the sky, the next morning at dawn when Willoughby was hit by friendly fire, his blood and brain matter sprayed in Stanley's face, the cuts of bone into his ear and neck, the scars still there like the graze of a meat tenderizer. And she knew, too, about Eden Gardens.

He could hear that music again, the same song from outside the bookstore. It had followed them, and for a moment he felt a pang of confusion.

> *When I touch your lips*
> *The world is golden*
> *You look in my eyes*

On a little table on the sidewalk, a teenager's plastic record player sat impossibly, spinning a black platter. When had she turned it on? She went to it now and shut it off, and then the streets went silent but the song remained. He felt dizzy, his vision fading. "I'm sorry," she said. "I can't get enough of that song. Isn't it something?"

> *And if I were to see you tonight*
> *In my blue Acapulco dreams?*
> *Would you dance so close and tight?*

With a jerk, they sat across from each other at the little Chinese place Wozniak regulared, blowing over bowls of noodles in broth. Painted in garish yellow and red, with a wall of windows facing the sidewalk, the restaurant had room for only three tables. "You had to find me," she said, stirring her food. "Otherwise it wouldn't be the same."

They ate. A woman in an orange raincoat stopped at the window and stared in as if she knew them, then wandered away. Then a man in a brown suit appeared, skinny, skull-faced. Stanley's heart pounded again, like a jackhammer. It was Penrod, watching them, only a pane of glass away. Soon the whole restaurant was clouded with steam. Penrod used the sleeve of his coat to wipe a circle through which he could stare. Now it was only the two of them, a clear line of sight, Stanley and Penrod, looking at each other as if through a ship's porthole. He expected him to speak, to finish Theda's message. But this never came. "I don't follow," Stanley said to him. "What do you want from me? What were you doing there?"

Then he and Theda were walking on the sidewalk side by side, her smiling like a queen in a parade, Penrod nowhere to be found. Without thinking about it, he had taken her arm. He held her lightly, just keeping pace, but now something had changed. On the way to Wozniak's bookstore, he kept his hand on her arm, noting the occasional stare from passersby. At least a half-dozen people, mostly men, white men, gave them varying degrees of serious looks on every block. Some spit in their path. The thought crossed his mind that the woman next to him wasn't Theda at all, but Marlene. But he couldn't bring himself to look.

He went into the dark store without flipping a switch. His bag glowed in a shaft of streetlamp light, piped along its edges in silver. When he looked back, he was unsurprised to find that she had gone. He was alone again, surrounded by books.

Behind him, a man cleared his throat. Wozniak. Or no, turning to see the hunched, dark silhouette moving toward him, it was his uncle Frederick, still alive, coming his way from the philosophy aisle. "Stanley?" the old man said. "Did you come back for me?"

"Yes," he said. "This where you been?"

"Me? I love books. I'm always here."

"But tonight," Stanley said. "Tonight I found you—"

His uncle approached him, a single hand outstretched. He hadn't noticed the man's eyes weren't open until now, when as their lids parted, a bright white light shot out in two tight beams. Then his mouth, a gushing *O* of unquiet glare. The sound of that Ornette Coleman, wandering and conversational, a racket, and finally silence.

He woke with the train squealing all around him, his body gone cold to the bones. There was no cigar box, no money, no letters. No Theda, either. And that damned song. Max's summer hit. The boy crooner, not twenty years old with his face plastered on record sleeves. And such a ridiculous tune. Standing up, reaching for the pole, all the fiction drained from him. He was at the 125th Street station, dazed like a man hit over the head with a hammer.

Awake now, stumbling out onto the platform, rubbing his face with his hand, another sensibility layered onto him. He missed his uncle.

Up the real stairs and into the real apartment, he knew that he wasn't going to chase west after Theda. That time had passed. And though it had been good to see Marlene living out what she wanted of life, he didn't see any romance with her, either. All those old connections had to be set adrift. What he needed, really, was to settle on good old Stanley himself, the fellow he had set out to be. Uncle Frederick had pulled him back together after Ridge Landing, had kept him afloat mentally after he wrecked things with Theda. Now he'd have to go it alone. He'd have to free himself to do the work that needed to be done, to make a face to meet the faces you meet and all that. And he knew he *would* now. Knew he would write until his parents arrived and then after they left, write until someone came to the door to throw him out, write until he found somewhere else to go, some other home, and there he would write again.

That evening with the phone pulled to the end of its cord and set on the hallway floor, he sat at his typewriter in the back bedroom. After a minute, he took the Douglas down from his uncle's wall and set it on his desk like a holy object. There had been no epiphany, no sudden rush to understanding, just that evil image of Penrod before him, the sainted form of his uncle, the curled shape of that little girl bleeding in the snow, the painting with its royal purple star fading through iterations of history. He would write about what happened that day; he would let it flood into his work. It was just his way to survive, his way to keep swimming forward. In truth it felt like the only way to cling to what he really was, to shed the boy from Mississippi, the intellectual's nephew, the soldier, the poseur. He'd hang on. He'd cling.

Hours passed like this, they must have, with him just hammering away at the keys letting little rhymes and half rhymes play out sloppily across the page, telling the story of some cartoonish him, beset by a chorus of white folks always at his heels, a dialogue of sorts, something like a play performed just in his head. Morning came again and he still hadn't gotten the call. By late afternoon he read through a few sheets. There were funny bits, clever bits, but there was no denying this thing was a mess. It didn't matter. Night had fallen again and everyone here but him was dead and he didn't have any other choices but to keep working.

Pacing the quiet apartment, circling with a pen this line and that, he realized no one had called from Hattiesburg. So he set down his work. His temples throbbed. When the operator patched him through, he'd expected his sister to answer. Instead it was his father. "Couldn't get away," he said. "The Covingtons had a dinner party planned, so Mama's helping out and I went into the shop. Ain't she called?"

"No," Stanley said. "I thought I'd hear from you at the station last night."

"Maybe tomorrow," his father said. But there was a distraction. Television. "Anyway, it sounds like you got things settled down up there? Sad thing, sad thing."

A minute later they were off the phone, two strangers. He'd wanted to tell him how he'd found himself, always here after all, Stanley. But his father might not have understood him. Funny how a man sees in his son a better self—until he doesn't anymore. Then what does he see? Some odd boy with the mendacity to drag his name around like it was his own. Well, better not to try curing everything at once. Better not to get a family visit in this maelstrom. He'd settled things down, all right. Let the machine of his uncle's life swallow up his death, too. Tomorrow he would call the pastor first thing. He'd call the pastor and then all his uncle's friends and then he'd right the ship. Everything in its place. For now he needed a walk. He needed to clear his head.

Collar turned up against the October chill, he met with the crowds shuffling home from work, restaurants filling up, cars packed in tight, lurching and braking, honking their horns. It was the city in autumn with night blazing in the streets, and with that strange woman Marlene on his mind, he felt a freedom in his legs, like someone just relieved of a debilitating cramp. But the city's verve wasn't the same as that clanging around in his chest. Something was wrong. Through half-fogged windows he could see the troubled faces of cabbies. A middle-aged woman came running from a group of folks standing together outside a store, her hand over her mouth, her eyes wild with tears. It was the appliance shop, where he'd told Uncle Frederick a dozen times, threatened him, really, that he'd one day buy a television and haul it up the stairs so the two of them could join the twentieth century.

He could see now, between the heads of those gathered, President Kennedy, sharp as ever, turned slightly leftward, his face too somber, like he'd come down with something awful, his stomach gone to pieces. He was saying something about Cuba, about the Soviets, and then turning from one of the dozen screens there was Billy Washington, in a scarf and hat, his eyes, too, looking a little sick. He stalked free of the clump, leading his way with the black leather case of his saxophone. "Say hey, Billy," Stanley called out. "What's all this noise?"

And then Billy turned to him without any signal of recognition. It was someone else who shouted the news before Billy could even speak, and right there on the sidewalk the world went rushing headlong toward its end.

"Missiles," the person said. "We're all finished."

THE MIDDLEMAN

SKIP MICHAELS—1967

Let me tell you about this night, one of those cool damp autumn nights in Florida, the grass still shimmering from the evening's rain. I'd come out onto the landing for some fresh air. I was staying at one of these roadside motels, U-shaped, with a little courtyard and pool in the center. For the hour prior I'd been minding my own business inside, my head in a book, smoking cigarettes and waiting for sleep. Now I'd come out to stretch and air the place out with the door open behind me and to look up at the faint stars. The sky wasn't necessarily cloudy, but it wasn't clear, either. This was 1967. The days then felt like they were about to explode, the whole country scratching at a scabby itch, not a lot of trust in anyone's eyes. So the cooling night and the quiet felt like a visitation from the past.

I can even remember the book I was reading. Stendhal's *The Red and the Black*. Don't ask me for a synopsis. It's enough to remember that I read it, and that I'd been reading it the night I met Charlie Ranagan.

Those days I sold fine leather-bound volumes with gilt pages as a representative of the Great Works of Literature Subscription Service, Incorporated, known to just about everybody as Great Books. So I had plenty around to read, half a dozen show copies to let the customers finger through, and as long as

I was careful with the pages, nobody at headquarters seemed to mind my self-education. Every couple of months I had a new set of books. This way they stayed new, and nobody could tell you that you'd shown them that same copy of *Huck Finn* the last time you swung through town. It didn't take me long to start using this system like a library. You see, I felt I had some catching up to do if I wanted to talk up the product line. In high school I never much went in for English class, couldn't make heads or tails of Robert Browning's poetry, and when I had the offer of college through the G.I. Bill, I had a baby and another on the way and a wife and a house to pay for, so instead I'd gone into sales. Luckily my cousin Trudy on my mother's side, a big-boned woman who knew how to get her way, just happened to be secretary to Great Books' vice president of sales, Mr. Asa Knopfler. She set up the interview at their Paterson, New Jersey, headquarters just two months after I'd returned from Korea. I sweated it, lost sleep, rambled incoherently at the pink-faced middle-management schlub who conducted the inquisition, but it all turned out to be a formality. They just needed proof that I was a breathing, English-speaking white man who could ambulate on both legs. The pink-faced schlub let me know as much about ten minutes into his questioning. "You'd be surprised the fellas think they can sell books," he told me. And then, though it seemed to be a contradiction to me, "But you seem like just our type."

When I went in for the gig I thought I'd be out again within the year. Me, a door-to-door salesman? Aside from the desperate need for a paycheck, I thought at the time I was doing ol' Trudy a favor. My mother had been on the phone haranguing me to call the girl up since the day I was discharged. I still had

ticker tape in my hair when she pulled me over the barrel.
"You remember your sweet cousin Trudy, don't you?" Sweet
cousin? When I was in grade school she used to pummel me
with her outsize dirty-knuckled fists when nobody was looking.
I used to dread visiting Grandma and Grandpa Hofstedtler
out of fear that hippopotamus would be waiting for me around
a dark corner. Here I was, a goddamn decorated war hero, my
eyes full of girls, with one of my own waiting at home with the
child we'd conceived during my one weekend of leave before
being shipped off to the other edge of the world, and I was
quaking in my boots to hear about how I just had to call up
Trudy and wrangle a job from her. I did, of course. I got
around to it. But only after Irene came back from the doctor's
office two months later all smiles and tears to tell me our family had, by some ridiculous luck of biology, just expanded.

So six years went by, or seven. Irene and I sold the house
outside Philly to move down to Jacksonville, when after I'd
been on the job two years, Great Books gave me all of Florida
and the southern portions of Georgia and Alabama as my very
own sales district. This was before the retirement boom really
hit Florida, so my excitement over having such a large district
handed to me quickly fizzled out. That part of the South wasn't
necessarily a bastion of freethinking and literary conversation.
In fact it wasn't even middle class. A lot of the small towns and
suburbs around there looked pretty much as they had at the
turn of the century. People had cars and telephones and TV
antennas, sure, but otherwise it was another country. Here I
came up the drive with my suitcase heavy with classic literature
and my mouth full of Yankee talk; it's a wonder I wasn't greeted
with a shotgun at every doorstep. But I give the South a rough

time. Things were changing. Modern life was coming. The bell of civil rights was ringing, and though they stuffed their ears as long as they could, most of them got around to hearing it. At the time I didn't have the softheartedness to see any change in the air, though. I imagine nobody from outside the place would have. Me, I felt a constant sense of disgust over the poverty and desperation and bigotry I ran across every day. When I made a sale down there, it would be to aristocratic white families with whole retinues of black folks working every lever of their household, or to white shop owners who cursed and grew red-faced at the slightest mention of a black citizen, or to school principals with severe buzz cuts and eyes that trusted me only as far as the reach of the paddles hanging threateningly on their office walls. At home with Irene and the boys I worried what they were learning in school and cautioned her against making friends with the neighborhood wives. On the road I thought of little else but returning north at the earliest possible minute.

Back in town, we had only Pat and Jenny Riley. And thank god we had them. They were transplant Philadelphians like us, and just as lost as we were in the tropical South. The pair had made a small fortune in Tupperware sales, moved down to work at the headquarters in Kissimmee, and then moved up to Jacksonville after not getting along with the new management following Earl Tupper's departure. By the time we met them, they owned a string of car washes, five or six of them, all called Life of Riley's Auto Bath. Many a Friday evening I would be traveling back home, feeling the headache of the screaming, messy kids and Irene's week's worth of complaints already building between my ears, when I would think of Pat and Jenny, of cocktails, of intelligible conversation. These were classy people for us, far more successful if money is your measure of success, and still quite a bit more successful if you're measuring by any other standard. Then again, they were twenty or twenty-five years older than us. Pat's first job had been in FDR's Civilian Conservation Corps, and Jenny, if you can believe this, worked as a taxi dancer in some little upstairs joint on Philly's north side—a job that taught her how to carry a knife under her skirt and make it look like nothing. These were stories they were fond of telling us, I guess to remind us that even they went through rough years. These days they were made of money and swimming in time, but they never came off as upper-crust Main Liners. Just folks.

Aside from them, sure, I had some acquaintances, especially out on the road. I saw the same waitresses and cooks and motel night clerks in a cycle just about every month, so they knew my name and I knew theirs. Got to know more than a few of my fellow salesmen, too. There was no dodging it. I'd see Benny Hargrove with United Plumbing Supply and Ralph Bellamy (not that Ralph Bellamy) from North American Siding, and little Pete Dickson, that hunched-over shrimp, representing some sporting goods concern the name of which escapes me—I'd see these fellows and we'd have a drink or two, play cards, laugh at old jokes.

But mostly it was me and the books.

Irene and I (I might as well tell you, she was my first wife) hadn't really gotten along since the beginning, when we were young and in a hurry and President Truman had determined it best to send me, along with another two million or so other boys, off to the Korean peninsula to defend the world from

Reds on the march. Even our love letters during my deploy-
ment amounted to one extended back-and-forth argument set
down in ink for posterity and peppered with the necessary
occurrences of words like *sweetheart, dearest,* and *honey bear* to
keep me from getting hauled up on spy charges, simply because nobody in charge of any war would ever believe a pair of
newlyweds could possibly communicate to each other in this
way. I had it out with her so bad over a haircut she got that I
remember staying up all night in the frigid snow composing
new strings of curse words for her by cigarette lighter. It's a
wonder I wasn't shelled to kingdom come that very night. And
of course at every opportunity she trotted out this guy Nick
Winstone, who sold Cadillacs and who, even though he was
married to a buxom blonde, seemed to be the object of all my
young wife's romantic longing. Why couldn't I be more like
Nick Winstone? When I got back, would I consider wearing a
suit the way he does? Why is it I had that weaselly voice and not
his rocky tenor? Was I aware that Nick Winstone exercises with
weights and even used to fight semiprofessionally before he
broke his nose? Wasn't it a fine nose? Maybe I should break my
nose while I'm off at the war. That would be a swell idea. In
fact if I wanted to just turn myself in to the enemy and stay in
Korea, she wouldn't complain, either. I dreamed of taking a
tire iron to this Nick Winstone. Then after coming back, I
heard from her sister that Winstone had been Irene's crush
back in junior high school, that he'd been married three years,
that he lived in Wyoming. All of it was fiction, then. That didn't
make me forgive her. But really the whole Winstone affair was
small potatoes compared to all the ways I didn't measure up to
what she'd expected of me, or what her mother had expected,

or even what my own parents—she had them over to visit every other Sunday—had expected.

What had I done to warrant all this disappointment? Search me. All I could think of at the time was that before Korea I'd taken things a little slow. I worked part time at a mechanic's shop, carrying tires, taking money, filling out paperwork. And I'd spent the rest of my time, when I wasn't wooing Irene, listening to the radio or stooped over in one of the listening booths at Childress's Record Shop, humming along to every song I liked, jotting down the lyrics in a little notepad I kept in my back pocket. What I thought I was doing had become a mystery worth talking about in our circle. It drew a lot of attention. When one of Irene's girlfriends would ask me, I'd shrug and tell her I didn't know. I had the same answer for my nosy uncle Gerald and my parents and my teachers and Irene herself, who finally came up with the explanation that I had a screw loose and couldn't tell one song from the next. Hence taking the notes and memorizing the melody. For goodness sake, he can't sing. He couldn't possibly be thinking of singing.

I believe for a time I was thought to be "touched." At least among members of her family, this was a prevalent attitude. Even when I was at basic training I'd get letters from Irene reminding me that her father thought I was a crackpot, or at least slow, and that the United States military didn't have any business putting me in uniform. This man, tall as a basketball player, worked the leather goods department at Macy's for thirty-two years, and during the first eight years of my marriage with his daughter, he never gave up on the idea of getting me a job with him. Why he thought that was a good idea, I'll never know. He clearly hated my guts. Anytime we were over with the kids, even during our years down in Florida when a visit really meant something, he'd be dressed in a ribbed undershirt with the dark tufts of black hair poking up from his chest and out his armpits, a pair of slacks with the belt slipped out, and dark dress socks, the nails of his big toes sticking out of eternal holes. He came to the dinner table like this, without conversation, often eating behind a newspaper. My father-in-law. When he heard via Irene upon my return stateside that I planned to make a career writing songs, he told her it wasn't too late in our son's life to adjust to another father, and that despite their family's Catholicism, he believed even the priests would consider divorce the proper, even righteous, decision. Only Irene's sweet mother, that progenitor of eight previous substandard models before my blessed wife, had the faith in my ultimate failure to say, "Let him do what he wants. He's a young man. He'll learn to take responsibility for his family one day." This she said right in front of me as she poured me a cup of coffee—on Christmas Day, no less. To which her slob of a husband, that other grand producer of humanity, ruffled his newspaper and set about finishing his cheesecake.

My career as a songwriter up to this point—up to the night I want to tell you about—could hardly be called a success. In fact, Irene's mother had pretty much called it. I scribbled in my spare time, sent manila envelopes to all the publishing houses and talent agents, made a point of meeting every bandleader I could—even the nobodies performing at upstate hotels. Managing to build up a little interest around '61, with two songs getting performed by a couple of different nightclub acts and one orchestrator telling me I might just be onto something with a lyric I called "Moonlight in Brooklyn," I took a chance and entered a songwriting contest put on by Capitol Records. The winner would get the chance to meet with Nelson Riddle and a check for a hundred dollars, and the record company would have the option to put one of its contract artists in the studio with the song. My head filled with wild dreams of Sinatra belting out my words. I was sure this was going to be my break. Instead I received honorable mention, meaning my name was read over the radio and a paper award came in the mail a few weeks later: *Skip Michaels is hereby bestowed the distinction of Honorable Mention by the judges of the 1961 Capitol Records Songwriting Contest for his song "Moonlight in Brooklyn."* By that time, the post office had to forward the creased-up envelope, as I'd taken the job down in Florida and, at least as far as my in-laws were concerned, given up this pipe dream of being a songwriter.

I run through all these things so it's understood the situation I was in as I stepped out onto the motel landing and gazed at the silvery rectangular pool, the mismatched lawn chairs, the glistening grass leading down to the lake. I wouldn't say I was at a crossroads. At least I wasn't aware of being at one. It was a day like many others over the last several years, and as is my nature, I was still getting used to it.

Really, you could say that in spite of this stuff, I was actually in a state of relative peace. My sales were up, I was getting a free education, and only occasionally did I spend a few hours in a coffee shop "looking for a rhyme for orange," as my astute father-in-law used to say. I breathed in the cool damp air, thought something or other about Stendhal's book, and rested my weight on the railing, slippery and chilling to the touch. The motel stood near Orlando, on the outskirts of one of those little townships that would later become suburbs to Disney World, still under construction at the time. The next morning I'd be headed west to Tampa–St. Pete, where I would make the rounds before driving back up to Jacksonville for the weekend. That makes it a Monday night, around ten. Bedtime.

Cars whizzed by on the highway, their tires *shush-shush*ing over the wet asphalt. The ice machine buzzed. From a couple of doors down, a radio played "Ode to Billie Joe." A woman in a yellow dress clacked across the courtyard, skirted the pool, and made for one of the rooms below me. The big moon, a white blob in the gauzy air, shone down a palling light.

A vague awareness of something happening off to my left built up like the elements of a melody: feet padding on concrete, the railing vibrating in my palms, the squeak of some unoiled hinge, and finally the growled mammalian harrumph that added a belch-like tastelessness to the calm night. Of course I looked. Only a minute or two later I would think the looking, the inquisitiveness, had been my first big mistake. But I did. I couldn't help it. I looked.

An egg-shaped man, dressed in boxer shorts and a sports coat, without socks or shoes, stood before the open door of the ice machine.

He had his back turned to me and his attention drawn toward the black insides of the machine. Still, I could see from my perspective, some five or six rooms away from the corner where the machine hummed, that the top of his head was as bald and nearly as pointed as an elbow. A thin mat of dark hair ran above one ear and connected around to the other. He held aloft the little blue plastic bucket provided by the motel's management, designed to match the headboard and curtains. His free hand was clenched into a fist next to one of his mostly naked legs. Again he harrumphed.

At this point my gut reaction was to go back inside. It's not that I thought this guy was going to be trouble. Only that I wanted quiet.

But then with one swift, ungraceful movement he propelled his upper body—head, shoulders, both arms—into the ice machine. Instantly the door slapped down on his back. His hairy white legs kicked about. He wriggled, cursed. Stuck. The machine rocked a little, side to side. But he didn't come free.

I leaned over the railing to get another look at the courtyard. The woman in the yellow dress long gone. Most of the lights off. Nobody around. From the radio two doors down, Sonny and Cher warmed up "The Beat Goes On." He hadn't seen me. Could I with a clear conscience slip back into my room and let this half-clothed halfwit work himself free? I did a little physics calculation in my mind: with most of him hanging outside the machine, it should be a cinch that he'd fall out, eventually. But that end was flailing in the moonlight, in white boxer shorts no less, and by his girth around the soft middle he could very well be wedged in there permanently. So I went to his aid.

"Hey, buddy," I called out. "You want some help?"

His response sounded like it had come from the back of a deep cave. Its contents were nothing more than a string of grunts and curse words. Up close I had to back away from those wild legs. It looked like he was trying to swim inside. "Fuck!" he shouted. "Aw, fuck."

I opened the flap door off his back. "Hold still a minute," I said. Then I circled my arms around his belly. My fingers didn't meet. He jiggled and squeezed in my arms. "I said hold still."

With some considerable effort, I lifted him up an inch or two. But then his kicking legs flipped upward. I think he may have believed he was jumping from a great height. His heels whacked the flap door and again it dropped, this time on my head. I weathered the crack, but now we were both cursing and spitting. I lifted. I told him to hold still. I lifted again. On the third try he came flying out like a champagne cork. Both of us dropped to the concrete landing. The ice machine door flopped closed.

Now I could get a clear look at him. For one thing, he was shirtless. That sports coat and those boxer shorts were all he had on save his silver wristwatch. His fat white belly, a spitting image for the moon, sat between his thighs like he was a woman with child. A red line crossed his chest from where he'd been wedged against the lip of the machine's door. His face was fleshy, long, with a cauliflower nose and dark lines running down from his inset eyes. It was a severe face, an angular face. Too narrow. Something Picasso about it. I couldn't understand how it fit with the rounded-off rest of him.

He was breathing heavily, gasping. And instead of looking at the person who had just rescued him, he stared into the empty ice bucket.

"Shit," he said. "Just my luck."

My ass hurt. With my arms around him I'd had no time to catch my fall. Standing upright was a bit of a challenge. Still, I did so, then flipped open the ice machine's door and looked inside. Dark, cavernous. A pungent smell of mold. The machine went on buzzing but nothing dropped from the freezer. I leaned inside and reached for the bottom. Empty air. "It's out of order," I said.

"What?"

I pulled my head out. "Out of order. The thing doesn't work."

"No ice?"

In spite of what he'd just been through, this concept seemed to baffle him. He wagged his head back and forth with the disappointment of a lousy gambler at the dog track. I was beginning at this point to wish I spoke another language so I could pretend not to understand him and walk away. Instead I said, "You okay?"

He looked up at me, perturbed. You'd have thought I'd interrupted him in the middle of doing his taxes. "What do you mean, okay?"

"Are you hurt?"

"I need a drink, all right? I need ice."

This didn't have much of anything to do with what I was asking, but I didn't feel like following up on it. I rounded his outstretched legs and started down the walkway. "Good night then, pal."

I'd only taken a few steps before he said, "Hey, hold up." And when I turned around he was scuffling his feet on the concrete to pivot himself in my direction, still sitting, his scuffed knees pointed at me. "You got any ice?"

"No."

"Damn bottle's been in the back of the car all day."

"That's swell," I said. "Drink it hot. Good night."

He grunted, rocked back and forth, not yet ready to let me leave. "Lend me a hand, will you?"

The guy couldn't have put more weight on my arm if he'd had another man on his shoulders. Pulling him up was like lifting the back end of a car. "C'mon," I said. "Push."

"I'm pushing."

"Drop the damn ice bucket."

He did. Then, with the freed-up hand, he found some force to aid in his rise. "Whew. Oh, boy." He dusted off the back of his boxer shorts and the elbows of his sports coat. "Sheesh. What a mess, huh?"

I realized now that I'd been smelling bourbon ever since I came over to help. Maybe the moldy ice machine had masked it. "You ought to sleep it off," I told him.

"Ah, don't be a square."

Coming from him, the word just didn't fit. I wondered for a moment where he'd picked it up. Likely from the movies. Then again, maybe he was some hip college professor, the type of jerk who listened to a Beatles album one day, joined his students in the streets with a Vietnam sign, and learned to roll his own marijuana cigarettes. Maybe at night these types roam around seething for a drink, wearing next to nothing. But that silver watch. That was no would-be longhair's watch. *This guy has a real job,* I thought. Or had one.

Suddenly he put out his hand. "Charlie Ranagan," he announced. "Metropolitan Life and Accident."

This fellow, this egg, stood to about my chin. And I'm not a tall man. I'd put him at around five-two. I watched him totter back and forth a moment as I tried to come up with a civilized way to divorce myself from his presence without any further ties. Finally I just shook his hand. "Skip Michaels. Great Books."

After some forgotten small talk on the subjects of door-to-door sales and life on the road, I excused myself successfully from this ill-clad stranger and hightailed it back to my room. The oddball nature of our meeting, not to mention the physical outlay involved, had wiped out my earlier sleepiness. Still I felt it necessary to shut out all the lights, bolt the door, and stretch out on top of the bed in the proper sleep position. I was worried he would drop in if even the slightest hint of my being awake was evident from the outside, and I was more than a little worried he would try the door either way. The man didn't seem to have a full grasp on himself. Maybe it was the booze. But he could just as well be a loon. You meet all kinds out on the road like this, and it doesn't hurt to keep up your guard.

So I lay on the bed, sleepless, listening for the padding of feet outside, and though I heard nothing, I kept thinking of myself as a victim, a powerless rube, left open to the pestering of a pantsless and quite possibly dangerous dipsomaniac. But the padding never came.

Apparently I dozed off just before dawn. When I woke in the morning with my travel alarm clanging, I hadn't yet been aware of sleep. During the short interval of my unconsciousness, a folded sheet of paper had appeared on the carpet right in front of my door. I didn't have to look to know Charlie Ranagan had slid it inside. Still I retrieved it and flopped back onto the bed. *Dear Pal,* it began. *Had breakfast yet? Going to*

Elroy's on the highway south around seven. My treat. C.R. (the guy with the ice)

It was already a quarter after seven. I showered, shaved, put on a clean shirt. But the whole time I knew I'd be going to Elroy's. I'd already planned on doing so. It was my regular stop here, the regular stop for all the salesmen, apparently Charlie Ranagan included. Finding another spot for breakfast and coffee sounded like too much trouble. Especially given how tired I was. So I went.

No surprise Ranagan hadn't left, even by five after eight when I arrived. "Over here, pal," he called to me from the corner booth. Only his eyes and bald forehead showed over the seats. Those, and one of his short paws. "Glad you came," he barked. "Glad you came."

The waitress made a zigzag to meet me halfway to the booth. "That bum's been over there since six-thirty," she said. "You want any coffee, honey?"

"Yes," I said. And when she asked if I wanted my regular two scrambled eggs and toast I said again, with a sigh of defeat, "Yes."

Ranagan looked like a man who'd already downed a pot of coffee. He sort of bounced in his seat like a child as I neared. The table showed signs of three or more unfinished courses to his breakfast: half-eaten pancakes, tooth-trimmed crusts, bent sticks of bacon, two different kinds of egg, a steaming untouched bowl of oatmeal.

"You had guests already?" I said, pointing at the spread.

"Nah," he said. "I've got a big appetite in the morning. My doctor says it's healthy. Eat more in the beginning of the day and less at night, he says. He and the new wife have been trying to get me to take off a few pounds, you see." He patted his belly. "Doing the best I can. What about you? Hungry?"

"Already ordered," I said.

"They know you here."

"I'd say."

He bounced in his seat again. "Been in the game long? Sales?"

"A few years. You?"

He'd been in sales since the end of the war, he said. The real war. Hardware, safety equipment, fallout shelters. Now insurance. The only type of work he'd ever known aside from assembly work in a boot factory as part of his wartime service. That's his terminology. *Wartime service.* What he meant by that was that he stayed stateside with a 4-F and ran a machine that pressed boot soles in a plant in Jersey.

"You look put together to me," I said. And though my own wartime service had been to train South Korean soldiers how to make conversation with their American counterparts, I felt like needling him. "What's with the 4-F?"

"Bad eyes," he said, "flat feet, one bowed leg, and some trouble I got into as a kid. Went to a home for delinquents and malcontents."

I knew there was something off-balance about this guy. But I didn't want to know any more about it. In fact I never should have asked. "What about fallout shelters? How's that market?"

He grimaced, didn't look comfortable answering. Luckily the waitress came with my coffee. "It was a short-term thing," he said after she left. "After that, I moved up to Metropolitan. Don't think I'll ever leave this gig, either."

"Been down here long?"

"In Florida? Nah." He gazed out the window like he needed to take a good look at it before saying any more. "Only two, maybe three weeks." He shrugged, noncommittal. "I like it good enough."

Not the most compelling conversation being had in the Western Hemisphere that morning, I'm sure. Hell, there was probably something more interesting going on right there in Elroy's. But I got his story and he asked me for mine. So I told him about Korea and my songwriting and my cousin Trudy, about the wife and kids up in Jacksonville, about my habitual perusal of the company's goods.

"You ever get back to the songwriting?"

"Not often." It occurred to me about this time, after the dishes were cleared and we were working on yet another cup of coffee, that I hadn't told another soul out on the road about my songwriting. And here I was spilling out my guts to this complete stranger. Why? Because he'd wedged himself in an ice machine? Because he reminded me of a squat, bald Lou Costello? "But I want to get back to it. If you care for the truth, I want to quit this line as soon as I can and head back to New York."

"You're young. Why not?"

I didn't need any human gumdrop telling me I was young and I should shirk my responsibilities to follow a dream. I'm no dolt. "I got a few tunes to send up there. If I can get somebody interested." I deliberately trailed off, trying to kill the discussion.

It seemed to have worked. Charlie Ranagan leaned to his right and yanked his billfold from a back pants pocket. He counted out six dollar bills, placed two quarters on top, and slid out of the booth. Then he showed me a little picture of the woman he called "the new wife," a handsome enough creature if you're looking to marry a football player. "Time to hit the road if we're going to make any money," he said. In the parking lot he reached out a hand for me to shake. "What did you say that song of yours was? The prizewinner?"

"So the kid's band is playing it," Ranagan said the next time I saw him. We were in the lobby of a Holiday Inn in Daytona, nearly a month since the incident with the ice machine. "'Moonlight in Brooklyn.' Says it has girls swooning."

"I don't follow. What kid?"

"My nephew. Didn't I tell you?" Ranagan dropped his suitcase so that he could mime playing a guitar. "He's in one of those rock 'n' roll bands. Little Maxie Felt?"

"Max Felt?" I said. "The crooner in the sweaters? 'Blue Acapulco Dreams'? I thought that kid was through."

But as Charlie Ranagan slapped his knee laughing, the more important question hit me.

"Max Felt's your nephew? The kid that sang 'Icing on the Cake'?" I was a little humbled, if you have to know. A little humbled and then again a little miffed. That kid's music wasn't really my cup of tea.

"Sheesh," Ranagan said. "I can't believe I didn't tell you about him. He's only my favorite nephew. Real swell kid."

But here's the thing in case you missed it, as I did. The trap was set. From here on it would be Max at every step of the way, crumpling up my old life, opening up possibilities I never would have had, and yeah, of course, all that would happen in

159

that damned warehouse, all the human toll of a man allowed to lead others without any check on his wants, all that I did to make it happen. My tremendous and sleepless guilt.

We agreed to meet for a drink in the cocktail lounge down the street. I beat him there because I wasn't looking forward to rekindling our passing friendship and thought a belt or two would at least make it tolerable. The place had a stage with the lights on in the corner, a record player seated on a wooden chair just like those at every table. A real high-class joint, in other words. Christmas lights hanging from the bar. A couple of pale-looking young women in bright-colored skirts who may or may not have worked for the lounge stood chatting at the far end of the bar top, filling up an ashtray as they complained about men. The bartender wore a paper hat like a short-order cook and kept giving me the eye and looking over toward the women, from me to the women like that, as if I were missing the point. From the record player came the voice of Gladys Knight, tinny and distant without amplification. The other fellows around looked about like you'd imagine, old dusty-shouldered drunks out of Central Casting.

Luckily I brought a copy of Turgenev's *Fathers and Sons*, translated by Constance Garnett, a book I would eventually buy at my employee's discount. I kept my nose aimed at the book as best I could. By the time Ranagan arrived I was getting tight, and Arkady and Bazarov had just met Madame Odintsova, and the Gladys Knight record had been turned three times. "So my nephew," Ranagan shouted before he even reached the bar. "I can't believe I didn't bend your ear about him already."

And so he did. He told me a story I would return to again

and again over the years, about a kittenishly shy and mesmerizingly bright kid, beloved by everyone, a stamp collector and avid reader of *Popular Mechanics*, with a good sense of humor, a fan of the Marx Brothers movies he'd seen on television and even more of Sid Caesar, who was his personal hero, a kid who worked part time at the little grocery on Main Street of some ideal Long Island suburb, a kid with a passion for science, a fun kid who liked rock 'n' roll and monster movies and ice cream sundaes, a kid as innocent and trustworthy as anything America had yet made. A kid who loved his sister, oh, his poor sister, Charlie didn't want to talk about the sister. He wiped a tear from his eye. "What they did to her," he said. "I should have done something. I should've kept her safe."

I was a little tipsy, as I said, a little off-balance. "What are you on about now?" I asked him. "What's this with the sister?"

He blew his nose like a character out of a newspaper cartoon, the handkerchief fluttering, a great honk bleating from his sinuses. "I said I didn't want to talk about her."

"Okay," I said, and later, years later, I would hear about this sister. Max in his amphetamine stage would rock in a chair gripping at his knees and clenching his jaw, the story of his little sister murdered in some unspeakable riot escaping the narrow space between his teeth like a leak. He had seen who did it, he always said, and kept the man's blood relation close to him, whatever in hell that was supposed to mean. His eyes then would be wild and he'd say how he wanted to finish the work of a robe-wearing kook with no hair that I just had to meet, a real genius apparently, gifted with visions from outer space. Of course I did meet that kook, and didn't believe a syllable out of his beatific face. He'd come to the warehouse in its heyday just like everyone: Tzadi Sophit. A sort of guru to Max, someone connected to what happened to the sister, maybe someone else to blame for all this.

Ranagan smiled at me like I'd forgiven him for whatever happened to this sister, like I was Peter giving him a thumbs-up at the pearly gates. "But Maxie's a heck of a kid," he went on. "You'd love him. Everybody loves him."

I pictured Max as something out of *Father Knows Best,* an aw-shucks type from a distant but also recent past with a sling-shot in his back pocket and a math textbook open in his hands, your general future-of-the-country type. In fact, Ranagan's portrait was filled with such electricity that it had a patriotic glow to it, like this kid, this Maxie, was the hope of his country-men. I'm almost positive that somewhere in my imagination I could see a flag whipping at the breeze.

Even later, when I knew the kid, or rather the man, all too well, when things got fully out of hand and he downright frightened me, I would seek out this early draft of him, try to project the innocent back onto him, look deeply into his eyes for some semblance of his uncle's beloved nephew. He would tell me how the whole idea for his warehouse had come from that more innocent time, when he'd seen how a single man had created a reality around himself to challenge the status quo, had made a different truth. But the real truth, he would say, was simple. I would ignore, then, how we were all con-nected to one sweep of badness and go instead to a dreamed-up picture rattled off by a sad, alcoholic insurance salesman, hold-ing it to me like a talisman.

In the long run, I have to say this was my mistake.

"So the kid has a band. Can you believe it?"

We were on our second round. I was munching peanuts and trying to sort out the least offensive way to extricate myself. Without knowing Max or what he would become, I didn't find this stroll through the family picture album to be particularly enthralling. The kid had a couple of hits a few years ago, slow-dancing numbers for the homecoming set. For all I knew, he was finished. The natural thing was to get a laugh and then call for my tab while spirits were high. "That's something," I said. "Now just tell him he owes me royalties on that song."

Ranagan laughed, sipped at his drink, and laughed again. One of those lurched-forward, shoulder-shaking laughs. Then he said, "You serious?"

I had my hand up for the bartender like a schoolchild. "Nah. Kidding you, Ranagan. I wish him and his band luck."

"They're playing small clubs and such," he said, still hunched over and smiling. "What I hear from his mother, they have their own recording studio in Manhattan, this empty warehouse, a place he bought with all that 'Blue Acapulco' money."

"Well, if he gets paid," I said, trying to keep up the joke in time to hook that bartender, "you tell him he's got to give me a cut."

Ranagan laughed once more, then didn't. "You're serious. You're really serious."

"Nah."

"You are."

I slapped Ranagan on the back and stood from the bar. The next morning I was off for Jacksonville and home and family. The thought of seeing Pat and Jenny, and yes, even Irene, filled me with a warmth toward humanity I hadn't quite expected to feel. It reminded me of a connection I'd felt, only briefly, with

Ranagan's story of his perfect nephew. "So he likes the song, huh?" I asked. "And the kids dig it?"

"They love it," he said. But he looked stricken, frightened. "He couldn't believe you were a friend of mine."

I set down my cash and gave the egg-shaped man another pat on the back. "That is hard to believe," I told him. "But tell him I said hey."

It must have been a month, month and a half later when I received the letter. *Dear Mr. Michaels*, it began. *My name is Maxwell Feldberg and you know my uncle.*

> *I wanted to write you because I found your song on sheet music at the Kleinhorn Music Shop on Broadway Avenue in Manhattan, New York. My new band, the Jet Clique, learned the song in my building and played it as part of our set at our first show earlier this year in a New Jersey nightclub. I changed the instrumentation to electric guitar, electric bass, and trap drum set, as those are the instruments we have and know how to play. We played this song in Jersey, as I said, and it was well received, and so we made it part of our set and have since played it in Cincinnati, Baltimore, and here in New York. I would like permission to play the song again in future sets and to inquire about rights to record it on our forthcoming album.*

> *I have enclosed with this letter a fifty-dollar bill, exactly ten percent of my take from this year's performances thus far. As we are just getting started and I am trying to shed my earlier fame as a solo act, we do not yet make a great deal of money on our*

shows. This may change with the album. Please let me know if this is an acceptable payment for royalties in the meantime.

I would also like to know if you have any other songs that would be good for our band. Thank you and I hope to meet you in person someday soon.

Sincerely,

Maxwell R. Feldberg

That was it, word for word. I'm only leaving out the address and phone number so his obsessive fans don't start hassling the strangers who now live there. I'd saved the letter first because it was comical and later because it came to signify the turning point in my life, which followed soon after. The young Mr. Feldberg's handwriting was impeccable. Each letter was fully formed in a smooth cursive and leaned elegantly rightward, with carefully matched flourishes at tails and points. Before I could even make sense of the message I first had to make sense of the script, which, in its aesthetic perfection, was like watching a futuristic machine dance the ballet from *Swan Lake*. Its precision, I determined after reading the signature, had to have been helped along by someone with an eye for detail, a feminine someone, I imagined, but not a manager. No manager would ever send such a junk letter, no matter how good the handwriting.

"Look," said Irene. She was dressed in her orange party dress, her hair back in a black kerchief. We had been on our way out the door. "You dropped some money."

At my feet lay the fifty-dollar bill, exactly ten percent of

Maxwell R. Feldberg's payment from some unnamed number of performances with a band nobody had heard of, a band led by what I could picture then only as a slighter, more sugary Bobby Darin. I didn't crouch to pick up the bill in any hurry. Apparently my face must have betrayed some deep confusion.

"What?" said Irene. "What's the matter?"

"Nothing."

She squinted. "Well, what is it?"

It wasn't that I had anything to hide from her. It's just that getting a fifty-dollar bill for royalties from a pop singer I didn't know living a thousand miles away was something of a shock, especially for a book salesman whose songwriting days had otherwise slipped into his past. Mechanisms in my head had to recalibrate. My throat, also, felt the need to swallow numerous times before I could work anything out in the way of words. A faint buzz called my ears.

These weren't inner workings Irene had any privy to, so it was no wonder she leaned over, snatched up the bill, and placed it firmly—accusatorially—in my palm. "You don't have to go and lie to me, Skip. For god's sake. Is it for work? If it's for work, just say it."

Like I said, we were on our way out. On our way to meet Pat and Jenny at McKinley's, this fancy surf-and-turf place downtown, in fact, and not just for dinner, either. Irene had been talking with Jenny about us investing in one of their car washes. We would be partners, in a sense. So dinner had an added bit of stress hanging over it. Especially, I think, for Irene. She'd been talking about getting me out of sales for a while now, and had let herself be convinced the car wash business was just the thing for our future.

"It's for work," I said.

She turned for the door. "You're lying. I know when you're lying, Skip, and you're lying."

I stood in the doorway holding the crumpled bill.

From the sidewalk outside she said, "Why tonight? is all I ask you. Why tonight?"

This was in front of the wide-eyed babysitter, who had seen enough of our fighting to know better than we did, I imagine, just where our marriage was going.

McKinley's faced the street, with a modernist exterior of concrete-block powder-blue walls. Its sign had a swordfish stabbed through a T-bone steak above big red lettering reminding customers that the back patio was available for party reservations. At the door a man in a tuxedo greeted you from behind a glossy black stand. The staff wore little tux jackets straight out of Bugs Bunny. Classy stuff for Jacksonville, and we liked it. Pat and Jenny sat at the semicircular bar in the back corner. They weren't too uptight not to shout over the heads of diners when they saw us. We held drinks, martinis, hovering beside them on foot, talking weather and sports, until a waiter glided past asking us to follow him to our table.

Once seated, the small talk ended. "I'd like to propose a toast," Irene started in. "To good company and to a growing business."

"Irene," I said.

But Jenny wasn't embarrassed. Her eyes glinted happily in the yellowy light raining down on us from a sculptural chandelier. "To us," she said. "To all of us."

We clinked our glasses together. Irene's had only a thumbnail-sized slosh left. She tipped it back and flagged the waiter in one graceful maneuver. Pat leaned heavily on the table with both elbows. "I've got this round," he said. Then he made a circle with his finger. "One more for everybody. On me."

So we were tipsy when the details of the transaction passed, and to make matters worse, we were interrupted twice by the waiter, understandably trying to take our order. When he returned a third time Pat said we should all just decide right now, and the poor man had to stand there biting at his lip while we oohed and aahed over the menu. Once we'd finished with that bit of discomfort, another round was ordered, this time by Irene. I tried giving her the "let's not" eyes, but she wasn't looking. "How soon can we break ground?" she asked.

Irene was a short woman, round in the face but with a rather slim figure, with farm-girl cheeks that were often blushing. She didn't even have to be embarrassed for them to flare right up, red as roses. When she got excited, she talked in a rapid and unnatural style reminiscent of Shirley MacLaine. At times she got so excited she would have to go be alone and cry. I never understood these bouts; they weren't necessarily tied to the reception of bad news. As I watched her take charge of the discussion, as I began to realize I had very little interest in its outcome, I felt distinctly worried that she would reach that pitch of excitement which clearly hurt her. This wasn't out of shame, but pity. I hated the thought of her being hurt for any reason. I was never cold.

But I knew then, even in this sharp moment of empathy, that this whole idea with the car wash wasn't for me. I'd been trying for weeks to get myself behind it. I knew she needed something, wanted something, and that she never had been comfortable in the role of a housewife. She was too big a personality. She had her own prerogatives. I'm pretty sure that's one of the reasons I was attracted to her in the first place. But the idea of being tied down to Florida with a commercial property nearly made my heart stop. Hell, even our house was a rental. To own, and to own a place of business—this meant sticking it out. It meant something more than sticking it out. To me, it meant surrendering.

After all, today I had received that stupid letter from Charlie Ranagan's favorite nephew. And though I knew it would sound foolish if I said it out loud, I felt suddenly that this kid knew me in a way I'd forgotten to know myself.

Imagine! A grown man with a family being swayed back toward his childish dreams by a teenybopper he'd never met sending him a fifty-dollar bill. Maybe it was that Max's letter reminded me of the letters I'd sent in my own youth to Tommy Dorsey, Kay Kyser, and Glenn Miller. Only Kyser ever responded, and he sent a signed photograph with a short note: *Hiya, Skip. Make every day a song.* I couldn't tell at the time if this was advice or not. But I determined it was the Yiddish backward grammar I'd heard from radio comedians, and what the bandleader was telling me was to write a new song every single day. So I tried this. I churned out song lyrics on everything around me: erasers, sparrows, falling leaves, tape measures, pots and pans, my father's Chevrolet, the cracks in the sidewalk in our neighborhood, the fall of China to the communists. Each one a love song. They were miserable, but good practice. Still, what I'd wanted was a leg up, some advice, a little guidance into the songwriter's life. What did a dull boy from Harrisburg, Pennsylvania, know about being a song-writer? It was all I could do to try to rhyme words and think about holding a girl in my arms at the same time. Even with all the hormones coursing through my veins, I knew this wouldn't be enough. But how I tried.

Now this kid nearly twenty years later was sending me a fifty in the mail because he played a song of mine he must have found in the dusty back bins of the music shop, probably something the owner didn't even recognize. *"Moonlight in Brooklyn"? "Moonlight in Brooklyn"? I don't know, kid. Maybe a dime? Fifteen cents.*

At the table I tried my best to come off as a man with an interest in what was being discussed. I nodded, *uh-huh*ed, went through the motions. At some point it became clear that every red cent of the savings I'd built up in ten years humping books up and down the state was about to get sunk into soap and water hoses on the west side of Tallahassee, that we'd see only half the profits from the venture, and that we'd never in our lives walk away from this swampy southern hell, and with a single jerk I stood up and said simply, "No."

"Skip," Irene said, her face apple-red in an instant, her hands splayed out flat on the table like she was surrendering to a stickup artist. "Sit down."

I looked at Pat and Jenny. They'd gone slack. "Forget it," I told them. "The Michaels don't wash cars. Got it?" And here I rapped my knuckles on the table like something I'd seen in a movie. I felt for the life of me like a youth movement leader, like I was standing up to the war machine, like I was about to burn a draft card. "The Michaels. Don't. Wash. Cars."

Pat stood, too, I guess to be on my level. "Skip, let's talk this over."

But I had already decided. "Forget this harebrained nonsense. I won't do it."

There's more to it, of course, more to that night, more to the dinner even. Somehow our food arrived and we all actually tried to eat, though all I remember was pushing steak and potatoes around while Irene took turns grinding a heel into my foot and whispering curse words at my shoulder. And there was more to our argument, a rager in the car on the way home and then a blowout once we'd paid the babysitter and sent her on her way. Dishes were broken. Irene threw my best suit out onto the lawn, and when that didn't seem like enough, went outside and jumped up and down on it like she was killing a snake. I slept on the couch that night and in the morning had to hit the road again anyway. I kissed the kids. I told Irene I still loved her.

But really I'd made a decision, and it was one about as big as any other in my life. Later, after what happened in the warehouse with Max, I would blame myself, sure, and I would look back on my decision to leave Irene and the kids and see that I'd hurt them beyond repair and that the only good I'd made was more hurt. Some would say more hurt and a few albums that changed the course of pop music forever, but more hurt nonetheless. Max's plan for a world without moralists breathing down your neck sounded good to a lot of folks for a little while. And what could I know then? Not even this much. I was a man possessed. And like anyone, when I saw the trail of my failures, I did all I could to right things. At least I did some.

I drove to the interstate and headed north. I took things slow. I drove three days, really seeing the country, but I had a purpose, a clear goal. I wasn't going to accept anything but a yes. At the end of three days I was back in New York, back in the town that was supposed to have made me a success in the first place, tapping on the metal door of a big nondescript brick building south of Houston, the address Max Felt had written on his letter.

A young woman answered after a few minutes. She was dressed in a black turtleneck and tight black pants, her long hair in two loose pigtails, her Latin features hogged up by the biggest pair of spectacles I'd ever seen. Spectacles tinted a goldish red, like a setting sun. Her feet were bare. "Yeah?"

Here I was in my horn-rimmed glasses, my gray flannel suit, my checked tie, my hair cut like a Marine's, suddenly aware of the fact that I must look like a square citizen standing in line to meet Barry Goldwater, while the young woman at the door had walked out of a nervy French film. "I'm looking for Max," I said. "Maxwell Feldberg?"

She set one of her feet on top of the other and leaned into the jamb, then looked up at me and said, "What? Are you from the IRS or something?"

I introduced myself, but when I extended my hand, she didn't reach for it. Instead she said listlessly that she'd heard of me and that Max was inside. So I followed. "What is this place?" I said. "Some kind of warehouse?"

"Used to be," she said. Then a little girl maybe two or three years old appeared at her side, a little munchkin, her face jerking out of its playful smile into a wide-eyed shyness. She hid herself against the young woman's thigh. Her hands were noticeably dirty. "We threw out all these ancient sewing machines," the young woman went on, as if nothing had happened. "Now it's just where the band plays."

She led me down a narrow dusty hallway with high ceilings and a row of yellowed windows at about the level of a second story. I could hear now the sound of an electric guitar doodling around with scales. Then came a long uncertain creak from a cello. "Ah," I said. "I hear them now."

"Of course we live here too," she said, about as disinterested in her own words as she could get without just not saying them. "Are you a fan of the Jet Clique?"

"Not sure."

We came to the end of the hall, where she pushed a heavy door opening onto the wide, high-ceilinged space of an old warehouse floor. Here and there chains still hung from crossbeams. The cement floor was pocked with black squares that must have been left behind by old machines or storage pallets. In the far back corner was a glassed-in office, the foreman's, and in there stood four hazy figures, the band. "I think they're changing the name," she said. "Something peppier. Or darker. One or the other."

Her name was Rebecca Vasquez. Her parents were Mexican by way of California, and she'd first known Max on Long Island, in that town where his sister had been murdered, where she'd lived only a very short time. And this little girl hiding her face, clinging to her leg, was their daughter, Debbie, named after Max's late sister. These two would matter to me, later. I'd learn through them that I had the capability to put everything on the line, to put others ahead of myself. I'd bring down this whole warehouse and all it had become to save them.

"We met again after 'Cuddle Me Girl,'" she said as we crossed the wide empty warehouse floor, the band making more and more noise. "Then he wrote 'Blue Acapulco Dreams' for me. He told me all about the shock therapy then. You know his parents are just monsters. They were trying to control his career."

"What shock therapy?" I said.

But she ignored me and reached for the office door. "That's why I told him to quit the Max Felt act and start a band."

The band, it must be said, looked nothing like the bands of that year. They had none of the Sgt. Pepper's marching-band-on-a-drunk look, none of the Indian thing all the hippie groups were doing, none of that earthy Dylan vibe. Instead they were dressed in matching black T-shirts and pants, Italian boots, black sunglasses—modeled, I would eventually learn, after the Velvet Underground, a band they rejected later that year when its singer cursed Max out in a radio interview, calling him nothing but a leech without a personality of his own. For now they all had short hair. One of them, a girl, had shaved her head to look like the friar from Robin Hood. And Max, who glared at me hatefully from a stool with his guitar, wore a dog collar around his neck and a pricey silver watch on his right wrist. Nobody could have known then that he was a genius. "Who the fuck is this, Becky?"

The little girl, Debbie, squealing in mock terror, went running back across the wide empty warehouse floor, waving her hands in the air. In just about any other scenario this would have been cute. All that would happen here seemed to already leak from the walls. This would be his pleasure dome, and I would be the crier announcing his decree.

Rebecca gestured at me. "Somebody," she said. "I forgot his name. You know him."

So I strode in, with no knowledge of the future, offering again my salesman's hand. I'd been planning what I'd say all the way up the coast, and only my delirium and the fact that I'd thrown out my family and career to say it kept me from thinking it was foolish.

"Skip Michaels," I said. "I'm here to make this band a success."

LISTEN UP

ALICE LINWOOD—1972

Alice "Listen Up, People" Linwood. That was her, on the poster wheat-pasted to the radio station's stucco walls, facing all of Phoenix and America, her hexagonal glasses and the little chain Jeff bought for her years ago, now dangling loose behind her ears, under the wool helmet of her hair. If she'd known they were going to use that picture, she would have taken off her glasses, would have smiled. She would, for heaven's sake, have gotten a new perm. She looked like someone's crazed grandmother.

But that nickname of hers, that catchphrase. It was something, wasn't it? Emblazoned there in a tilted cursive between her name and the one she'd taken for marrying Jeff a lifetime ago. She'd been a different woman then, as different as she'd been playing dolls with Suzanne back in Minneapolis. Now she was the hottest radio personality in the counterculture, according to the station manager, Grant, who only a year ago had laughed at her idea until he sat up with a jolt, the epiphany of ad revenue lighting up his eyes. The hottest radio personality, and at forty-eight years old, no less. A housewife. Two kids in college. She'd been at this six months, talking JFK and RFK and what Kissinger was really up to in Vietnam and the FBI's war on freedom and all the dirty laundry Nixon had ever tried to hide away when the bell struck: the story to end all stories, the most brazen conspiracy in American history, the break-in at the Watergate Hotel.

Since then Grant, with his horsehair mustache and his perpetually stained mug of coffee, had put her on twice a week. Now not only did she have her regular Sunday-night show, *Listen Up with Alice Linwood,* but a call-in program Wednesday afternoons; "Watergate Wednesdays," Grant called them, officially dubbed *Alice Linwood Live.* And both shows had been picked up in L.A. and San Francisco and Denver and the Sunday-night show all the way in New York as of last week. To think her voice—her mousy mom voice—was being heard across the country. Even celebrities were talking about her— well, one celebrity, but it was that handsome Warren Beatty, and on *The Dick Cavett Show,* no less. "Everybody should listen to her," he'd said. "She's onto something."

When Jeff heard about that, when he came home from the bowling alley and shrugged off his jacket, he said, "So you're leaving me for movie stars next?"

Jeff.

The kids, Anna and Mike, seemed embarrassed their mother was getting any attention. They wanted to know where she got her information. They wanted her to stop saying such nutty things on the radio. They wanted, really, for her to go back to stirring brownie mix in the big yellow Pyrex bowl, to spreading ketchup on meatloaf, to pushing around a vacuum. "If the president wanted to steal information from the Democrats," Anna had said over the phone just this morning. "Oh, never mind, Mom. Never mind."

Now when they came to town for Thanksgiving she planned

to drive them by the station to see this very poster, with her face eight feet tall, no less. "Look, kids, there's your mother," she planned to say, and they would groan and sigh from the back seat like she'd asked if they wanted to go to the antiques store.

She'd known the minute she saw the Watergate news on Cronkite. Known immediately that this was the turning point, the hinge. She could feel it like she felt the memories of her past lives. All that had been going on in this country since Eden Gardens, since the assassination in Dallas, since MLK, all the shadow government's little and big lies, they were aimed at this single target, getting the country to this very point, where an election could be stolen and all of it could be hushed up and then what? Martial law? The mass locking-up of any citizen unhappy with the way the war in Southeast Asia was being conducted? More civil rights leaders gunned down in the streets? More CIA-led "riots" in Watts and on college campuses? And then of course the final move, the one she knew would be coming on the other end of the hinge, something only someone as evil as Nixon and his CIA cronies and big-oil puppet masters could plan for—a populace completely under their control, a country of walking potatoes.

This was it. This was the only time to strike. The last gasp to get the truth out there before it was all replaced by double-speak and flag-waving. Listen up, people.

The surprising thing—although not that surprising, or, okay, a little bit surprising—was that so many out there wanted to hear what she had to say. Not only wanted to hear it but believed her, had actually been thinking the same thing. How many of them had started thinking about these dark connections, these unexplainable phenomena, these assassinations and lies and disappearances, but at some point had shrugged, had said they understood enough, or even worse, had feared for what they would understand? For a long time it was better for everyone, she thought, or at least more comfortable, just to try to ignore what we all sort of knew was going on around us, that fear of a Big Lie working on us every day. But things had changed. People wanted to listen up. They wanted to hear and they'd had enough.

"Well, I'm glad you're getting it off your chest," Jeff told her a few weeks ago. "Just don't go so hard on Nixon, okay? Some of the guys at work—"

"Nixon's the architect, dear," she'd said. They were sitting in the living room with TV dinners, *Mary Tyler Moore* just coming on. "I've told you a million times it all goes back to Nixon. At Eden Gardens, that was all Nixon. And John Kennedy? I never believed Johnson—"

"Nobody's saying LBJ killed Kennedy."

"Plenty are saying it," she said. "On Wednesdays I get half a dozen calls—"

"Nobody's saying that."

She cut a bite of turkey roast and dipped it in the little square of gravy. "Plenty," she said. "And my information points to Nixon. He wanted Kennedy out of the way so that—"

"Okay," Jeff said. "All right. Can we watch the show?"

He was like that now, Jeff. Ready to skate off into old age. Nothing like how he'd been when they were young, when they had ideals, or rather when they shared ideals. If she'd changed, it was the fire in her growing brighter. Jeff had spent the years since they moved to Phoenix doing all he could to snuff his out.

Sometimes she thought they'd already gotten to him.

His eyes now always aimed straight ahead, shielded a little by his wincing brow. Even in the days when she knew there were other women, he would at least look her in the eye when they spoke. Now that happened only when he left for work in the morning, giving her that sad look like she was a stranger, her on the recliner with the coffee table pulled close and all her papers, all her letters and manuscripts, the phone already ringing at her elbow. "Have a good day," he'd say. And then not look at her again, not really look at her, unless he was a little tipsy, home from the bowling alley or a late meeting, laughing about coworkers she'd never met in person.

To think of who they were in the beginning, a handsome young couple in sweater vests, at Yale and Vassar respectively, courting and then necking and then that summer suddenly rushing into marriage, the wedding on a little island in the James River in Richmond, Virginia, near where his family still lived, and back to school a married couple. She'd finished only one more semester of her English degree, and even though it broke Professor Ronkowski's heart, she'd stayed home to wait on their first child, all the misery of being pregnant, all those long days stuck in the apartment desperate for a little more space and his coming home in the evening to study or staying out all night, and even if he was always such a sweetheart, she already knew there were other girls. Girls whose attention he wanted. Girls whom she hoped he didn't go far with, maybe just a smile or even a kiss—after all, what does a kiss hurt?— but still, the other girls. Their names accidentally mentioned.

Her friends reporting back about his talking at the grocery store or a coffee shop, or flirting with others in class. She was already changing then, becoming the housewife, the full character of Alice Linwood that someone else, not even Jeff, had written. Her body changing around her, widening, like an item of clothing she didn't recall buying. Soon Jeff graduated, and with his engineering degree took a job in San Diego, halfway around the world to her, and in the Oldsmobile with everything they owned piled alongside them and baby Anna in her arms and Mike on the way they had driven across the great country in five days, seeing what sights they could, over mountains and plains and deserts and mountains again.

She had loved his restlessness, his caffeinated explosiveness. To know Jeff in those early years was to feel always swept up in something, always looking over the next horizon. He had a way about him that excited his coworkers, their neighbors, even the few friends she'd made after uprooting and settling. Janie from down the street told her once, maybe a little drunk, "You're lucky, Alice. I'd follow that man off a cliff." Forever there was something more to be done, and when people were around Jeff, they thought it could be. Impossibilities appeared to be right around the corner. She told him once in their garage as he changed a spark plug, rambling as he did about fixing segregation by making every American citizen go out into the street each day and shake hands, that he ought to run for governor. He'd given her a look like she'd said they were eating raw alligator for dinner. "That's a hell of a job," he said, and wiped oil on his new trousers. "No thanks."

It was Jeff who discovered the Sophit. Ran across one of his pamphlets in a bookstore downtown where she knew a pretty brunette with a pug nose worked the front desk, and came home not only with the pamphlet but also a little telescope he'd purchased from a hobby shop, claiming that the skies were full of other beings, sentient creatures with intelligence greater than ours, and that if we were to contact them, we, too, would have their intelligence. "He's right up the coast," he said. "Says here we're welcome to visit anytime."

Even twenty years later she could remember the squinty light in his eyes. He was so excited that really she had nothing to do but say yes, even if it did seem strange, and by the following weekend they were loaded up, all four of them now, on their way to a beachside town known only for horse racing. There, near the beach, they parked next to a big tin warehouse with faded lettering and some old wartime use. A hand-painted sign reading LOOK TO THE STARS invited them inside, and for the first time she had doubts.

"It doesn't look on the level," she'd said.

His arms crossed over the wheel, Jeff squinted. She could tell that he, too, wasn't feeling altogether great about this idea. "We'll just go in and see," he said. "Half an hour."

A little farther up the road shone a roadside diner with chrome trim and windows that slanted forward, reflecting a bright skirt onto the parking lot. "I'll take the kids in there," she said. "For lunch. You can meet us after."

He was angry now, that vein in his forehead bulging. She knew in a moment this would boil over and he would say "Alice" in that tone of voice that meant she would have to do what he said, not because of any threat of malice but only out of guilt, out of some unspoken or perhaps too-spoken obligation. Her duty as a wife. "Alice," he would say. And then, up a register but with a note of sadness, "Alice."

And so rather than wait for this chain of events she gathered Anna up from the floorboard where she'd been playing with her wooden horse and opened the door and said to her, "Come on, honey, we're going inside."

Of course inside were all those beautiful people of every skin tone and age all in flowing white gowns and candles hanging from the ceiling and a lilting, haunting form of music she'd never heard before, humming from their smiling lips and accompanied by an organ in the corner, where a very old man met eyes with them, glimmering and hopeful. She would learn his name later as Saul, and the woman who came to them with gowns, even for the children, as Eileen, and the towering man who appeared at the end of the song in a green gown and no hair at all even where his eyebrows should have been as the Tzadi Sophit, a sort of prophet, a man said to have communicated with beings from another solar system.

Even as all this was happening, as they stumbled through their first visit and talked into the night for weeks about *The Vision at Mount Shasta,* the book the Sophit had given them, about the Seekers, about their belief in a better, more equitable world where human beings were judged entirely by the good they brought their fellow man, where all the divisions of race and class and even sex would disappear, labeled as logical fallacies, unnecessary—according to the Sophit's knowledge—to the beings in all solar systems but our own. To think of it now. Building a better world because of UFOs! She hadn't been so sure. Even after meeting the Seekers and finding them lovely and yes, of course yes, agreeing with the effects of their philosophy, she couldn't at first take that extra step of believing in people from other planets skimming the night sky looking to solve our ancient problems of blood and kin. No, she told Jeff, it was too much. Weren't there other ways to go about it? A church? A letter-writing campaign? A volunteer organization? Why, her very own sister spent her Sundays in a Buffalo soup kitchen for no other reason than to help the needy. They could do something like that, couldn't they?

And, stretched out in his blue pajamas, with his hands clasped together over his chest, he'd said, "Alice."

Funny thing was she started to believe. Belief, she liked to say later, infected her. At first it didn't matter what the root of the issue was, whether the Sophit's ideas came from alien beings or Moses or Dwight D. Eisenhower. What mattered was the end product. Well, that and what lay in between: the long days visiting their new friends in Del Mar, long days that became weekends sleeping on cots with the kids wrapped up in sleeping bags, weekends that became week-long and two-week-long visits with Jeff driving back and forth to work, and finally just life with the Seekers. After that slob at the diner called the police on them one night, they'd all moved together into the desert, to a ranch outside Palm Springs. Those had been the days of light and hope. By the time Jeff volunteered to act as the Sophit's advance guard in Long Island, by the time they'd agreed to move as a family all the way to a suburb called Ridge Landing, she was a true believer, watching the skies, waiting for the moment when she, too, like the Sophit and a handful of others, would be contacted, perhaps even chosen as one of the select few to board one of their ships and see the universe outside this small planet.

The adjustment to suburban life after living in such close quarters with her fellow Seekers had been a shock. Even the children, Anna school age and Mike ready to begin, cried miserably in the new house. They hated Long Island, hated the cold, hated the wide fenceless yards, hated the now-strange whiteness of the people there, that off-kilter awareness that simply by living in a place they'd joined an exclusive club that they'd never wanted to be members of. But they were in contact with Eileen and the Sophit, and their letters often included crayon-drawn pictures and notes from Mike's and Anna's friends. And the work was important. A purchase of land was being made. Planning and construction. All without anyone finding out that Jeff was a part of it. They were tasked as a family, too, with softening the ground, with making manifest a general sense of racial harmony and progress. They held parties and coffee klatsches, went to town meetings, talked and talked like concerned average citizens hoping to change the minds of those around them. They even joined the Feldbergs' Human Relations group, meeting every other Tuesday evening to talk about justice and voting rights and desegregation.

The poor Feldbergs. Poor Deborah. That mob, their red faces and saliva, their bloodshot eyes. Like something out of a Frankenstein picture. They hadn't been there to kill a monster. They'd come to put down a whole town. And they had put it down, only a week after everyone had moved into their new homes. Like animals, all teeth and swinging arms, they killed that little girl and put a dozen others in the hospital. God, those poor Feldbergs. Little innocent Deborah, the smartest in her class, someone for Anna to look up to. And even the Feldbergs' son from what she knew had been in an institution, and now look at him, a drugged-out rock singer famously disappeared from public view. She'd seen his early success as a balance in the scale. But now she imagined Ira and Rose Feldberg alone, two decent people betrayed by the life they'd put so much effort into.

It wasn't just the child, though. There had been dear old Saul, one of the founders of the group, as close to the Sophit as Eileen. She had seen him in that electric terror, his face down in the shallow slushy water of that pond, still dressed in his ecclesiastical robe, a single arm bent back in a way that wasn't natural, unable to wrap her head around why he wasn't moving. And kneeling next to him, his jeans wet with snow and slush, the last person she would have expected. There, with tears streaming down his bony face, was Paul Penrod, that snake from uphill, for the life of him screaming out a curse to god and anyone else who would listen. Jeff had to pull her away from them by the arm. She had just frozen there, baffled.

After that, after the mob and the fires and the terrifying nightmare of those first days after Eden Gardens, Alice stopped believing. Stopped, and in doing so, forced Jeff's hand to also stop. He'd walked around for a week looking stunned and confused, unable to speak, the four of them in a cheap motel room with no changes of clothes and nothing to eat but sandwiches and a view of the rushing highway outside and not a word from the Sophit or anyone. Right there in front of the children she'd said, "Jeff, these people aren't coming for us.

Jeff, they lied. Jeff, there aren't any people in flying saucers at all. Don't you understand this is just real life and we're here and we've got to move on? Jeff, we've got to do something. We can't just wait."

Then came their stay in Buffalo with her sister and after that Brookline with Jeff's younger brother and later the job offer in Phoenix. As the weeks piled onto weeks and some semblance of a normal family's life was reconstituted, that stretch of time with the Seekers began to seem like a distant vacation or a long drunken jag or the story of some other people's lives they'd read about in *Life* magazine, and she'd put the faces and names involved away, jars in a cellar, best to be forgotten until necessary.

But a few years later on a sunny November afternoon the man on the radio interrupted her hanging the laundry to say that the president had been shot in Dallas, and after that, she was another person altogether.

She was, it seemed clear to her now, that image on the poster: a tough, smart, squint-eyed woman reaching deep into her middle age, with a voice and people who wanted to hear what she had to say. *Coast to coast,* they used to say. She had a voice that was coast to coast. In the station wagon, gazing through the windshield with the late-afternoon sun in her eyes, she felt powerful. The woman who could bring down a presidency. A dangerous woman.

She'd come by to look because Grant had called that morning to tell her the poster was being hung and because she was already headed across town to meet with one of her sources for the first time, a man she'd received letters from since 1965, since she published her first copy of *The Truth!*, her newsletter on the assassination and later on all things underhanded and illegal being done by the shadow government right behind the thin veil of official news. He was a high-level federal employee, the type of official whose skill and intelligence could be used in this department and then another as needed, and all along he'd known more about the shadow government's movements than anyone else who had sent her tips and leads over the years. And it was only to her that he had spoken about these issues, or written, his letters always on U.S. government letterhead, sometimes including grainy black-and-white photographic evidence or pages out of official paperwork, many lines marked out black and unreadable.

He'd signed his letters for a long time as Concerned Citizen—the first arriving out of the blue, addressed "Dear editor of *The Truth!*"—but on the day of Nixon's inauguration he'd written by hand to tell her that things would be worse than they appeared, that he would soon be in possession of knowledge that would put him in great jeopardy, and that while the natural thing to do would be to remain anonymous in such circumstances, he wanted someone to know who he was, to be able to find him, to understand what had happened to him if he went missing. His name was Gary Reynolds and he could be reached via post office box in Bethesda, Maryland. In the three and a half years since then, they had exchanged letters at least every couple of months, hers full of theories and interpretations, his full of new information. Nearly all of his notes pushed her onward, told her she was asking the right questions. Only now and again did he say that she was going in a wrong direction, did he correct her aim. Combined with all she was hearing from her other sources, he had become invaluable, the linchpin of what she presented in *The Truth!* and later on the radio.

Now, after a long silence, after ignoring three of her letters since the break-in, to think he was here *in person,* in Phoenix, with something urgent. He'd said as much over the phone late last night, ringing her at home somehow, saying that he was on the run, that he'd be in town for only twenty-four hours, could she meet him? And so a diner was chosen across town, frequented by Mexican workers, a shabby little place she'd only seen before from the street. Ten in the morning. Late enough for Jeff to be gone to work and early enough to avoid a crowd.

When she arrived at the stucco building she saw him through the wide glass window. A short, narrow-faced man with the mustache and chin beard of an old beatnik, his salt-and-pepper hair combed back tight and out of fashion, his eyes behind dark sunglasses. He didn't look at her until she had stepped out of the car and then only for a flash before hunching his shoulders and looking down at the table. Then she could see his deeply inset eyes, a familiar something to his face. *He is,* she thought, *shy. Or maybe just afraid.* Inside, she gestured to the waitress that she was here to meet the man huddled over his coffee in the corner, and as she neared him, she said his name very softly: "Gary?"

He looked up with a jerk. "Don't say that," he said. "No names."

"Then you know who I am?"

"Of course I do," he said, speaking in a sort of rasp. "Sit down."

It was all very clandestine, very much like she'd imagined such a meeting, though it surprised her anyway. Somehow she'd convinced herself overnight that they were simply old friends getting together for an early lunch, a chat, a little gossip. She slid into the booth opposite him. "Are you in a hurry?" she said.

He tilted his head up and squinted at her through those dark glasses. For a moment he looked half-familiar, or more than half-familiar, like a TV actor, nobody famous, just a man cramped behind a desk answering questions delivered by a more handsome and deep-voiced detective. "I have only an hour," he said. He looked to the side, into the rest of the café, where at the only other occupied table, the waitress poured coffee for two Chicana women in long dresses. "I have reason to believe they've tracked me down."

She thought for a moment he was talking about the women. "But you can talk?" she said. "Or should we go elsewhere?"

"This is good," he said. And then, absurdly, "Besides, I ordered the tuna fish sandwich."

From the kitchen she could faintly hear a radio playing: a man speaking rapidly in Spanish. When the waitress came by, she ordered only coffee with cream and sugar, and after this was delivered along with the tuna fish sandwich a minute or two later, Alice leaned forward and said, "What did you want to tell me? Is it about—"

His eyes stopped her. "The break-in?" he said. "Yes. But you've got to promise me you won't say anything about it. Not now. Not until I'm out of the country."

"You're leaving the country?"

"Yes," he said, and it seemed by the way he looked at his

sandwich that he'd lost his appetite. "You'll understand once I tell you. I've got no choice."

It occurred to her that since she'd arrived, her hands had been sweating, and this only furthered her sense of alarm. She hadn't even told Jeff she was meeting this man. This man was wanted by the government. What if they came here now, men in trim black suits, what if they appeared from the kitchen where they'd been waiting all along? What if two black cars squealed to a stop in the parking lot, blocking the exit? What if there was a gun trained on each of them now from across the street? She'd agreed to come here with a sense of relief, a sense—she hadn't wanted to admit to herself—of romance. Here was Gary Reynolds, in Phoenix, to see her. And like a daring wife in a French movie she'd dressed smartly, she'd worn lipstick, she'd left her glasses in the car.

She had to set all that aside. All her ridiculousness and all her fear. She owed it to her audience, she owed it to her countrymen, to tamp her damp palms on her skirt, to breathe easily, to take out her pen and pad. "Go ahead," she said. "Tell me."

What he told her was that the break-in was only a ruse, a cover-up that would warrant a greater cover-up, all to turn the attention of the press and the American people away from what was really going on. That, he said, was a conspiracy so unfathomable that even if a big newspaper saw the facts he'd seen, they wouldn't report it. Because Nixon was no longer president. He'd been replaced by an actor working for a secretive group founded by former leaders in the Nazi Party who had been carefully staging coups and clandestine takeovers of nations around the world, some of them masked as communist, such as in Cuba, and others as anti-imperial, such as the multiple countries in Africa now under their control. OPEC, Yugoslavia, the IRA, France under de Gaulle? This group had its hands in all of it, and now, as of exactly twenty-four hours before the faked arrest of the so-called Watergate burglars, they were in control of the executive branch of the U.S. government. With a bit of tuna fish sandwich half chewed in his mouth, he said, "I know because I was on the crack squad monitoring their activities. Watergate was the signal to their coconspirators. It's all in their playbook."

Alice sipped at her coffee. It had gone cold, and really, she'd stirred in too much sugar. She'd been listening in dreamlike terror to this ludicrous tale, delivered like a practiced speech. It was nonsense. He was lying. He hadn't even gotten the names of the burglars right, or the dates of events. He'd said three different times that the man at the head of this conspiracy was named Thurman Munson, who she knew from Jeff was the catcher for the New York Yankees.

Or maybe this Gary Reynolds wasn't necessarily lying but was simply a deeply troubled man. Suffering. A suffering and troubled man connecting dots in a child's comic book, his face behind the beard and mustache growing ever more familiar, a person she'd known, and this troubled her. Maybe she was meant to recognize him. Maybe at some point she'd known him in some passing way. She watched him eat, watched him swallow painfully, cough, take a drink of water. "And now you're here," she said finally. "You came to tell *me*."

She hadn't meant to emphasize the word *me*. Doing so made her seem frightened, she knew, and so knew, too, that she really *was* frightened.

"I left the minute I saw the story on television," he said. His face hadn't changed. He hadn't registered that she didn't believe him. "I've been hiding ever since. Town to town. You know the drill."

His performance, she thought now as he raised the other triangle of sandwich to his mouth, had been like a parody of her broadcast. A satirical cartoon. Was he making fun of her? Making fun of her listeners? But there was nothing funny about this man. Troubled, then. A sick man who had traveled all the way from Bethesda, Maryland, to meet with her here at this little diner where she knew nobody on a side of town she'd normally never be. And for years he had fed her information, sent her leads. Had he always been like this, so hard to believe?

Then another thought occurred to her. This might not be Gary Reynolds at all. He could be pretending. He could have intercepted one of Gary's letters. He could have been listening to the broadcast. He could have come from Nixon himself. She scrambled for something personal to ask him, something only he could answer. The cocker spaniel. "Did you bring your dog?"

His eyes softened. "Oh, Maryanne? She was ill. I didn't want to say anything in my last letter." He gazed out the window. "The vet thought it was time."

"I'm sorry," she said, guilty for asking. That was his dog's name. Still, she had to get away. "But I really should be going. I need to prepare for tonight's show."

And then he did it. He lunged and gripped her wrist across

the table. "You're not going to say anything about this, right? Not until I'm out of the country?"

In reaching for her, he'd dropped his sandwich on the table. It lay splayed open, tuna fish scattered next to her elbow. "Of course not," she said.

He kept their eyes locked another moment and then released her wrist. "Then I should go as well," he said, and slid out of the booth. He didn't reach for his wallet, didn't say anything more. He just turned toward the door and walked away. No goodbye, no wave, not another look. Just out the door, his eyes straight ahead. She craned around to watch him pass by the front window and disappear around the corner.

When the waitress asked suddenly if everything was all right, Alice jumped. The waitress was standing over the table now, appearing out of nowhere, glaring down at the dropped sandwich, no less. "Yes," Alice replied. "He just had to leave in a hurry."

In the station building, in the glass-walled conference room, Alice couldn't remember driving back across town. It was as if she'd reached into her purse with her hands shaking and counted out a few bills to pay for the food and coffee and then reappeared, genie-like, at the head of this narrow rectangular table, her papers and legal pads set out neatly before her. At her side, Grant sat with his arms crossed, his face mushed into a doubtful look. "Tell you the truth?" he said. "I don't believe half or more of what you say on this show. What I believe in is ad revenue. Market share. You've got something here and you can't drive it into the ditch now."

"But I can't trust him," she said.

Grant shrugged. "Then don't. But you've got a show in six hours and somebody's going to be answering those calls."

"I can't go on today. I don't know what's what anymore." Staring at her clasped hands, at the blue vein running along her thumb, she'd never felt more foolish. "Don't you see, Grant? He's been a source for years."

For the second time today a man put his hand on her wrist. This time she pulled away. Grant looked flustered by the reaction. "Look," he said. "Nixon's a son of a bitch. I don't like him. You don't like him. The goddamn listeners sure as hell don't like him. Nobody's going to make you say this bullshit you heard today. But you've got to say something. You've got to go on the air."

The idea of facing the microphone, of taking questions on live radio, today of all days, felt like an insurmountable challenge. How many of her theories had been informed directly by this Gary Reynolds? How much of her thinking had he infected? What she needed was to dig through all her notes and files, to compare what he'd told her with her other sources, to find out where along the line his input had turned her in a direction she wouldn't naturally have gone.

"When your government spins so many lies," she said, "what's even true?"

Grant grimaced at her. "What?"

"Confusion," she said. "Crossed wires. Maybe even some fiction. But what's under it?"

He seemed pleased by this set of words. "That's the old Alice," he said, pushing out his chair and standing. "Now you're talking some sense. The show must go on and all that."

She wasn't certain what he meant. "Grant," she said as he was about to leave the conference room, "I'll need to run home for my notes."

He didn't respond with any words, didn't even turn around. Instead he raised a fist in the air, black-power style, and left. A putz in a loud tie, his tan trousers frowning under love handles, a blackened diamond of sweat creasing the spine of his gray shirt. She watched him recede, his mind clearly having moved on to another subject, and said aloud to no one but herself, "I fucking quit."

Driving again across town, this time fully conscious, she could remember Gary Reynolds with a clarity she wasn't aware of at the time she was seated across from him. He'd said that he'd been on the run for what would amount to months, peripatetic and looking over his shoulder. Yet his suit and shirt were pressed and clean, his collar shiningly white, his narrow black tie uncreased. When he'd stood and walked past the short barstools in front of the café's kitchen, his wool trousers and wing-tip shoes looked like they had just been taken off a mannequin.

It was entirely possible that he'd packed and preserved this outfit during all his travels. And some men are careful with their garments, with the clean shave of their chin and neck, maintaining an overall appearance that could at no time warrant aspersions of their character. But in hindsight she saw that these details had unsettled her, and like a painting viewed in a museum and understood only on the second pass, the clean-cut neatness of this Gary Reynolds hinted at something theatrical, something fictive, a well-crafted scene that was at its heart only a scene.

Add to this the very nature of that scene, with its dialogue ripped directly from a detective movie, the absurd paranoia of his performance, the well-chosen setting meant to keep her back on her heels. Even his sudden departure felt calculated now, as a way to leave her gasping, on the hook for the bill, certain he was running from trouble.

She'd thought he looked familiar. Had even thought he could be an actor. But then she placed him. Or at least placed who he looked like. He looked—didn't he?—just like that man she'd seen kneeling next to Saul's body in the snow in the last moments before Jeff grabbed her hand and they took off running with the kids. Fifteen years ago. That little man, that so-and-so who was always with Rob Halford back in Ridge Landing, always trying to start something, always kicking up dust about the town's racial covenant. If you subtract the little beard and mustache, he had the bony face for him, if older, and he had the build, too. Short, thin, with narrow shoulders. The head just a little too big for that slight body, skull-like, all forehead and cheekbones, narrow as a trowel at the mouth.

She'd never seen Gary Reynolds and never asked the man at the diner for any sort of identification. She'd known him only because he looked nervous. A man in a suit at a diner. What if Gary Reynolds was still out there, or what if he had been arrested? What if that man at the diner really was an actor, a federal agent? And now—oh, *wait* a second here— what if Penrod from Ridge Landing was a federal agent? What if it was all connected, as she'd long suspected? What if it had never been about her meeting Gary Reynolds but instead about Nixon's men meeting her? Putting a face to her name, and to that a home, a car, parked and idling in the late-afternoon sun?

Pulled into her drive, she realized she might have been followed. They could be watching her this minute. They could be inside, waiting, black ski masks pulled down over their faces. One of them could be in the rhododendron there by the front door.

Alice, she thought. Jeff's voice was there in her head, as it had been for more than twenty years now. *Alice. You're getting away from yourself.*

Instinctually, she slid the transmission into reverse. She looked into the rearview. Just the shiny blacktop. She released the brake.

Her best girlfriend, Kathleen, cut hair weekdays in a converted double-wide trailer with a sign outside that read PAM'S FAMILY SALON. The Pam in question, Pam Doblin, had moved away three years ago, selling the place to Kathleen and three other women in equal shares. This basically meant they were free agents billed for upkeep and on the hook for a mortgage. If someone didn't show up, they didn't show up, but no profits were shared. "I'd say it's basically the definition of free enterprise," Kathleen had told her when she first signed on. "And it's not like I tell Uncle Sam about every strand of hair I cut."

But to Alice it always seemed like Kathleen was getting scammed, that she would have been better off in an establishment not her own. As soon as she opened the door, a diagonal of light stretched over Kathleen and the old woman whose gray hair she was curling, then shrunk back to a sliver at Alice's feet. Her old friend launched into a chattery complaint about having to fork over money for a new water heater for all four women to share—this after spending all her money on an unplanned trip to Vegas the weekend before last.

When the old woman went to rest her beady eyes under the dryer chair's plastic dome, Alice and Kathleen went out for a cigarette. "No," Alice said, waving off the cigarette itself, "I'm still quitting. But go ahead."

Kathleen lit her Pall Mall and blew a cone of smoke at the desert air. She'd left her apron on, tight over her heavy breasts, hairs glistening on its black surface like a carpet of slash marks. She was a tall woman, big-shouldered, always in makeup that would have terrified Alice to be seen in out in public. On Kathleen it looked good, made her seem like Ava Gardner in her heftier days, in *Night of the Iguana*. Or was that Elizabeth Taylor? She couldn't recall.

Alice told her everything. She always told her everything. And when she came to the part about how she thought this supposed Gary Reynolds was a fake meant to throw her off the scent, maybe even a guy from this town where she and Jeff used to live, Kathleen flicked the filter of her cigarette into the parking lot and said, "You need to sit down with this man and tell him how you really feel."

"I don't want to sleep with him, Kathleen."

"Who said that?"

"I mean I'm not attracted to him. I'm not interested in him like you said before."

Kathleen shook her head. "Girl, you need to get your head

out of the gutter." She jabbed Alice's arm with two fingers. "I mean push him a little. Find out if he's really on our side or one of Nixon's plumbers."

It's true that she could have been more forthright, less caught unawares. Thinking about that meeting at the diner, she saw herself as a starstruck kid, not at all the hard-hitting personality she played on the radio. Embarrassing. So she started to put together a line of questions in her head, visualizing herself at the microphone, the tape machine going. "Still," she said, "I don't even know where he's staying."

"So we ask Robert," Kathleen said. "Then I take you over."

Robert, Kathleen's ex-husband, was also an ex-cop, and though now he spent his days selling pools and hot tubs out on I-10, he still had the connections to call around at a few hotels and ask about the arrival of a strange well-dressed man from the East Coast, maybe signing in with a Maryland license plate, maybe wearing his hair slicked back in an old-timey way. "He stayed at the Plaza del Sol on the 101 loop north of town," he told Alice over the phone two hours later. Waiting on him, she'd had nothing to do but read magazines and listen to Kathleen go on about how she needed to just see *The Godfather* already. "Him or somebody like him," Robert said. "Going by the name Reynolds."

"That's him," she said. She was standing at the salon's magazine-strewn front desk, and when she spoke, everyone turned her way, their eyes conveying the same know-it-all judgment. She sounded, stupidly, like a woman in love. It occurred to her all too late that Kathleen had told them everything. So she turned, embarrassed, and cupped her hand over the mouthpiece. "Is he still there?"

Robert appeared to be chewing on something. "If he's planning on staying," he said. "All I know is, he checked in around eleven last night."

"What time's checkout?"

He laughed a very satisfied laugh. "I ain't the manager, Alice."

"Right," she said. "I'll just go."

"Want me to come along?"

She glanced behind her at the women, half a dozen of them if you count Kathleen, all feigning a lack of interest. "No, I'll take care of it."

When she sat in the car and saw Kathleen through the windshield with her arms akimbo, a cigarette dangling from her mouth, she thought distinctly and clearly that this was the sort of story a woman told the police after her best friend went missing. *I tried to go with her, Officer. But she wouldn't listen.*

She'd backed out, righted the wheel, and rolled down the window. "He's probably not even there," she'd said. And when nothing changed on Kathleen's rumpled face, "Don't worry."

But he was there. The thin, tanned hippie at the front desk, wearing a beaded leather vest over a Dodgers T-shirt, hadn't even had to look at the register. "Mr. Reynolds? Room 215." He pointed over his shoulder, a glass partition between them. "Up the stairs and all the way at the end."

She thanked him and turned toward the stairs, and only af-

ter a moment did she realize she wasn't walking. Something
had frozen her in place. The idea of going to that door, of
knocking, of going inside room 215. Back at the glass partition,
the hippie's fingers tooled with the dials of a small radio on the
desk. She cleared her throat to get his attention. "I wonder if
you could call him? If you could ask him to meet me here?"

The hippie's face went through a series of quizzical gestures
before a relieved smile stretched wide. "Oh, sure," he said.
"Not a thing at all."

A little out of herself, she watched him ring the telephone,
and when he said that no one had answered, she asked him,
though she didn't want to smoke, for a cigarette. "What was
your name again?"

"Adam," he said. Then, giggling at something significant to
only himself, "I just moved here. From Minneapolis?"

She accepted a match under the glass divider as well, and
after lighting up, she took the cigarette out to the parking lot,
where she could get a good look at room 215. As if on a timer,
as she gingerly inhaled, the curtains up there parted. She
could see only a hand and then the curtain fell closed. As she
blew out the smoke, she felt impenetrable, in spite of the itch-
iness in her chest, and thought briefly of marching up the
stairs to knock on the door after all. He would answer in his
ribbed undershirt, his armpit hairs showing, sweaty and nervous. He would be Penrod then. She'd tell him she knew. She'd
demand to know what he was doing here after all these years,
why he was fooling around with her. Instead she stood there
inhaling and exhaling. Time passed. Then the hippie, Adam,
joined her. "I called again," he said. "No answer."

He was taller than she'd thought. A tall, bent-shouldered

young man in need of a shave, smelling a little rancid and a little like oregano, his eyes unfocused and orange-rimmed. "It's okay," she said. "I don't think I need to see him after all."

They stood a minute or two, smoking.

"You're that chick from the radio," he said after an unending silence. "*Listen Up, Alice* or whatever."

"I am," she said.

"I'm your biggest fan. Or one of them. I thought it was you but I needed to hear your voice."

He was laughing, embarrassed apparently, a little shocked to be in her presence. She extended her hand. "Alice Linwood," she said.

"I'm Adam. Can I, like, buy you a drink?"

He was a good twenty years younger than her, a married woman. Besides that, she was here to confront this so-called Gary Reynolds, not get picked up by long-haired motel clerks. Still, the situation rattled excitement down her spine. "I've got my show in a couple of hours," she said. "I really just needed to meet with Mr.—"

It occurred to her, perhaps too late, that she was drawing attention to Gary Reynolds, or Penrod, or whomever. Here was one of her listeners, maybe a little stoned but certainly aware enough to have taken her measure. She'd arrived nervous and secretive in the middle of the day looking for a man this same clerk must have been asked about by a retired cop only an hour ago. He didn't have to ask her why she was here. It could only be a couple of reasons, and his forwardness in asking her for a drink told her that one of them had been crossed out in his mind. As if the idea needed any more clarification, Adam gazed up at room 215 and said, "He seemed a little funny to me when he came downstairs this morning. Said he needed another day. I said, 'Dude, the place is all yours.' I mean, we're half-empty, you know?" Then, pointing his chin at the window, "Is he, like, FBI or something?"

For a lot of reasons, she knew she needed to get away from here. One of them, the most important, was that Gary Reynolds had peeked through those curtains and still hadn't come downstairs. The others were reasons she shouldn't have come in the first place. "Hey," she said. "I'm on live tonight. Will you call in if anything changes? If he leaves?"

He squinted at her. "My shift's over in, like, half an hour."

"Can't you stay?" she said, touching his warm forearm. "Can't you help the cause?"

She said that on air as well: *help the cause*. It was something she said near her sign-off. *Call or write in. Do your part. Help the cause.* A twinge of guilt passed through her, but then was immediately replaced with a sense of fortitude. This *was* helping the cause. Nothing could help it more. He held his face scrunched up a moment before saying, "Yeah, I'll call."

"If he's left, just ask me about Martha Mitchell. If he's still in his room, say anything else."

"Martha Mitchell," he said. "Got it."

At home the phone was ringing. Somehow it seemed more urgent, more insistent than usual, and she had the irrational thought that it would be the police on the line, calling to tell her Gary Reynolds was in custody. For what? She didn't know.

Without setting down her purse, she lifted the kitchen phone and put it to her ear. She couldn't bring herself to speak. "Mom?"

It was Mike, her son, calling from Fresno State. The sound of his voice was like someone interrupting sleep. "Mike?" she said. "What's going on?"

"Nothing, Mom. Sheesh." He laughed. Mike had his father's easygoing laugh, that sound of a man untroubled by the world, untouched by even the things he himself had done. She didn't like it. The first time she'd heard him laugh that way, that condescending way, she'd wanted to slap him. He'd been sixteen then, showing her a picture of a Mustang in a magazine, telling her that was the car he wanted, and when she'd said they weren't made of money, he'd laughed just like his father, just like Jeff, and it had been all she could do not to slap him. "Are you going on the radio tonight?"

"Why?" she said.

"Just asking," he said, offended. "Anna called me. She says this Watergate thing has pushed you over the edge."

"Edge?" she said. "What edge?"

In the white kitchen with the late-afternoon light glinting in the windows, she wished now she could remember the kids at that table, in those chairs, in their voices. She shouldn't have come home. Then again, where else would she have gone?

"Mom, we're worried about you," Mike said. "I mean, I voted for McGovern. You know that. But this thing. It's—"

"It's worse than it looks," she said. And then, feeling a little drunk, a little not herself, "I don't really have time for this right now, Mikey. I've got to get ready for the show."

He was saying something else, something condescending

again, something starting with the word *Mom,* so she hung up. Of all people in the world, she couldn't have her very own children turning against her, not today of all days, not when it felt like everything she'd believed for the last six or seven years had been thrown into question.

She dropped into one of the plastic-cushion dining chairs, not her usual seat but Jeff's. She normally sat opposite him, trying to regain his attention as he fingered the morning paper, listening to his complaints about work on nights they actually ate dinner together. The seat felt warm. She knew this was all in her mind.

The phone began ringing again.

Only after the fourth ring did she stand up to answer it. "Mikey," she said, "I'll call you tomorrow."

"Mikey?"

It was Grant, incredulous, bothered.

"Listen, I had a guy call here a minute ago," he said. "He was calling for you. He didn't make any sense. Just said Martha Mitchell. That's it. Martha Mitchell, like, five times."

When she cradled the phone again, she felt cold all over. She thought about getting in the car and driving away. Thought about showing up in Fresno to see Mike or Albuquerque to see Anna. Thought about driving all the way to Buffalo to her sister. Instead she walked to the living room and turned on the television. A game show was on. A man in a burgundy suit with wide lapels held a long thin microphone, smiling. The sound was off. She thought about everything and nothing, and both categories felt the same: a jumble of words and feelings and substance, none of which had ever really connected. She looked at the patterns in the carpet going this way and that. She'd wanted a dog. She'd asked Jeff to get them a dog. A cocker spaniel. One just like Gary Reynolds had described in his letters. That's what she'd wanted. But he hadn't. He said the hairs would be in everything, would be in the carpet. He said puppies pee on everything, too. She recalled with clarity the gray oval rug they'd had in Ridge Landing, saw the face of Deborah Feldberg, that sweet girl, smelled the sweat and bodies of Mike and Anna when they were children in the summertime here in the desert. Their minds had been so open, their lives empty pages. Today would mark something in all of that. Even Jeff would remember. Even he would see today as a wave turned back toward the empty, lifeless sea.

The doorbell rang. She waited a moment. Breathed in the stale air of this home of hers, this place that might as well have been her own. Then she stood. When she was younger she could still communicate with her past lives, could still see with her eyes closed those whole lifetimes she'd once inhabited. Now, today, she could see ahead to the writhing darkness just around the corner, and past that to a silence like the astronauts had heard on the surface of the moon. She went to greet Paul Penrod, who she knew would be waiting for her, though she wanted so much for it to be someone—anyone—else.

THE MATTER OF THE LAWN

JOAN HALFORD—1977

What did it matter? Oh, what did it matter? The boy out on the lawn cutting grass when she'd told him, told him straight to his face just last week, that she wouldn't pay him, that she didn't need the grass cut in the first place. Her son was coming home, would be here any minute. She didn't need the lawn cut. And so she'd gone out there, she'd talked to him, and he'd said that wouldn't her son like it even better if the lawn was cut when he got home, if he didn't have that little chore to do, if things looked all nice and neat when he parked there in the driveway. The boy, the Mexican boy, had pointed at the drive where Scott would be parking his car later that day. All right, she'd said. But down the hall she'd stalked from one window to the other. What did it matter? There was the boy now, his mower glinting in the noontime sun, his elbow on its handle. There was the boy fanning himself with his ball cap and taking a long drink from the soda bottle she'd brought out to him when he had ignored her and started up the mower. And now he was taking a break, shining wet in the August heat, a blotch of sweat darkening his T-shirt. He was some relative of that Vasquez girl down the street, her cousin or second cousin or something. Scott knew. Scott had told her. Told her, "Hey, Mom, do you remember Vasquez and his kids

you ran out of town? Well, that boy right there's his nephew."
Said it out loud the last time he visited, years ago, and said it
to hurt her right in the middle of the pharmacy with Olive
Dunning looking at them and Dr. Raeburn up in his white suit
looking, too, and they remembered Vasquez, of course they
did, they'd been there that night.

This boy, then, this Mexican boy, just out of a stroller, clinging to his mother's arm, walking like his legs belonged to a
stranger.

That is how long it'd been since Scott was home. He didn't
even come when Rob died. Only her and Jason, who of course
had come, who always came, the younger son, the respectful
son. Jason had only moved to Hempstead, a couple of towns
over, ran a successful plumbing business of his own there,
Halford's Plumbing, his father so proud to see that name on
the van every time he came home, and he was there, at home,
before the doctor had even lifted Rob out of his chair. It had
been Jason who had the self-possession to walk up to his father
and close his eyes, to shut off the television, to pull the front
curtains. She had been slumped in the dining room crying
in hysterics by then for nearly an hour, blubbering into the
phone, leaving a message with some unnamed woman at the
phone number Scott had given them when he last called for
money. Oh, and it had been Jason, cleaned up in a suit and a
shave, along with all of Rob's old bowling buddies, who had
carried the coffin from the church, who had lowered it into
the ground at Green Lawn Cemetery. For that, even Paul Penrod had shown up, followed sheepishly around by his young
son, Bradley, his face blotchy with acne, his hair as shaggy as
one of the Beatles'.

At first she'd expected to be haunted by Rob, to walk into rooms to find him there, to catch the familiar smell of his Lucky Strikes in the garage, to hear him muttering into the refrigerator about how there was never anything to eat. Instead, these years of quiet, none of Rob's harrumphing and cooing, or his socked feet up on the coffee table leaving white patches in the wood, none of his cigarettes in bed and his deep raspy laughter at Johnny Carson. She would still imagine him, often, his over-tall presence in doorways and his strong hairy arms and the horseshoe-shaped scar from the war just under his left eye. None of his complaining about the blacks and Puerto Ricans during the blackout, though, none of his carping on Jimmy Carter's weak hand when it came to OPEC, none of him, none of Rob. Just this house where they'd been forever. Her friends at church told her time and again to be sure to leave on the radio or a record or the television. A silent empty house could drive a woman mad, they said. But often she forgot their advice, and listened instead to the refrigerator's meandering wheezes and churns, to the dog barking three doors down, to the long approach of the mailman as he clomped up the sidewalk and onto her porch.

Or as today, listened to the growl of that mower and its silence.

The boy had pushed his machine out into the road next to the curb and set to raking. How old was he now? Twelve? Thirteen? Still a very young boy, but reaching that cusp of development in which his body takes on the rail-thin dimensions of manhood. By now his eyes were lingering on girls in his classes, and they, too, must be looking back with some measure of longing. His drooping black hair brushed back over one ear, his angle of a jaw, those surprised eyes. She could remember Scott at that age with clarity, spending all his time over at the Feldbergs' house with Max, that damned Max, whom Rob wouldn't allow Scott to speak to again. Of course he did, though. He spoke to him at school and then surreptitiously over the phone when his parents sent him off to that institution in Connecticut. She'd seen the telephone bill, after all. And later, after high school, when Scott was at NYU on his father's dime, she'd discovered and not told Rob that he was letting the boy live on the floor of his dorm room. Soon after that time it didn't matter anyway. Max Feldberg, through some Jewish channels even Rob couldn't understand, had been made into a rock 'n' roll star, a heartthrob wearing a tan sweater, his hair like a thick cloud on top of his head. He was always pictured snapping his fingers, mouth open, eyes dreaming into the distance. Scott, instead of going to law school, ran off to join him, first as a hanger-on and later as a member of his band, whatever that nuisance had been called, playing the drums.

Scott with a stick and a block keeping rhythm in the first-grade music assembly. Scott drumming pencils on the narrow desk Rob had built him, a portable record player in the corner. Scott going out for marching band, and they were so proud to see him in his uniform with that gleaming drum, the sin and sickness of Max and all that meant so clearly behind them all. But with Max it had been a cycle, like everything in this life, an endless process of return. Adult Scott, "adult" Scott, dressed in black on a television program, hammering away at the back of the stage while Max in sunglasses snaked before a microphone, singing something about meeting a woman in a parking lot with all the lights out. The Mercy Trips, they called themselves. A name that made no sense at all.

She was a wreck. Of course it was because Scott was coming. She hadn't been like this since that first winter, or certainly not since the year after when she watched the bicentennial events on television with Jason and his wife and kids and started crying like a child there in the very chair where Rob had died. No, she hadn't been this sort of wreck in quite a while, not in a year. She'd been doing better.

On the radio she tuned in to the gospel station. She left it audible only until a choir finished "Rock of Ages," and when the preacher came to the microphone, she turned down the volume so that only the whispered rhythm of his voice, its precipitous rising and falling, sounded to her like water running in another room. She turned it back up a notch when she heard the distant notes of a singing woman, a woman she pictured in blue flowing robes, her face an ivory pillow, her eyes exhibiting a pained sort of joy.

She thought of this, the imagined woman, seated with a child on her knee, a painting, really, one of those Renaissance pictures she'd seen that year she and Rob went to Italy, their big trip, the boys both moved out, American tourists with cameras about their necks finally getting the payoff they'd worked so long for. The people there had been rude, not only in Florence, where almost every work of art brought her nearly to tears, torn as they were from a book of color prints her mother had given her on her wedding day, but in Rome and Paris and even London, where Rob nearly got his wallet stolen by a red-bearded hoodlum dressed up like a beatnik. Rob had struck him hard, ignoring the flickering knife, and sent the criminal backpedaling into the street holding his face and cursing. What a terrible place, Europe. What a nasty place. But she had seen Italy as one is told to do, she'd seen the Colosseum in Rome and the Leaning Tower of Pisa and the canals of Venice. And she'd seen the painting of the blessed mother in blue and the child with the face of a man but the hands of a baby, grasping grapes and stuffing them into his awkward mouth. She'd thought of Scott then, too, newly minted as a college graduate, not yet drifted into whatever his life had become in Max Feldberg's circle. She'd thought of little Scott in that old apartment in Birmingham, the two of them waiting for Rob to come back from the war, seated at a card table with the window open and the hot miserable Alabama summer washing over them. It had been a special treat then to chill grapes in the icebox and eat them together, laughing as the radio played. Everything had seemed possible then, her heart broken with love for this little boy. Her husband, still mostly a stranger, shipping eastward in victory.

She knew something of what had become of Scott's life over the last ten years. Everyone in America knew something of it, especially of the last five or so, when reporters on television and in the newspapers said that Max Feldberg, known to them only as Max Felt, had holed up in an old warehouse in Manhattan and collected around himself a harem of young women and men, all of them on drugs and playing rock 'n' roll, a final sinful gasp of all that hippie nonsense she'd thought the country would have put behind itself by now. If Rob had still been around, it would have killed him. *My son,* he would have said. *Practically in the Manson Family.*

She'd read about it in *Life* magazine, the dreary color pictures of young people living without jobs, bone-thin and drug-
eyed, their clothes the same tatters they'd likely walked in
with, a caption reading *Gave Herself to Rock 'n' Roll* under a
vacant-looking girl with frizzy hair and bags under her eyes.
That's exactly how it was explained, without a note of absur-
dity. These young people, some of them runaways who had
disappeared from high schools, most of them girls, had surrendered their lives to a cult without any religious structure
but the worship of music and dancing and sex and drugs. They
put on shows every night that ran into the early morning
hours, Max Felt and his band, including Scott, but other bands
as well, seemingly any who wanted to drop by, some of them
famous on Top 40 radio, and in the hours they weren't sleeping or dancing in front of a band these poor wayward kids
were out on the street panhandling and pickpocketing and, in
one case, holding up a jewelry store, another picture of Ha-
sidic men looking wide-eyed and intruded upon by the pho-
tographer. They were living hand-to-mouth, over two hundred
of them, sharing two bathrooms and nothing but pallets to
sleep on and only a few actual bedrooms.

She'd watched the television report with Morley Safer on
60 Minutes, walking through the abandoned warehouse, showing the stage and the speakers and lights and posters, the refuse everywhere, old clothes and newspaper and whatnot, and
upstairs down a narrow hallway what used to be offices, which
he said were the dwelling places of the elect, Max and his band-
mates, as well as Max's common-law wife, the Vasquez girl, and
their daughter.

To think a child had been living there, had been raised

there. It was a nightmare, and her stomach squeezed over the idea and the necessity to look Scott in the eyes, knowing about that little girl, the ruckus of rock music all around her, the hundreds of irresponsible strangers.

She'd watched, too, when Morley Safer, whom Rob never trusted, never liked, calling him nothing but a Jew and a Canadian at that, against the Vietnam War and all, she'd watched Morley Safer interview a boy from Ohio who said there was no god but Max Felt and a girl from Washington State who said she'd slept with Max Felt at least a dozen times and why did it matter to anyone and then finally Max himself, little Maxie Feldberg, looking for the life of him like a cartoon villain, dressed in black and what looked like a dog collar and sunglasses and just as ice-cold as anything, clenching his jaw, answering only a few questions and then having provided very little in the way of information, finally telling Morley Safer to his face right there in front of the camera that rock 'n' roll meant naked bodies and pleasure and blow up all the system around us that makes us into people we aren't and why didn't he go and get something out of life instead of nosing around in other people's business. Everyone was always telling other people how to get off, he'd said. But here was a place outside all those dichotomies. Here you got off how you wanted. Was Max sleeping with the girls? Safer had asked. And the boys? Do you breath air, Max said back to him. Do you eat food?

Terrifying, really. *Outside all those dichotomies?* The boy had been a monster as long as she could remember, a child with no moral center. After Eden Gardens, before the Feldbergs left town nearly twenty years ago now, there had been the incident with Scott, when she'd walked into her elder son's room and seen something unspeakable, both of them with their pants down, Max kneeling between Scott's pale and quaking knees, her son's eyes closed and head rolled back onto the bed. She had screamed. She couldn't remember what she'd said. But she'd said something, strung together a series of words through the door once she'd slammed it closed, and then she'd left her house, driven up and down every street in Ridge Landing, muttering to herself, crying, seeing the image behind that door as if it were projected onto a screen just in front of the car wherever she went. When she returned, determined to tell Rob nothing about what she'd seen, neither of the boys were at home, and later when Scott came in just in time for dinner, he wouldn't meet eyes with her. The next day she went to Rose, she sat her down, she said she knew that the families didn't get along since what had happened downhill, but that now she had even worse news. And then she told her. *My Max?* Rose wanted to know. She told her, yes, it was Max, she knew that for sure, no doubt about it, and that there was also no doubt this behavior didn't stem from her Scott. It was Max's idea, she was positive. He was always getting into some kind of trouble. He was the mopey one. The likelihood of his being in some way perverted—sexually perverted, that is—shouldn't surprise either of them. Then Rose was standing, pointing at the door, shouting, and she left. It was after the Feldbergs had moved to Hicksville that she heard about them sending Max to that institution, where she'd heard doctors tried electroshock therapy to work some sense into him. He'd done the same as with Scott with another boy at his new school, so she had been right.

She had always been right.

Nowadays, she knew, these people were—like everyone else who was different, everyone who wanted to stand out in some way—demanding they be taken seriously by decent Christian people, demanding others bend their morals to accept them, demanding even that they be celebrated and seen on television and in the movies as if what they were doing with their lives wasn't wrong. Again with the cycle, the return of what shouldn't return, the bad dream you kept falling back into, an ungodly perversion and contamination. Communism, Rob would call it. And Max Felt took it even a step further, right there on *60 Minutes*, saying he went to bed with men and women both, and shrugging at the shock and gasp he knew to be on the other end of the camera. This was the company Scott had been keeping. This was the place. This was the behavior.

Without knowing it, she'd been pacing the house, walking from the back bedroom to the kitchen to the back bedroom, passing the mumbling radio, virtually sleepwalking in daylight. Now she shook herself free of the path and went again to the front window. The Mexican boy was gone, his work done, and she felt a cold chill. The air conditioner was set too low. She needed her sweater.

And just as she registered this, still gazing at the clean and neatly cut grass, as if called from the street by bells, a long brown sports car rumbled into the drive, its chrome bumper glinting stars out of the afternoon sun. Scott was here.

There was someone else, too, a slender column in the passenger seat, a face darkened by shadow, a woman's arm, a hand—perhaps by reflex alone—raising up a small greeting with slender musical fingers.

Scott had brought home a girl, here, today, and before she

could prepare herself for this new situation, before she could catch her breath, here was this girl, this woman, my god, Chinese or something like it, as thin-armed and tall as a model, her black hair straight down and cut at a harsh angle to her shoulders, displayed as it were in front of the car on the concrete driveway near the crack she'd meant for so long to have repaired, waiting for Scott, smiling, this beautiful Chinese woman, smiling at the approaching Scott, who appeared for the first time around the corner of the garage and didn't look at his mother in the window, no, but at this woman, touched her arm, kissed her lightly on the lips. Scott, wearing a beard and a denim shirt untucked from his fray-hemmed jeans. He seemed strong, more muscular and erect than she'd imagined, especially after the moral dissipation of where he'd been, and it was unmistakable the woman loved him. In the instant of their touch, that became clear. Then there was something else, too, something she didn't at first want to believe she was seeing, the rounded jut of the woman's belly, and then, yes, the telltale crossing of her arm over its humped top.

The story was told, then. Even before Scott's eyes flashed up to meet his mother's in the front window where she used to watch him leave in the mornings for school, where she'd been waiting for him to return all these tortured years, she understood who this woman would be to her son and what was to come for them all—another life, here before her, stretching tight the woman's sleeveless shirt, bulging out her jeans, splitting undone her top buttons.

She could have been drowned. That's what she thought of. She thought of falling through the pond that frozen day so many years ago, how she'd stayed at the top of the hill with the other wives, screaming for Rob and Paul Penrod to come back, not to go down there, to leave those people alone, even if they were a bunch of communists, even if the women all wore pants, even if a good half or more of them were blacks and Mexicans. Well, she didn't scream all that. She'd said it before, at Penrod's house, where they'd all been gathered, where Rob had made his case that it wasn't just the Negro family in the Linwoods' old home that mattered as much as that whole new addition downhill. *Those people,* he'd said, and the others had growled their assent. Those people showed up here all at once with the single purpose of changing our town, of forcing their ways on us. It was violence, really, and the only way to fight back was with more violence. They'd already put a brick through the window of the Negro family's house and played "Dixie" at them with half the high school band and shouted and held signs for a week even when the television cameras came. But now it was Eden Gardens. *Those people.* They'd be sending their kids to our school and driving down property values and pushing all sorts of un-American ideas on everyone and Rob and Penrod and the whole Civil Defense League had had enough. Were they with him? They were. And her pleas to take it easy—to sleep it off, to wait, to write their congressman, to have a drink or just a cigarette before going through with this, to do anything but raise arms against the people downhill—were all drowned out. Even the wives who stayed with her at the top of the hill had said yes, had said go, it was now or no time at all to take a stand.

And then, at the top of the snow-banked hill, she had screamed Rob's name, or at least had screamed the word *stop!* But she was held back like a fence with the wives. The men with their shotguns and tire irons and baseball bats and Rob with his golf club, for god's sake, they had descended fast and shouting like wild Indians and split along the water and come at that crowd gathered and their strange priest in the robes and what was Charlie Ranagan doing down there, and the Feldbergs, what were the Feldbergs doing down there, too, and then the promised violence, Rob taller than all of them, all muscle swinging that golf club. She saw it hit the poor girl's head. Saw her fly through the air lifted by the impact and the blood in the snow. And Rob reeled back, surprised at himself. He paused just long enough that even at that distance she knew he was horrified, but then came the blow to his face and another and then another and he, too, was down on the snow being hit. She remembered careening down that hill, her knees out ahead of her feet, reeling and screaming, and Rob was in the snow, his head pouring blood, and then she was on the frozen pond practically skating until she wasn't, and cold, and underwater, and desperately grasping her fingers, and sinking, the dark cold of that dark, and then fingers wrenching her up by the hair out of the water into the cold impossibility of gray daylight—was it daylight or just the moon reflected in the snow?—with ice crisping on her skin and her eyes already icicles and Charlie Ranagan yelling at her head—was she all right? was she breathing?—and he'd saved her, stretched her body out on the bank and saved her.

But she could have drowned.

And now here, with this young woman, this Chinese woman, and not only that, but her own son whom she hadn't seen in a decade, she might as well have drowned but to see it and know that Rob was better dead, better in that silk-lined box, and she hated him for it and hated him for everything else and still she had to screw her stomach down tight enough to go to the door, to pull it open, to press the flimsy little metal handle of the storm door and step out onto the patio and meet their eyes and near tears say, "Scott, oh, sweetie, Scott."

He swung toward her, dipping his knees, and raised her heels, holding her around the back behind her pinned arms, making her feel small.

The Chinese woman laughed.

She tried her best to sing at the happy level of a good host. "And who is your friend?"

Scott had released her. Had, in fact, taken an appraising step back to look at both of them, back and forth. "This is Ha-yoon," he said. "But you can call her Janice."

This Ha-yoon or Janice extended one of those thin hands and said, "Janice, please, Mrs. Halford."

"Oh, goodness," she said, "it's Joan."

Scott looked around the edges of the ceiling as if he were measuring it for removal. "The place looks just the same," he said. "But that's a new television, huh?"

The television—she didn't have to look at it—had been delivered in the Johnson administration. Even since Rob died, she'd had the repairman in twice. Still she said, "Yes. A brand-new color set."

"You have a beautiful house, Mrs. Halford," said Janice. Her voice, she noted only now, sounded as American as anyone's.

What followed felt like being drunk, though she'd stopped drinking so many years ago. In no time at all they were standing around in the kitchen making small talk, everyone's face stretched into pained smiles. The woman, Janice, had grown up in California, a Korean, her father having worked in some job or another in Hollywood. She had said, mysteriously, that she was from the Valley, and this place simply by its naming seemed a source of comedy. She laughed along.

Her throat catching, trying her best to stay focused on the roast she'd only just pulled from the oven, she said, "And how did you meet Scott?"

This sent a little quake between the two of them. "It was at the warehouse," Scott said. "Janice came in a couple of years ago and we met eyes and it was all over. Mom, we're married. I mean, not married for the state yet, but we're married."

Her heart left her. Or at least it felt that it must have left her because it did nothing, said nothing, reacted to nothing. "How wonderful. And you're so in love."

"Yes," said Janice. The woman looked fearful as she laughed, as she slapped Scott on the shoulder playfully, as she shook her head in disbelief. "After what Scott told me, I never would have thought—"

"We didn't know you'd approve," Scott said.

She knew that she was smiling, and this smiling must have been what sent the pair of them into their talking over each other, telling the story of a sham wedding performed by none other than Max Felt only a few months before the police came into the warehouse and scattered them all and then the weeks and weeks and nearly half a year they had been living at various friends' homes while Scott, her son Scott, was hounding his band's manager for money and finally getting that money and deciding together then and there that they would move to Austin, where another band needed a drummer, where a machine shop might need his hands, where Janice or Ha-yoon would stay at home with the child until it was school age. They rattled all this at her without once acknowledging that her smile was only a product of her upbringing, her good manners, and that behind its tensed muscles, her jaw had fallen open. She thought of Rob, of what Rob would say, what he would do. He'd be shouting to the ceiling already. He'd be telling this Chinese vixen to go wait in the car. He'd be stomping around ruffling the newspaper he'd been trying to read before they came in the door.

"Austin," she managed. "Texas?"

"Yeah, Mom."

She looked back and forth at them. "I thought you were staying awhile. I made up your room."

Janice wrinkled her eyes and pouted her lips to say, "We're leaving tonight. I can't believe Scott didn't tell you. We can only stay for dinner."

"Ah, Mom," Scott said, "I didn't mean to make you think . . ." And instead of saying more, he did what any son would do in the situation. He stepped forward again and embraced her. "We were in a rush, but I wanted you to meet Janice. And I wanted to see you again. It's been so long, you know? And we really want you to visit when the kid's born."

She looked instinctively at Janice's belly. "Of course," she said. "I wouldn't miss it. When's the baby due, my dear?"

Finally Scott let go of her. No man had held her in two years and suddenly she didn't want one to do so, especially this grown boy who had come to her home only to break her heart.

"A month and a half," Janice said. "Well, more like forty days. On September fourteenth."

"Then I'll come at the beginning of September. I'll take a plane."

Scott reached for her again, but she held up a hand. "The two of you should relax," she said, and gestured them toward the living room. "Dinner's nearly ready."

When they'd left the kitchen, glowing, looking for the life of them like winners on some hippie game show, she thought for a moment of collapsing on the linoleum floor, of stopping her heart by force, of the juicy irony to be had when news got around that she'd died in front of a roast while her long-haired son and his Korean not-yet-wife lounged on the sofa watching television. Too bad that's not how life worked. No, instead she was fully conscious, suffering from only a slight headache, her hands no more shaky than they'd been for years. How could they have come here? How is it they could have brought this sinful life of theirs to her house? And only for dinner, at that? To be living as they were, not married by the state, he'd said, but more important, not married in the eyes of the Lord. Just two young people cavorting, making a child, and to do so in such an unnatural way. That girl had her own people, her own men. Probably her Oriental morals had taught her that she could do what she wanted with a good American woman's son. Probably they'd taught her to take advantage of him. What was this money he'd talked about? But god, it wasn't just this girl, this Ha-yoon. It was Scott. It had always been Scott. The boy was trouble to the core. Greedy with his toys as a child. Fights in school. All that business with Max. Oh, it was Scott, all right. And he wasn't a child anymore. Wasn't a boy. At his same age, Rob had already fought in the war and moved them to Long

Island and bought them a house and started his own company and become the president of the Civil Defense League of Ridge Landing. What had Scott done but behave as if everyone still thought of him as a little boy? Play in a band? Live in a filthy warehouse? Impregnate some Korean whore? He wasn't a boy at all. He was nearly middle-aged.

In no time, paying little attention to her actions, she had the table set with plates and glasses of ice water and napkins and utensils and all the food set out across the countertop and she was standing at the edge of the living room looking at these two strangers on her sofa: the man with his hand and head resting on the woman's round belly and the woman leaning her black-haired head with an elbow on the sofa's arm and the television playing Walter Cronkite and she wanted so much to burst into tears that she did, she just started crying, and when Scott and the woman came to her with their pleading and soft and cloying voices she was smashing wadded paper towels into her eyes and saying, "I'm sorry, I'm just so sorry, it's just too much, I'm sorry," and when they sat her down at the table they pulled their chairs around close to her and all three of them huddled as she blew her nose and laughed at herself or tried to laugh and finally realized that they *were* strangers and that soon they would be gone and she would be off the hook for it all and so why not just make it through and go back to smiling. But then something ticked in her neck and she said, "I just hate you both for this. I can't believe you've done this to me."

And in the quiet that followed, Scott didn't so much as look in his mother's direction. Instead he touched that ugly beard of his and stared at the floor.

Dinner was eaten anyway. They scooted away and filled their

plates. Walter Cronkite went on in the background about the president making a whole new department of government and that killer in New York City and the Senate talking about mind control and they all chewed their food. The roast wasn't as soft as she would have liked it to be. Since Rob died, she'd let it cook longer so it wasn't even stringy in her teeth. She'd bought a microwave oven as well, and after making her Thursday roast would freeze half of it, sliced into inch-wide servings she separated with waxed paper. Then, following the same schedule she'd had before she was a widow, the roast would last her a month and sometimes more. This seemed like the kind of information they should know about as seeming newlyweds, and so she told them, though their eyes stayed focused on their plates. "One day one of you will be alone," she said, feeling quite good about it. "And when that happens, you'll need to adjust."

She was finished eating before they were, but she took up their plates anyway. "I'm sorry," she said. "I've been a terrible hostess."

Then with the plates in the sink she went down the hallway to her bedroom and closed the door. She thought they would understand that she wanted them to leave, but after sitting on the corner of the bed, she heard them mumbling and washing the dishes. The familiar slosh and scrape. Oh, how hideous. The pair of them, unmarried, a baby on the way, living all those years in filth, washing her dishes. She'd have to go back and do it all again. She'd have to scrub every plate and fork.

After a few minutes, a knock came at the front door and she stood. With her ear at the bedroom door she listened first to a tense silence and then the soft footfalls of someone—she thought it must be Scott. He wasn't coming down the hall but was rather going to the door. Then came the gentle sound of its opening and another voice and Scott's saying something about his mother resting and the other voice sounding confused and then the door's closing again. She went to the window. It was the boy, the Mexican boy, gazing at the brown sports car, god knows who could afford the gas these days. The boy had come, nobody needed to tell her, to collect for his work on the lawn, even after she'd said she wouldn't pay him.

She saw them off in the driveway. She couldn't stay in her room all night even if she wanted to, and after the boy had come to the door, it seemed they would never leave, so she'd shuffled back to them and without saying anything about what she'd said before—without even mentioning it—she asked them what they knew about Austin and how far the trip would be and would they send her a postcard when they arrived with their new address, and out in the drive she kissed them both on the cheek, these strangers, and watched their tepid smiles as Scott backed his brown sports car out into the street where he'd taught his little brother to ride a bike a whole lifetime ago.

The kitchen was surprisingly clean. Their communal life in that warehouse must have taught them a thing or two. She didn't turn the radio back on, but rather stood near the table in the new silence they'd left behind. She had meant to send them off with that old book of Florentine painters, had thought of it down the hall, had meant to pull it from the shelf when she'd realized they weren't just going to leave. But there it was, its spine brown and worn, a gift from her mother that she

could pass along, maybe those Bible images instilling something of Christ in their unnatural child. She would send it by
post. Tomorrow, yes, she would take it down and wrap it in
paper, and once she had their address, she would send it.

Her knees hurt. Earlier, before the boy had come about the
lawn, she had been down on all fours cleaning under the cab-
inets with a rag, up since dawn straightening every room, putting on the finishing touches. She was tired. This day was
supposed to have gone otherwise. When he'd called, when his
voice came over the phone, she'd been playing bridge with
Carol, right here at this table. Carol, in her faded yellow sweater
and hippie jeans, just back from a beach trip with Larry, smoking one of her long cigarettes, had watched her with growing
alarm as the fact of his voice on the phone took shape. *Who is
it?* she wanted to know. *Don't tell me it's Scott. Don't tell me.* She'd
put her hand over the receiver to tell her it was, indeed, Scott,
and Carol broke her cigarette in half, snuffing it out, cackling
with glee, so loud that Scott had asked, "Mom, who's that?"
And she'd said, "Carol. Do you remember Carol?" After she
got off the phone she told Carol that Scott was coming home,
and because she thought it was true, she said, "He's coming
home for good." And then they cleared the cards from the
table and went together down the hall to his old room, which
no longer had a bed but only Rob's old desk and a bookcase
and in the middle of the floor for no reason but that she lived
alone, the vacuum. They'd set to work clearing things out, the
room ablaze in a light she'd not known its bulbs to contain.
Carol had called Larry and Larry had shown up half an hour
later with one of their boys' old beds and bolted together the
headboard and side rails and then she and Carol dropped the

box springs and mattress in place and stretched the sheets and by ten o'clock the work was done.

That had been three . . . no, four days ago. What would she tell Carol now? How could she begin to explain it? It was a wonder, already, that she hadn't called. It would be just like Carol to call in the middle of dinner with her son just to see how things were going. And what would she tell her? That Scott had shown up with a pregnant Korean woman? That really he had never planned to stay? That she had been so hurt by them that she'd hurt them back? That she'd gone to hide in her room like a child? She could see Carol's face now, sympathetic but a little disappointed, disappointed in her, saying with her eyes that she should have held her tongue, that these were grown adults, that she'd ruined her one and only chance to settle things with Scott and become a part of his life. She should be running down the street after them, calling his name. But no, she wouldn't.

To him, it was clear now that she was nothing more than a mother, something everyone has, a station to stop by on their journey, a checkpoint that would validate their togetherness. In Birmingham so many years ago Rob had taken her to his parents' home as well, in uniform, to introduce the girl he said would be his wife. She could still recall with photographic clarity the looks on her future in-laws' faces. A girl he'd met at the soda fountain in Conway's. A girl with drooping socks and pigtailed hair and still in high school and with a last name they'd never heard. A girl he'd talked to for an hour and a half in a blue streak on his only leave from basic training before he'd even troubled himself to come home. Here was their son about to go off to war, dragging in some girl he'd picked up in a department store café. They'd watched her stone-faced and screw-eyed until finally his mother stood from the table and threw her arms around her and wept and called her her daughter, and the next morning they were all together with her parents as well in line at the justice of the peace.

Oh, she was that woman, all right. Mrs. Halford. A second Mrs. Halford.

From her purse she counted two five-dollar bills and only after crossing the living room floor did she return to put one of them back. She would pay him five, that was plenty, and she would ask him to come back in a week. Outside, the late-summer air was cooling off. The sky had been bright, the humidity down.

Everything had changed here over the years. Nothing since Eden Gardens remained as it was. The covenant had been thrown out, of course. All sorts of people were allowed to move into town, and every year another good family had left. She and Rob had stayed. They'd put too much into it to give up. But after what happened down the hill that day, Rob had changed. He went to church more, he sat in confession, he did all he could to make things better for the Feldbergs. Of course no one knew about Deborah, about who had hit her. Things had been so chaotic. Who could see anything all that clearly? Who could remember? And she had talked to Rob about it only once, that night, both of them in tears, the noise of sirens and the red lights still flashing in their windows. Scott had come to the door and looked into their bedroom, his eyes wide. "How long have you been there?" his father had asked. "Why are you eavesdropping?"

Scott had run down the hall and out the door and down the street. They'd had to drive around town all night looking for him, knocking on doors and peering into backyards. When they found him without a coat outside the Vasquez house in Eden Gardens, huddled with that family, some shabby Mexican blanket over his shoulders and Max Feldberg at his side for some reason, Rob hadn't shouted at them. He didn't say a word. No one but the girl, Rebecca, did. "He was cold," she said. "He was scared."

The Mexican boy's family lived only two blocks away, where the Bellsons used to live, on Oak Street, and it was only as she came in sight of their van and the two small children playing on the front lawn did it occur to her that she had never been to their home, had certainly never walked there. As she approached, the children watched her, a boy and a girl, dressed in matching striped shirts and denim shorts, their brown legs folded in the grass. They held in their hands brightly colored racing cars, and one of them, the girl, was still making engine noises as she walked up the concrete driveway next to the van.

She found the storm door closed to keep out insects but the door standing open, and inside on the sofa was the boy, stretched out with his feet hanging over the arm, reading a book. Rock music played from the radio. In the kitchen, in yellow light, his mother stirred a pot. Out the back window the boy's father manned a smoking grill on the back patio. It was, with the children behind her included, a living diorama, a pristine snapshot of life at its most basic and familial. Could they have known how exemplary this moment was? Or was it arranged so only because it was being seen? Watching in this way, she felt connected to them, and with a sharp breath understood that she was a part of this image, not just its viewer. Like stepping free of herself and onto the stage with the actors. She was a dear aunt, come to visit, her hands weighed down with bags. A silly idea. Many silly ideas, really. She was only lonely, a lonely woman at the door.

"Hello?" she called into the home. At once the boy popped up, dropping his book to the floor. His mother spoke first.

"Mrs. Halford? You okay?"

Then the boy was at the storm door, for some reason apologizing, trying to push the door open. It took her a moment to realize that she was in the way, or rather her foot was in the way, jammed against the flimsy metal frame. She took a step back. "I've got your money," she said. "May I come in?"

Inside, things were messy, but only in the way all families are messy. Toys here and there on the floor, a few too many dishes still in the sink, a pile of half-folded laundry in the living room chair. The television played without sound that sitcom about the young man living with two women. She'd tried watching it once and found it upsetting filth. The boy guided her over to the sofa and she dutifully sat. The book he had been reading, *The Great Gatsby*, was at her feet. She picked it up for him. "Assignment for school," he said. "It's pretty good, I guess."

The two smaller children came in with a ruckus and then the mother was standing over her, behind her, asking in a slight accent whether she was hungry. She'd cooked a pot of beans and her husband was grilling chicken. It seemed so incredibly late to be eating dinner. A summer darkness was about to fall.

"No," she said, placing the boy's book on the coffee table. "I only just ate."

Then she produced from her hand, folded and a little sweaty, the five-dollar bill.

"You did a very good job," she said. "I'll need you back next weekend. My son isn't coming home after all."

The boy reached for the bill with a worried expression. It was clear he had something more he wanted to say, some understanding of her anguish, a young person's oversize capacity for love. Instead of speaking, he gave her a tight smile, his eyes squashed as if he were near tears.

"Miguel," his mother said, and whapped the back of the couch with a towel. "You thank Mrs. Halford right now."

She hadn't known his name. Miguel. And his family name? That she didn't know either.

"Thank you," Miguel said.

She smiled and nodded. Then she asked them, both of them, if they were related to a Vasquez family who used to live here in Ridge Landing for a short time, many years ago.

"Vasquez?" the mother said. "I don't know them. My husband and I come from Chicago. Before that, Texas, where we met. I knew a Vasquez there. Is a very common name."

So now she understood. A little joke on Scott's part all those years ago in the pharmacy. A jab meant to remind her of her sin. And she'd been thinking all this time they were really part of that girl's family. She'd, yes, lost sleep thinking of what they had done, what they'd all done. And here these people knew nothing of that at all. It was like a blessing, a note of grace, and for a moment she closed her eyes praying that she would find a way to be good, to be truly good, so that the scales would balance.

Then the two children were at her knees. "Do we know you?" the girl asked. And the boy said, "Don't be rude."

On the television, the man, dressed in a lady's bathrobe, spilled a carafe of orange juice with shaking hands. She looked back at the children and told them she lived down the street and that she was a friend of Miguel's, that she had come only to say hello, and that she hoped to see them all again soon.

She was standing now, uncertain as to when she'd stood, and maybe it was a rush of blood to her head, but an idea struck her as pleasant that wouldn't have before. She would have them all over to visit, she told them. And looking at the mother, stout and short, with doubt glazing her eyes, she said, "Next weekend. I'll make dinner and invite a few of the neighbors. It will be like old times. A welcome party. To you."

"But, Mrs. Halford," the woman said, and it was clear she was about to remind her that they'd lived here for years. Instead she wiped her hands on her towel and said, "That is so kind. My husband will be very pleased."

"Just like old times," she said again, scooting now for the door. "You know, a long time ago Rob and I used to hold such fun parties. That was a lifetime ago." And then, nearly out again in the cooling summer air, she said, "I can't wait. Friday night. Seven o'clock."

"Friday night," the mother said. "Sounds wonderful."

She walked home in a rush, her mind busy with the future. She would have to call Carol. And the Brams from down the street. And Luke Tisdale wouldn't miss it. Not the way he'd eyed her at the grocery store only last week. Of course Jason and his wife would come from Hempstead. And they would all be friends. They would listen to the Glenn Miller Orchestra. She'd have the turntable repaired and they would listen to Glenn Miller and even Louis Armstrong and maybe after a few drinks some rock 'n' roll. And they would dance. They would all dance. They would all be friends, dancing as if time had never passed.

And Scott would call her from Austin then. He would have to shout into the phone to be heard above their music and dancing. But she would hear him. He would be saying, *Mom. Hey, Mom. It's me.*

AFTER THE PLAZA

DEBBIE VASQUEZ—1982

It was Wolfboy because of course it was Wolfboy and anyone hovering there behind her like a blob while she was trying to best YUK on *Ms. Pac-Man* could be nobody but fucking Wolfboy because Wolfboy was always there and "Jesus, can you step back already?"

"Sorry," said Wolfboy.

With his stupid long hair and his stupid almost beard and his stupid—oh god, how stupid—bead necklace he said he got off some dude at a Dead concert. Wolfboy the hippie. Wolfboy who she'd named Wolfboy only last year. Wolfboy her neighbor since Mom brought her here, this place where she was somebody, where she'd been the pride and joy. "You smell," she told him, stirruping the greasy joystick in the crook between her thumb and forefinger, waiting a moment as the flashing ghosts made their turn around the upper-right corner of the maze. "You reek like a skunk."

In the globby reflection he was so close that she could tell he ducked his nose and silently sniffed at his pit. "Do not."

"Shut up," she said. "What do you not understand about the words *shut* and *up*?"

Just in time, she caught the third blue ghost, ate him, and hightailed it the fuck out of there. She'd come here to get away from Mom, who'd spent the whole day freaking out on the phone, first with her parents, then even with Dad, all because that creepy old man Tzadi Sophit had been shot in a Safeway parking lot in Cleveland the day before. The same jerk who'd taken all her grandparents' money back in the fifties and still sent Mom a birthday card every year telling her she was part of the first generation of the Vision. *Had* sent. Whatever. He'd died in the ambulance without so much as his precious sister around. None of his old followers. Now, in the safety and familiar darkness of Crazy Eight arcade, the last thing she needed was Wolfboy breathing his potmouth down her neck, and really—no, really—he hadn't moved an inch.

"Wolfboy," she said, "get out of here already."

He chuckled like this was something fun to be doing. "How's it going?"

For a moment her rage got the best of her and she made a stupid move: flicked the stick so Ms. Pac-Man took the upper tunnel, appearing almost immediately at the bottom of the screen, right in front of a ghost, no longer blinking, no longer weak. *Bue-nue-nue.* "You fucked me," she said. "See what you did?"

He leaned in closer to her then, his smelly reflection a darker swab. "Sorry, Deb."

"Don't call me that," she said, and stepping back, she didn't mind at all that her shoulder caught the middle of his scrawny arm like a punch. "What are you hanging on me for, anyway?"

Looking at him now, shy-faced and dumb-smiled, his eyes on The Crazy Eight's shitty worn-down carpet, she knew he was going to say something miserable she didn't want to hear. "You want to go to Ted's?"

A rankle of irritation twisted her neck. "Ted *Macklemore's?*"

He muttered out a half-remembered description of the party to be held that night at Brain-Dead Ted Macklemore's parents' place, the unremembered half a collage of movie scenes involving nerds and preppies and sporties and weirdos, boozed up by every older brother in town, the upstairs bed-rooms sex initiation camps from which girls stomped dazed and unsure of themselves with half a six-pack dangling from the hand not fixing their hair. Alice Cooper playing on Dad's hi-fi, folks out of town, the whole house a wreck from floor to basement. Somehow this was supposed to appeal to her. The last person on earth she wanted to see was Brain-Dead Ted, too. She'd rather dig out her eyeballs with sporks.

"Fuck no," she said.

"I was just thinking if you want to go for a while," said Wolfboy.

"So I can lose my virginity to a stinky hippie?"

He pulled back then, puffing out an embarrassed mouthful of air, his eyes for an instant right on hers, wide and damp and terrified. All around them the *ch-ching*ing and beeping and zapping and darkness and flashing lights of The Crazy Eight on a Friday night, that whole Colonial Plaza vibe, the smell of hot dogs and nachos, dudes strutting and girls chatting and the music going with, Jesus, some kind of Stevie Wonder sap. "Man, I didn't say—"

"Don't worry," she said. It was "Ebony and Ivory." No joke. "Ebony and gross-me-out Ivory" playing on the overhead speakers like they were at a corny high school dance. For a second she felt sorry for Wolfboy, so sorry she thought of tell-ing him she'd already lost her virginity, and to that dull guy she called Turd out at his parents' cabin in a tent with every-one else inside, but then again, why would she tell Wolfboy this and how would it make anything better? So instead she said, "I'd rather choke on dog dookie."

Then she saw the fat guy who ran the place or acted like he ran the place step away from *Q*bert*. "C'mon," she said. "I'll let you cheerlead me."

He followed alongside her like a pup. "You really don't want to go to Ted's tonight?"

She stopped, her fist clenching the last of her money—well, the last of her allowance, the last of the money other than those checks Dad sent every couple of weeks, the most recent still magnetized to the fridge, ready to go to the bank and the deep black hole of her so-called college account. Seventy-five cents. "Give me one reason I should go to Brain-Dead Ted's stupid party. Can you do that? Can you give me a single reason?"

He really did reek of pot, and with his eyes now hovering over her Chuck Taylors, she wanted to give him a good swift kick in the zambonis just to put a bookend on their pointless little conversation. Two weekends ago he'd been hanging out at her house, uninvited again, and when she pulled off her socks and he'd seen that she didn't shave her legs, his face had gone bright red and his words started coming out backward. Now he seemed about the same.

Then he said what she would never have expected. "The band's playing."

The band he meant, the only band he could mean, was Tooth and Hammer, the screechiest, keyboardiest, punks-not-deadest shitty little high schooler band that had ever dared to put on leather jackets. And the slim connection Wolfboy had to them was the genetic happenstance of being the younger brother and polar opposite to Chris Cowper, who played bass and dressed in all black and wore his black hair down over his shoulders and bounced around the stage like a depressive tied to a pogo stick, his eyes seeming to never leave the floor. For half a month Debbie thought she had it for Chris, thought she would very consciously fall head over heels for him, thought she'd turn into one of those chicks who dangle off musicians and then wind up like Mom, smoking two packs a day and doing accounting work from home in a split-level outside Waterbury. But then after their last show in Hamilton Park, before the cops came to bust it all up, he'd put his lanky arm around her and said, "You know, your dad's like one of my fucking heroes."

She didn't like Chris anymore.

The band, on the other hand, was something else. Hearing them was like taking a pill that kept her brain from rotting out from the inside, a necessary act, a method for staving off the suffocating mediocrity of dumb old Waterbury and its dumb old clock tower. The thought of Tooth and Hammer stripping the wallpaper off some bourgeois house in the burbs and splitting the ears of all the dweebs assembled there set her reeling, made her legs disappear, caused her to float like gravity had surrendered. It didn't matter the fat guy had returned to *Q*bert* or that Wolfboy was smiling like she'd just accepted his hand in marriage. She was already gone.

What brought her back down to earth was that she'd ridden her bike to Colonial Plaza, chained it outside the lamp store where nobody would mess with it. She didn't have Mom's car. She had no choice but to ride with Wolfboy.

Wolfboy, whose real name was Nathan, whom she'd known since the third grade when Mom moved her here from New York, moved her back to her old hometown, moved her away from Dad and all the crazy shit Dad was up to back then, Nathan who lived down the block and showed up on their doorstep when they hadn't even finished unpacking all their boxes, and who still hadn't stopped showing up on their doorstep even though now she was a sophomore and they had nothing in common and she treated him like, well, like some kid you call Wolfboy because he's such a dumb hippie and won't leave you alone, this Nathan, this Wolfboy, she would have to accept a ride from to Brain-Dead Ted's stupid parents' house for a stupid party just to see Tooth and Hammer.

"All right," she told him. "Let's go."

Dusk was bluing the plaza. A final skim of gold light hovered across the valley, leaping from the tops of cars, setting the Ace Hardware sign aglow. Debbie looked around as she zipped up her jacket, hoping to spot a friend who would give her a ride, or even both of them a ride—after all, at least showing up in a group wouldn't mean showing up alone with Wolfboy. Not to mention it wouldn't mean getting stuck alone with him in his smelly car with his smelly music. For her birthday last year, uninvited, he'd shown up with an actual Cat Stevens LP, still shrink-wrapped with a Strawberries sticker on the corner, and then insisted that she listen to it on the old player Mom had stolen from Dad's freaky warehouse the night Skip came for

them, the night they left the city a million years ago. Of course
it was terrible, like the sound of someone vomiting in a mug
and then drinking it. But Mom, dear Mom, had nodded her
head. She'd tapped her foot. When Wolfboy left an hour later,
Debbie walked the record out to the backyard and stuffed it in
the trash can. "Don't tell me you threw that away," Mom said
when she came in the kitchen door. "That was a thoughtful
gift."

"It was awful."

Mom, beautiful Mom, like a woman in an advertisement for
diamonds or perfume, wearing a green muumuu and tapping
a Virginia Slim against the palm of her hand, said, "Go out
there, young lady, and bring that record back in the house."

And she had. Of course she had. It didn't matter that this
tough-mom act didn't fit and neither one of them believed it.
Mom had wiped the little banana stain off the corner and
brushed off some loose coffee grounds and then she'd slid it
between records of Dad's old band, the Mercy Trips, where at
least she knew she wouldn't have to look at it. Neither of them
listened to Dad, not anymore, neither his old stuff from the
sixties or the weird solo synthesizer shit he'd been doing since
that whole warehouse dream fell apart and all the newspapers
in the country called him the leader of a sex cult. Not since
they'd left, run away, the bleak nightmare of that life turned
into a story they would speak of only to each other. These days
on MTV, Dad was treated like an aging general who'd won the
war, could wear his hair short with sunglasses and a narrow tie
and a puffy jacket and mumble things about what a talent Mi-
chael Jackson was and how disco was making a comeback and
you'd think he was John Lennon returned from the grave.

Forget all the ODs, that guy from Wisconsin who leaped off the roof on acid right after kissing Mom on the mouth, Benjamin or whatever, and forget the powder and needles Debbie used to run across so often she'd just gather them in a leather satchel someone had given her and deliver them to the little glassed-in office where Dad slept, tapping on the door like a mouse. Forget all that. Ambulances and shit stench and that woman five men held down during one of Dad's shows and Mom pulling her by the arm from the warehouse floor and the woman screaming to stop and Mom crying later, and forget a few months after that, too, when the same woman had to help carry out the limp blue body of a long-haired dude Debbie had called the Pizza Guy, because he'd always come back with it— stolen, Mom said, from the delivery boy. Forget, forget. Dad like a loop on television saying how everyone needed to give Elvis Costello a second chance. "His new record's a blast," Dad had said. "He's better than ever."

Now, in Wolfboy's white hand-me-down Pinto, she wanted to scream what an asshole Max Felt was for everyone to hear but instead pinched up the raisin-sized roach left on a nickel on the green fuzz carpet in front of the console, punched in the lighter, and started digging in the glove compartment, where she knew he kept a tiny pair of cuticle scissors. As she waited for the lighter to pop, Wolfboy dug in a gym bag of clacking eight-tracks for something to listen to. "Neil Young," he said, pushing one of the tapes into his player. "I think you'll like it. He's sort of punk."

She gave a serious thought to getting back out of the car, but then he had it in reverse and there was the lighter ready anyway. "Nathan, I know who Neil Young is. And he's awful."

"He's not," he said, jerking the little car forward. "He's real good."

Headed south on Main Street with the clock tower phallusing into the sky, she held the smoke in her chest, the jangly country-mouthed first song whining into her ears—something about a lonely boy buying a truck and driving to Los Angeles—and it sounded so miserable she figured it must have been written just at the moment Neil Young realized how horrible and boring he was, just as he was ready to wrap it up and quit singing, but here he was anyway and so he kept going because somebody had the tape recorder running, and for all that, she was still lent a little sorrow, an edge of pity. She felt sorry for Wolfboy, of all people, and blew out a wet blob of smoke that sat in front of her like another passenger for half a minute. Sorry for him, sure, but also appreciative of this little nub of a joint. And taking another long inhale, she watched the Roller Magic pass by, with Stacy and Jennifer leaned against Stacy's boyfriend's van right there in the parking lot. "Wait," she said. "Stop."

"What?"

She pushed out the rest of the smoke still in her lungs. "Forget it. Never mind."

When Mom had moved her here as a kid, she'd thought of the place as every fairy tale's setting, its Union Station clock the high tower where the beautiful princess resides, its picturesque buildings creeping up the mountainsides all around like a newly discovered village. None of it reminded her of the brick and steel and glass city they had left behind, and the split-level house Mom was given by Debbie's grandparents was nothing like the little windowless room on the second floor of the old warehouse where they'd lived since before she could remember. She'd started to believe houses and yards and kids on school buses were all things made up for television, which she'd watched a few times in secrecy, Mom keeping the sound low, aiming the antenna just the right direction to pick up a grainy picture. She couldn't remember where the little set had come from, or where they kept it hidden when Dad visited. Really the new house had scared her as a child. All the extra rooms, the echoing space, the very fact that Mom wanted her to sleep overnight in an upstairs darkness down the hall from her. She would fall asleep only late into the night, rerun TV theme songs or Johnny Carson playing from the living room, the shadows creeping along the ceiling like one of Dad's hangers-on as she knew them now, one of his friends as she'd thought then. It must have taken a year or even two before she felt the place was her own, hers and Mom's, without sneaking down on her tiptoes even in the morning for breakfast, sure the whole house would have in the night been filled by all those strangers from before, their stinks and paranoias and sometimes naked bodies. After all, she'd grown up with all those boobs and balls and hair and belly buttons, all those cottage-cheese asses, all that constant music from one record player or another, and then nearly every Sunday, Dad with his band doing a show, with everyone weeping and drugged and screaming. Yes, here was better, even for the nightmares, even for the long nights and shadows and fear of what could return. And they were in this place of magic, with its storybook peacefulness and Mom doing real work and those grandparents dropping by every other day with candy and their long car and talk of how everything would be all right.

Then there were the years after that. Her grandparents moving away. Dad's so-called sobriety. And how this place turned from something new into something so very, very old. Fucking Waterbury.

"See," Wolfboy was saying, "it's all about us."

She was blowing out the last of what that shrunken roach had to give. "What?"

"The song. We're out on the weekend."

"Jesus," she said. "Can we just not talk awhile?"

She dropped the little nub of ash on the carpet and snuffed it out with her heel just as Wolfboy would have done. He lived like a stinking animal, after all.

"Hey," he said, "speaking of Jesus, did I tell you Chris and me went to Holy Land last weekend? Mom made us go. Caught Chris with a *Playboy* under his mattress and said we needed to learn about the Bible. I was toasted, of course. Totally."

She'd just told him to stop talking, but now, a little high, the flowing open valve of his words sent her into an inexplicable wave of laughter. "Oh, Wolfboy," she said, rubbing at the tears in her eyes. "Oh, shit."

He gripped the wheel along the top, awkward and stiff-armed, always afraid she was making fun of him. "What?"

Really, it had been nothing, but he wouldn't believe her if she said that. He was too sensitive, too sure everybody had it in for him. "Just imagining you two being pulled around Holy Land by the ear."

He huffed out a nervous laugh. "Yeah," he said. "That place is fucked up."

Her mom had dragged her there on two occasions. The first time she'd gone without complaint, instead excited at the opportunity to see stories from the Bible presented before her in modern times, and in Waterbury, no less. She was only starting middle school then, and her social life more or less centered around the Sacred Heart Church Hall on Wolcott Street. But something had happened since. Without her knowing that anything was on the move, she had realized one day that her belief in all that stuff had packed its bags and left town.

Mom's faith in the Church was doubtful, given the world she'd seen out there and everything that had happened with Dad, but it signified something to her, something about another life, an alternate, with a desert and palm trees and music and a view of the sea. For her it was important. All the trappings of Catholicism mattered to her and to her understanding of herself. Catholicism connected her to her parents, who left Mexico City right after getting married in the forties, and became American citizens when Debbie's grandfather was in the Korean conflict. It had been these grandparents, on Mom's side, who had been a part of Eden Gardens and the Seekers, had lost all their money in some shoddy investment before being run out of town anyway. Mom had met Dad there, but only briefly. She never really understood how they got together. Everything was a mystery when it came to Debbie's family, sickeningly so. She hadn't even met her grandparents until the night she and Mom showed up on their doorstep here in Waterbury, the two of them tying robes, spry but bleary-eyed, looking at Debbie like she was an escaped dog. They hadn't even heard of her existence. Then five years ago, they returned south to open a hotel of their own in Acapulco, just like in Dad's old song.

Before they left, she'd grown close with them, though she

remembered in those first months feeling dodgy about any new stranger. Their home was so quiet, their days so peacefully uninteresting. She learned they had never liked Dad, had found him grating even as a teenager, too hopped up on himself, too blabbermouthed. When they sold the convenience store they ran together and left for the Mexican seaside, she'd thought they would soon follow. But Mom wanted to stay. Instead she made annual promises to visit, promises that went nowhere, clues to Debbie that Mom had never really forgiven them for something, a feeling whose evidence she could never quite put her finger on. Even now, months before every Christmas Mom would get off the phone with Grandmother and with a tense expression march into Debbie's room, saying they were going to take a plane to Acapulco for the holidays. As the weeks passed, it would become more and more clear that no such trip was coming. There was no money. Mom couldn't get away from her work. Even with a free place to stay, they would need passports and better luggage and they would just try for next year. Debbie, pale and winterized, possessor of maybe a dozen Spanish words outside the numbers, whose whole picture of Mexico came from those cartoons with the sombrero-wearing mouse, would only shrug. She'd grown out of her sentimental phase.

Whatever. Her mind was wandering. They'd left the city center now, and as the car passed along South Main Street alongside the Naugatuck, night had fallen around them. At some point Wolfboy had begun very quietly singing along with his precious Neil Young, which had built into an overblown orchestral mess about a man needing a maid. Sometimes she thought the only redeeming thing about being saddled with

Wolfboy was that hippie connection for drugs. He'd gotten her LSD last March, which totally flipped her out, and over that summer he'd kept her and Stacy and Jennifer in ludes, which they were all into until Stacy's dumb boyfriend wrecked his van on them up on Woodtick Road and nearly killed them all. Tonight, though, it occurred to her that the pot he was always sharing with her always put her in the same mood: depressed and fuzzy. It would seem like a good idea as she was smoking it, and then she'd find herself wandering into a cavern of sad bullshit and regrets for how much she took Mom for granted while Wolfboy here whispered the lyrics to vague folk-music garbage.

The turn for Platts Mill Road came just in time so she didn't have to throw herself from the moving car. After what felt like a single eternal minute they were there, parked next to the row of trees that cut off their view of the river, right across from the dull yellow split-level with its rock walls and its two-car garage. They were early.

"We're not going in now, right?" she said. "I mean, nobody's here."

Wolfboy looked perplexed. "I told Chris I'd help set up the sound."

On his bony, oddly gray cheek, an orange stain hinted at pizza sauce or chili dogs, either way something gross she hadn't noticed in the dark arcade light of Crazy Eight. Now, with the light from a streetlamp in their faces, she felt miserably uncomfortable in his car. "That's fine," she said, and reached for the door handle.

Stepping out she felt too high, too dizzy, a little frightened. "You ever get the feeling," she said, finding her footing on the asphalt, "that somebody else already did all this shit? That we're, like, just watching it happen?"

Wolfboy laughed, then gave her a frightened sort of look as they crossed the lawn, and by the time they reached the patio he laughed again. "All the fucking time," he said. "Wait, what do you mean?"

She pressed in the bell. "Just forget it. I'm stoned."

Inside there were actually more than a dozen people from school already there, most of them dudes of the prep variety like Ted, all of them carrying around juice glasses of brass-colored fluid. On the open-plan kitchen counter stood two bottles of bourbon and an empty bottle of ginger ale. Three pizza boxes stacked next to this. The weed was making her more nervous than she'd expected. She felt a dangerous vibe here, like a nightmare rearing up, like that Stanley West poem Mrs. Popper assigned them to read in English class last year:

> And then who are these ill-dressed
> Ghosts out troubling their chains?
> No, Charles, sweet Charles, we is just white
> Folks puttin' this-here cross on a flame.

On television in the sunken den, where Ted Macklemore hunched making a jerk-off motion with his hand, an old man with a pouf of silver hair talked earnestly to a toupee'd newscaster. She knew that old man. Didn't *know* him, exactly. She'd heard of him. Seen his picture hanging in her grandparents' home. He'd led a church her grandparents had joined on the West Coast before returning to the big-C Church, as Mom called it. Knew, from behind the closed door of their little room in the warehouse, of the long weekend when he'd visited Dad and all the people who lived with Dad. The newscaster, now dressed in a different suit and facing the camera, was telling his audience that the old man had been the victim of a mysterious killing in broad daylight, that he'd been a major figure in the burn-out sixties, that he'd been born with the name Oliver Danville. "A whole generation of Americans looked to the sky and saw a bright future. I say we keep looking," said the newscaster. "And never ever stop."

She had the sneaking suspicion, especially today with Mom crying on the phone with everyone, that he had been to blame for all of this, that he had been the one to make her life into this miserable trash heap in stupid freaking Waterbury. Another creep, another total jerk, deemed by society a counterculture hero. Fuck that.

"Total bullshit," she said aloud, unluckily gaining the attention of Ted Macklemore, whose gaze fell on her, making all her insides squirm, though only long enough for him to yell at Wolfboy that he wasn't invited, then that he was only kidding, and finally that he wasn't allowed to sit on any of the furniture. In a situation like this, she actually felt sorry for Wolfboy, wanted to come to his defense. But it didn't seem necessary. He only chuckled, too stoned to care apparently, and opened wide the refrigerator door. Inside were more Coors cans than she'd imagined anyone being able to purchase in a single day. On the top shelf sitting alone in a clearing, a single red bell pepper accented the wall of tan.

"Wow," said Wolfboy.

He was so absorbed that it was nothing for her to reach past him for two cans. "Come on," she said. "Let's look around."

She wanted more than anything to get away from Ted, away from his joking eyes, away from his blabbering mouth, so she led the way up the carpeted half stairs next to the fridge to a hallway of wood paneling and family pictures: Ted in grade school, Ted at Disneyland, Ted tearing open presents. In most of these he wore his hair like he was a miniaturized Marine; only in the more recent did he sport the loose, shaggy bowl cut he and his crowd shared. It was a look decidedly between styles, conservative enough to wear to church and just long enough to suggest the guitar hooks of Foreigner and Boston. The first room they came to was a bathroom with a pink tub and sink and toilet, with pink rugs and towels. Tasteless, really. As garish as yard flamingos. Onward, then, to an office with a *Reagan '80* poster behind glass above the desk. Really, its presence made more sense than the pink bathroom. Of course Ted's parents would be Republicans.

Next was Ted's bedroom. She flicked on the light: unmade bed, tennis shoes on the floor, torn-out pictures of sports figures taped to the wall in place of decoration. Atop a short bookcase sat a turntable, headphones hanging nearly to the carpet. When she went to see what he'd been listening to, her breath caught at the sight of Gang of Four's *Entertainment.* It was literally her favorite album. "Look at this," she said, but Wolfboy wasn't there. She called his name and then she called his real name. In the doorway, she told the hallway, "Hey, I'm not kidding."

She popped open her beer. Something felt wrong now about being up here, about being in this house at all. But she tried laughing it off, tried taking a swig of Coors. It was the pot giving her that paranoid edge, that tickling intestinal uncertainty, and the old man on the television, that Sophit who she'd heard about all her life, it was like—no, no, it wasn't—but it was, it was just like he was outside this room somewhere, down the hall, meeting with Dad and the others, and Mom whispering, "You just stay right here, Deborah, don't answer if anyone knocks at the door. This is important and means a lot to your father, so just stay quiet." No. That wasn't happening again. And anyway, why would she be afraid of him? That day wasn't nearly as bad as others. She wasn't afraid. Who said anything about being afraid, anyway? She took another swig. The sharp tang of the beer slid down to her stomach, to its emptiness. She'd forgotten to eat. She should ask Wolfboy if he wanted to get something to—

"Wolfboy?" she said, and the crack in her voice alarmed her. "Are you up here? This isn't funny."

Something moved in the stairwell, some shifting of dark and light. It was Ted Macklemore. He was at the top of the stairs, brushing his hair back with a hand. "Hey, Debbie."

She took a step back into his room. "Hey."

"Wolfboy said you were up here?"

"Did he?"

"You call him that, right? Funny." He was in the light of the bedroom now, smiling at her, cute in his way, maybe trying to be nice. "He said you wanted to talk?"

She didn't answer. Instead she slammed his door closed and twisted the lock. He knocked. He rattled the handle. "Go away," she said. "I need to think."

"It's my room," he said. And then, after a moment, "Just come downstairs, okay?"

· · ·

She went to the window and threw it open, stepped out onto the lower roof line, and out there in the moonlight with her heart exploding and everything else trembling, she watched the blue curtains move subtly and waited for him to barge through the door after all and come barreling out after her and she waited to jump, waited to leap down into the backyard, and when nothing happened, she sat cross-legged and kept watching anyway.

She was stoned. No one crouched out onto the roof with her, not even the ghost she always felt to be traveling behind her, just out of view. Ted had gone downstairs. Fucking Wolfboy. Why did he tell Ted she was waiting for him? What did Wolfboy know about Ted, anyway? Probably they were both downstairs sniggering on the couch with all those idiot friends of Ted's. After a time, she relaxed. The terror subsided. Voices filled the night. People had begun to arrive for the party. She could hear music. Springsteen. Then Zeppelin. After a while there was nothing again but voices and the pop and hiss of beer cans, the occasional strum of amplified guitar, the rat-a-tat of a drummer warming up. Then the band started playing. Tooth and Hammer. She gazed into the night sky and it seemed for a moment that all the stars shook loose, bouncing to the rhythm, until she closed her eyes.

The white room with Mom in the warehouse settled over her, and it was like she was there. Not the terrifying times but those others. Mom reading to her from an alphabet book. Mom brushing her hair in the mirror, catching her look in the reflection, that pained little smile. Mom at night with her arm over her, holding her close, with only the thin fan of light under the door. Nothing had happened to Debbie there, nothing like what now she could imagine could have happened there with all those speed-nosed ex-hippies wandering the hallways and drilling their eyes at them in the cafeteria. Bad things had happened to Mom, of course, things she didn't want to talk about. Torn clothes. Black eyes. The night, lip bleeding, she'd blocked the door, with no pants on, no underwear, and some man's fist banging behind her, a voice that wasn't Dad's. Thank god Skip had come for them not long after that, shown up in the night, placing his hand over their mouths, whispering it was time, gripping their arms and running with them down the back stairs and out a door she'd never seen and onto the sidewalk, where the cops were just arriving. Dad's manager of all people, breaking them out. He'd saved them. He'd broken up that whole mess by calling in the cops.

And Dad. That infrequent host. His bobbed hair and sunglasses. His black clothes. His guitar crossed over his lap like a cat or a dog, his whole body collapsed under it, a king with a scepter asking Mom if Debbie, little Deborah, was keeping up on her studies. So like Dad to name her after his dead sister and then treat her like a doll stored in the attic for someone else. "She'll be a new generation," he would say nearly every time, his voice catching like Buddy Holly's, nearly using the same words as that creep Sophit. "She's like a living future."

Now he was the grand sober genius, the rebel of all rebels, a historical fixture still alive to comment on the mystical power of rock 'n' roll. Fuck him.

What she wanted was the old Mom back. Wanted that arm

over her here, protecting her from the frigid pull of chaos below. Wanted Mom to look her in the eyes once again in the dark of the night and say they would be fine, that no one could get to them, that together they were special and beautiful and smarter than everyone else.

She was lying on her back now, her behind scooted down to the lower edge of the roof, her knees aimed at the sky. With her arms crossed over her head, she listened again, listened to the driving crash of the beat, the temper tantrum of the keyboard, the shout and call and response of the vocals, the irritable gruff sighing and whining of all those idiots downstairs caught watching them. They had only four songs and then a spiteful cover of Bertie Higgins's "Key Largo," and when that was over, when the booing ended and some piece of glass or another was broken, another quiet pause was filled by a record, Queen's "Another One Bites the Dust."

Somehow that strange old man with his UFOs had died and she'd come in to see it reported on the news right in front of Ted Macklemore, of all people, and all of this had rushed back to her, all of the white room and Mom and everything and she didn't know what to do about it. Only to look at the faint stars.

Then a single voice, a girl's voice, Stacy's. "Debbie, what are you doing up there?"

She sat up, still at the edge of the roof, the toes of her Chuck Taylors pointed down at her two best friends, at Stacy and Jessica, who appeared by magic, glowing in an ethereal white fog, dressed in skirts and too-big boyfriend jackets.

"Debbie," said Jessica. "What the fuck are you doing?"

"You're here," she said.

They looked at each other. "Uh, yeah?" said Stacy. She

dropped her cigarette and smashed it on the patio. "Do you, I don't know, need a ladder?"

Instead they moved the Macklemores' charcoal grill under her, and with both of them holding it in place, Debbie slid with her elbows off the roof, gingerly toed the metal lid, and pushed off. For a moment she could have fallen forward or backward, but with her hands out like a surfer she found her balance. A crowd had gathered by this time, and when they clapped and shouted and laughed she added an extra bit of flair to the event by tipping back her last sip of Coors before hopping down to the patio.

She had done something, had gained the center of attention, but it had all been an accident, and the last thing she wanted to do was explain herself. So, channeling her best John Belushi, she announced, "I'm gonna need another beer."

A little later, inside, in the kitchen, Stacy gave her a serious look. "What's wrong with you?"

"What do you mean?"

"You're acting totally weird."

She took a long drink. Across the room, Jessica in her boyfriend's denim jacket was laughing at something her boyfriend had just said. The music was loud now. Zeppelin again. Ted Macklemore was still outside, and through the sliding-glass door he was looking at her again with his eyes all soft and not putting on the gross-dude act he put on for his friends, and as much as she didn't want to admit it to anyone, not even herself, he was the boy she called Turd from the tent down in Naugatuck—no, really, that's who he was; there was no Turd, only Brain-Dead Ted—and she'd never wanted to tell anyone, had even hoped here she'd just wander off and the crowd would drown them and it shouldn't have mattered because they hadn't talked anyway, not since summer, not since that night in the tent outside his parents' stupid fucking summer cabin. And here he was. A complete waste of humanity with this dumb party and all his empty popularity and she should have done anything to stay at Crazy Eight and not come here. Wolfboy had done this. He had brought her here, stoned, to Ted's. It wasn't an accident. Where was he?

"He's here?" Stacy said. She had her red hair back in a ponytail, still wearing her stupid boyfriend's jacket with flames painted on the back, her eye makeup two black slashes like she was a Japanese stage actor. Looking around the crowd, a little frantic. "I didn't see him."

"I bet he's upstairs," she said. And then, her gut squishy, "Come with me."

But upstairs they didn't find him. Not in the bathroom or the office or Ted's still-locked bedroom or even his parents' room, where a leather-trimmed waterbed faced a console television and another smattering of family pictures. "I bet he's with his brother," Debbie told her. "With the band."

"Oh, yeah," said Stacy. "They left. Like, in a fucking hurry? I think they were headed up to the bunkers to get stoned."

"Let's go," Debbie said, and for some reason had never felt more strongly about anything.

Stacy pursed her lips. "Why?"

"Because," Debbie said, searching her mind, "I told Wolfboy I'd get a ride from him."

"Wolfboy is a retard," Stacy said. "We'll take you home."

They were literally standing in Ted Macklemore's parents' bedroom, Debbie woozier than she'd expected to be. "Let's just go, okay?"

Finally, after another beer and an eternity of waiting, Stacy and Jessica and their grumbling boyfriends agreed to give her a ride back up to Hamilton Park. On the radio, the newscaster sounded relieved to explain that a trade war in agriculture had been avoided. A letter had been sent to the Soviets about making friends with the new leadership. Something had been decided about sending satellite TV stations to other countries. All of it made Debbie feel small, like the tiny problems she faced here in Waterbury didn't amount to enough to worry. Little Deborah. That's what Dad called her, after all. Little Deborah. Named after his sister who was killed in a riot on Long Island, all part of that stupid Seeker nonsense back in the fifties, a little girl trampled by big white men swinging baseball bats and garden hoes at their neighbors, years before anyone in this van was alive. She wished she could forget all that, forget everything, Dad and her name and all that had happened before this very minute. That's who she wanted to be. She wanted to be just this very minute.

Listen, she tried telling herself. *All you asked was to go find Wolfboy so you could get this straight, so you could ask what he knew and what he put in that weed and why he dragged you to Ted's party.* Had Ted told him to bring her? Had stupid Wolfboy made a deal, thinking Ted would be his friend if he brought that girl he screwed to the party? Is that why Tooth and Hammer were there? Ted and that Sophit in the same night, and on top of it all, being so stoned that even now her stomach churned and her eyes felt like they'd been sandblasted and she missed Mom. Maybe her problems were bigger than satellites and letters to the Soviets. Who does the measuring?

"You're lucky Roger grabbed all those beers on the way out," Stacy told her from the front seat as they crept along in the park, lights off, looking for somewhere to stop. She was handing her a sweaty can, in fact. "Here," she said. "C'mon."

Debbie took it, but she wanted her head to clear, so she set it discreetly down between her sneakers on the questionable floorboard. Everyone else in the car was plastered and getting on her nerves and talking too loud and for god's sake unable to figure out where the best place to park was if they were going to traipse to the bunkers. Finally, without any real sense of where they were, Debbie said, "Here. Here is good."

And, really, it was okay, because when she opened her door to the cold she could hear the chug of a generator going in the dark, and the riff-raff sounds of young people miles from their parents' watchful eyes. So she took off ahead, with Stacy and Jessica and their dumb boyfriends calling to her from behind. She was running. Why? Like, really, why was she running? But she was. Into the woods and low on breath and still a little too stoned to be exerting herself by anything but running, running, running.

Over the crest of a hill along a path leading steeply up, there was the bunker and the dozen or so punk and sort-of-punk kids, only very few of them from the party, gathered between a burning trash can and the long concrete wall of the half-buried bunker.

These places were a mystery to her. She'd been here a couple of times before, knew they had something to do with chemicals made during World War II, but now they were the hovels of homeless men, their walls graffitied, their flattened cardboard boxes and refuse the beds of teenage trysts. Occasionally, like tonight, they held parties, illegal get-togethers run on fire and gasoline, sometimes even with a band playing. The only music this time came from a turntable and speaker set up on the hood of a green sports car she didn't recognize, its fender flickering green reflected flames. They were listening to Kiss, of all things, a few of them singing along.

She'd once asked Mom about the bunkers and hadn't gotten an answer. Instead she'd heard about the watch factory in town where young women in the 1920s were poisoned with irradiated paint and died a few years later with football-sized growths splitting their necks. The Radium Girls, people called them. Hired to paint the clock faces so they glowed in the dark. Debbie imagined them walking barefoot on an assembly line, zapped now and again by green webs of Tesla lightning. Dead women. They may as well have worked here, in this no place, hidden in the nowhere along the edge of the park, the bunkers already enough of a mausoleum. Mom said their deaths were an embarrassment, the sort of thing you weren't supposed to talk about as a local. But last year in Mrs. Popper's English class she'd written her final paper on the subject. "Super good," Mrs. Popper had written in blue ink on the last page. "But spelling could use improvement."

Spelling could use improvement. Fuck Mrs. Popper. Go learn to read in a white room with your mom and nothing but wrinkled magazines, you old lizard. Then *your* spelling could use improvement.

"Wolfboy," she shouted when she saw his scrawny hippie frame step out of the bunker's open doorway. A few of the kids outside turned to look at her as she approached. "Where'd you go?"

Wolfboy sauntered toward her. "Hey, Deb."

"Don't call me that," she said. "Nobody calls me that."

"Your mom does," he said.

Apparently a couple of out-of-town girls thought this was funny. She flashed a look at them and then took Wolfboy by the elbow. In the flame's light his bashful face was orange as a jack-o'-lantern. "Why'd you take me to Ted's?"

"The party," he said. "Remember? I asked if you wanted to—"

"Shut up," she said, squeezing him tighter, shaking his arm like a rag. "Why, though?"

He yanked his arm free and took a step back. "He likes you, okay? He got Chris's band to play and he wanted you to go. So what?"

Somehow, hearing it, she felt like she'd already surmised as much. "That guy doesn't even talk to me," she said.

"He said you guys made out."

She'd left her jacket in the car, and only now, standing next to the whipping flames from the trash can with her arms crossed tight, did she realize how cold she'd gotten. "Bullshit," she said. "Why would he tell you that?"

Wolfboy pointed at her with a loose finger, measured her up and down. "He said before this. Before you were punk rock. He said you guys, uh, he said you guys did it."

"That's nobody's business," she said, and knew at once that he'd been telling everybody and that he thought because of this he had some kind of power over her and that she hated

269

him, hated Ted and hated Wolfboy and hated all the stupid boys in this stupid town. She was hitting Wolfboy with her fists and kicking his shins before she could force out another word. When he dropped to the grass she kicked him again and then she was down there with him, prying his hands from his face, trying to hit him.

It was Stacy and Jessica who pulled her up off the ground. By that time everyone was shouting and Chris was down on his knees next to his brother and everyone else had stopped frozen in place with the light of the fire making them all freaky-looking and she was yelling, "I hate you I fucking hate you," and when she stopped she was already being dragged away from the light and kids from school were yelling at her and pointing and calling her a bitch and somehow she could still hear that Kiss record playing and then Stacy's boyfriend was in front of her walking backward saying, "You need me to kick his ass?"

Stacy told him that was already taken care of, but that he could get down the hill and start the van. Then she asked her what had happened. "Yeah," Jessica said on her other side. "What'd we miss?"

"I need a ride to the Plaza," she said.

Stacy bent her head sideways so her big gold-colored earrings caught the moonlight. "But what happened?"

In the van everyone soured on her. She wouldn't answer their questions because she didn't want to answer them. And after a while she could tell that her presence was making them nervous. They could be transporting someone that all their friends might be hating by Monday morning, after all, and it's not like Debbie was so cool that she was worth the risk. Thinking about it made her want to puke but also, for at least the second time tonight, made her want to jump out of a moving vehicle. But she was tired. Too tired to be angry. Too tired to do anything stupid.

Stacy's boyfriend squealed the brakes at the edge of the near-empty Plaza parking lot and wrenched the wheel so that he nearly pulled a U-turn. There was no way to communicate more clearly that he wanted her out of his van. "Okay," she said. "Fuck."

Out on the asphalt the place looked even more depressing than usual. Pools of yellow light gathered under each of the poles. The stores, long closed, had shaped a new form of reflective darkness under their shared awning. Not a soul moved. Not even the homeless guy crashed in the walkway in front of Ace Hardware with his legs splayed out and a paper-bagged bottle next to his arm. This was dead Waterbury, zombie Waterbury. Nobody her age was supposed to be out at this hour, and certainly not in Colonial Plaza.

The van jerked toward the street but then squealed to a stop again. Debbie looked over her shoulder as Stacy pumped down the window. "Listen, will you just call me?" Stacy shouted. "Just tell me what the fuck is going on with you?"

She knew she would, or she would try to, or she would want to and then talk herself out of it. Instead of saying anything, she raised a hand and waved. Stacy shook her head, pumped the window back up, and the van shot out into Thomaston Avenue. If she had a choice, if she'd learned anything tonight, she would never speak to any of them again. But she knew here, too, that this wasn't how things would work out. She would find a way to call Stacy, and later find a way to ask Wolfboy's forgiveness. And inside she would hate them both a little for knowing her too long, for not letting her change, not letting her find who she really was. What she was, what she wanted to be, or what she wanted others to see in her was that song "Pretty Vacant" by the Sex Pistols, just emptied out and gone, and if someone better than Ted or Chris or anyone ever asked her, that's what she would say, and if they laughed, she would beat them to the ground like she had Wolfboy. Or she wouldn't. Of course she wouldn't.

She walked through the flat urban expanse and wanted to fall down into a heap. Why did everything have to come at her tonight? What kind of life was this? An absent dickweed for a dad, a mom working herself to death, all that lousy shit from New York that with each passing day felt more like abuse than just an old adventure. A life kids her age read about in fucking magazines. Read about and then looked at her and said things like "You're Deborah Vasquez. That's Max Felt's daughter, right? You must fucking party then, huh?" Only Brain-Dead Ted had ever told her he didn't know who Max Felt was. Only he listened to her cry that night out at the cabin and spill her guts about all the ugly shit that had happened and all the ugly shit she thought about herself. And only him, the following night, after the families had cooked out and danced to the radio and laughed at his dad acting out *Saturday Night Live* skits, when night was long fallen and everyone was asleep, only after that did she sneak out to the tent where he was still awake reading *The Stranger* by flashlight and kiss him hard on the lips, and then after that, everything else, all of it, as if there could be no more days ahead in the world and so she could deal with the embarrassment and pain and the way his face winced up and he'd pushed her off and they'd both stretched out there next to each other like two people from an accident waiting for an ambulance to come for them. And then he hadn't called and hadn't come to her house and when school started and she was—yeah, so fucking what—wearing black now and a little more edgy than she'd been before—but not really changed, not really—only then did he go a step further and not speak to her at school.

And now, stupid, stupid. She'd gone to his party. On the television, as impossible as anything had ever been impossible, the old man, dead. And always at some distance, Ted acting for the life of him like another of his shit-sack friends, his eyes had shot back at her, bullets, headlights, mirrors.

Passing along the shadowed concrete walkway she let her own eyes drift past the night-reflecting surface to what lay beyond: tools, furniture, clothes, lamps, the hulking blocks of arcade games in the murky dark of Crazy Eight. She could see herself inside alone playing *Ms. Pac-Man*, eating up ghosts, really doing what she'd always done, surviving on the see-through flesh of her haunt. Up ahead in the real world her red Schwinn leaned against a post waiting for her, chained, her faded *Don't Blow Up the Planet* sticker on the back mudguard.

She was squatted with her key when she noticed Mom's car. The gray station wagon. In it, with the seat leaned back, was Mom, sleeping hard, her mouth hanging open, her closed eyelids turned right at her. It was like she'd been struck dead looking at Debbie's bike, waiting for her, having come for her. The sight was enough to kill her and she didn't know what the best thing to do would be—whether she should get on her bike and ride home and act like she'd never seen her. She stood instead. Stood and walked slowly to the car and counted every second like she was counting her steps to the electric chair, and when she was close enough, there was nothing else to do, so she tapped lightly on the glass.

Mom opened her eyes. Her mouth closed. Then it opened again so she could take a deep breath. Even through the closed window she heard her say, "Deb, thank god."

At home on the couch Mom sat down next to her with a plate of food: a chicken cutlet, steamed broccoli, mashed potatoes. She'd heated them up in the new microwave bought at Stevenson's Appliance in Colonial Plaza, right next to The Crazy Eight, and just looking at the burnt-boiled edges of the potatoes made Debbie feel like the whole night had been circling her and attacking her for hours. "I don't understand why you didn't tell me you went to a party," Mom said.

"You'd be totally pissed."

Mom stared a minute at the TV. Nothing was on. The channels had long signed off and they hadn't gone in for cable. She'd seen Dad on MTV only at Stacy's house, and the thought of him in that fucking leather jacket and sunglasses filled her throat with fire.

Then Mom said, "I'd rather know where you are. I nearly called the cops. You're not eighteen. You know I can call the cops, right?"

"I'm sorry," she said. "And I'm sorry about that old man. I know he's somebody important."

Mom blinked and looked at the wall, somehow hurt by her bringing him up. "That's not enough," she said. "It's been a long day."

Neither of them spoke for a long time. She was hungry, starving, and beating up Wolfboy had only made the pit of her stomach sink lower. "I hit Nathan," she said. "I hit him a lot."

Mom tucked her chin and raised her eyebrows. She still looked like a magazine model. "Nathan Cowper?"

"Yeah."

Again a long silence allowed her to eat. Then, fluid and sensual, just that general really-too-perfect way of moving about the house, Mom went over to the record player. She slid out the first Mercy Trips LP, the one with Dad's face on the cover, packing tape over his eyes and mouth. She placed it on the turntable. Dropped the needle on the second-to-last song from side A. Everyone knew it. "Love Is Terrible."

> *Love is terrible*
> *Just about unbearable*
> *Could you walk away from me*
> *If I walk away from you*
> *You're just unbearable*
> *Because love is—*

Anyone with ears and taste knew the wandering liquid guitar line under it and the driving bass and drums and that manically plucked cello, that slap in the face when the rhyme didn't quite end and instead you just went on this jagged solo and then that jagged solo, none of them technically impressive but all of them stabbing you with that sense of cold repetition, like love itself really was terrible and unbearable and why should you bother because none of the lies pop music had told you were even remotely true, and the only thing holding you or anyone together may be just this song, this sense that you were in the know because you knew enough to like this song, which meant you knew enough to see your darkness and everyone's darkness and still see this song, and if there was a reason to hate and love Dad, it was this and only this.

Back when Debbie was in junior high, the song came on in the car. Mom had turned it up, and to maybe both of their surprise, she'd sung along. Afterward, wiping a thumb at her eyes as she steered along the interstate, she'd said, "Inside your dad there was somebody else. A good man. The boy I knew. But he saw a lot of bad things. He thought the only way to fix them was to make everybody feel everything. I can't explain. He thought it was a kind of freedom in the warehouse. He didn't know. He didn't see how it changed. He couldn't see himself anymore."

Now, as the final chord lifted in that oddly hopeful way, and before "Moonlight in Brooklyn" began, Mom said, "You need to call me if you're out. Don't ever lie to me again. Do you understand?"

By that time the night had moved on. Debbie felt like she was years away from Crazy Eight and the party and Wolfboy and Ted's stupid house, as if she'd skipped up into the future and could now remember only how she'd hurt her mom, with that tired look on her face, could only hear Dad singing, not on the record but at the warehouse, in another time, through the white and pounding walls. The sensation was that of a slide rule, with the future and the past and all the stupid people involved in it somehow lining right up with now, with Mom's disappointment, and then the memory of the present opened wide: their house, the precious house of their own, with the framed Frida Kahlo print in the hallway and the Simon & Garfunkel records leaned against the television and the crocheted owl-shaped coasters on the coffee table and the smell of TV dinner lingering and nearer between them the great pile of papers and the adding machine and everywhere all that desperation, that tension, all that they never talked about. She loved her, loved Mom, loved the creases around her eyes and the smooth point of her jaw and her black hair pinned back and even this town she'd brought her to, this Waterbury, godforsaken as it was. "I understand," she said.

And back in her bedroom with the lights out and Mom humming some fucking Eagles song under her breath in the bathroom they shared by two doors, she thought of the pictures out in the hallway of Mom in her New York days. A beautiful young woman in disco dresses and wide hats and big sunglasses, her lips seemingly always blowing a kiss. Last week, Mom had hung a Polaroid of Debbie standing outside school, dressed in black, sneering, her hand clenched in a threatening fist. They were two sides of something, sure. A cliché. Maybe even a family.

THE FOAL

JACK PENROD—1987

He had seen him before and known he wasn't seeing him, that he was dead and buried. He had spoken to him, knowing he wasn't speaking back. At first Opal thought he was just working through grief, that he wasn't really seeing anything but just pretending. She would ask him what they talked about, and Jack would tell her. These were simple conversations at first. "He's doing well," he'd tell her. Then, as she lost interest, when she began to worry, when she started talking about needing to see someone, a professional, he made up little jokes to excuse his behavior. "He says the food up there's better," he would say. "He told me to put money on the Oakland Athletics." And she humored him awhile longer. But nearly two years passed with Paul in the cemetery over the highway, close enough, as she told him one night in bed, that he could go look for himself. He didn't need to.

Then when he saw him, when he heard him, Jack would ignore his older brother, appeared like a gathering cloud at the table in his brown suit, his thin pale face and big eyes imploring him, saying, "Listen. Why don't you listen to me? You've got to make it good."

The minute Opal left the room, Jack would square toward

his brother and whisper, "I'm not cleaning up after you. Leave. Go on."

But the next day Paul would be back, leaning against the barn door in the vast empty sunshine, sitting in the truck next to him fiddling with a cigarette, lounged on the sofa watching the evening news. Then that late summer his brother was gone and Jack thought he was cured, that his imagination, once out of hand, had been folded and tucked back in its place.

Fall threatened its arrival and then backed off after a heavy rain, the warm weeks of an Indian summer returned, Jack's favorite time of year, especially now in his retirement, when he could enjoy it. He'd been on the new riding lawn mower evening out the straw-colored grass for the last time of the year when a car pulled to a stop at the end of the gravel drive stretching the length of the front acreage. A gray Lincoln Town Car, from what he could tell, with dark windows and shining chrome wheels. Not the sort of car you saw around Meeker all that often, and strange, too, that it would block the driveway, parallel with the road. He turned a corner of the lawn and, careful to veer around Opal's flower box, cut to the far edge. There he turned again, not exactly surprised to see the car still in place. Engine trouble. Maybe a blowout. He pulled the brake lever and shut off the engine. Under him, the whole machine rattled once and fell inert. When he looked up, the car was gone and a small thin man was left in its place. With a stooped gait, the man started down the drive.

Now this was something. Jack muttered curse words to the deaf wind and raised a gloved hand, thinking the best approach here was a friendly presentation. The other man, too, waved, and though a great distance of the long fenced drive remained, in a flash Jack recognized his brother. A spring jumped in his chest. "Paul?" he shouted, careless of Opal's hearing. "That you?"

The man walked a ways before calling back, "Who else?"

Nearing him was when the difference struck. The deeper-set eyes. The shiftiness there. The brown suit that didn't fit him, threadbare at the hems. Altogether a wiry drawing of what his brother used to be. The man had always been a little sparse, never shaking off the impoverished habits of eating they'd been raised with as kids in Idaho. But he had, it appeared, aged even thinner, worn out in the absence of his death, gone shabbier in these months without haunting.

Jack gave a look at the highway like he could conjure back that car. Only the unquiet wind and a view of the cemetery across the road. "You okay?" he said. "Everything all right?"

"Of course, of course," Paul said, though his body shuddered as if he were losing his balance on the gravel.

He couldn't help but reach to steady him by the elbow. Last he'd seen, his brother hadn't aged a year, maybe looked younger than the day he'd passed. "What brings you back now?"

Paul didn't shake off his hand as he would have anytime before. Older brother. The tough one. So independent that even when Paul was alive Jack wouldn't hear from him for half a year or more at a time, or in this case, long into the silence of his visitations, in the last warm gasp before winter. They walked between fences nearly to the front lawn before Paul said, "Listen, I need somewhere to stay awhile. Think you could help me out?"

Opal, needless to say, was shocked. "Honey, I thought you were through with this," she said when she found him in the bathroom testing the hot water for his brother's shower. "I thought we'd settled this was all over."

"Something's wrong with him," he said.

"Him?" she said, and shook her head.

"Let's give him a few days."

She put a stack of folded towels in the bathroom closet, her eyes watchful and concerned. "Why's he here now?" she said. "Did you ask yourself that?"

"Didn't think to," he said, but he could tell that she was growing alarmed. With the water running, he went to their bedroom to hunt up a change of clothes for his brother, a pair of gray sweat pants with a drawstring, an old T-shirt. When he turned around, she was in the doorway, her hand on her face like she was going to cry. "Don't worry," he told her. "I'll ask him to leave as soon as he's well."

"*Ask* him to leave?" she said. "My Lord."

He forced a chuckle. "I'll tell him."

She gave him a hard look, her brow skirting down at her blue eyes. "This isn't funny, you know," she said. "I think it's time you talked with Dr. Peterson."

Years ago he would have said something about his being his older brother, about Paul's holding the family farm together when Mom and Dad left, about being there when Dad died up in New York, about taking care of Mom after all that, about how whatever secrets Paul had they were kept for the government or something like the government and anyway necessary. A few months back he would have reminded her that his brother's son had died young and how that had changed everything and how he'd been out to make amends when time struck him, when his body left, unhealed, unfixed. But these were things he'd repeated and repeated. On top of all that, he had never in his life believed in ghosts. "I'm sorry," he said. "Honey, I swear this is the last time."

At the bathroom door he heard his brother talking through the spray. He put his ear close but couldn't make anything out. "Paul, I'm leaving some clothes here at the door," he said. "Opal's gonna heat up spaghetti, all right?"

"I just need a little time," his brother shouted back at him. "Then we'll fix everything."

And what was that supposed to mean? For a frightened moment, bent there at the door, he thought Paul had overheard them talking down the hall. But that was impossible. And besides, his brother went right back to talking to himself. He struggled again to listen, and when nothing came clear, he set the clothes on the floor as he'd intended. "Okay," he said. "They're right outside here."

Opal tried her best to make conversation over dinner, touching Jack's hand now and again as he filled Paul in on what the boys had been up to, Joshua living in Omaha now with his wife and kids, Terry in Dallas just named partner at his law firm, feeling as he did so that this vision of his brother was more and more real with each moment. Cleaned up, his hair combed back, and in Jack's baggy clothes, he looked even older. Liver spots had spread up his neck and one side of his face. The skin hung under his jaw. His nose seemed to be all flesh, a saggy thing like his ears. And those smart eyes of his were globby now, faded, like a man going blind. He would have turned sixty-three earlier in the summer, no age to spit at, but he looked frail and sick as someone in a nursing home, or worse, waiting out his last days in a hospital. The man was a troubling sight. He didn't touch his food.

On television a little later the news anchor said something about Fawn Hall, and when her picture appeared, Paul looked him in the eye and said, "Can't keep her damn mouth shut."

Jack laughed. "You saying you know that woman?"

"Do I know her?" Paul said, and then he stood up from the couch and walked down the hall to the boys' old room, where Opal had let Jack make up a bed for him.

After a long silence, Opal primly cleared her throat. "Well," she said, "are we done playing this game now?"

Jack switched the channel to a science program. "Let him rest," he said. "I'll talk to him tomorrow and see."

Later that night he slipped on his jacket and boots and went to the barn to check on the horses. The foal was there, still unsteady on his legs, messing about in the straw like a child on stilts. "Whoa there," Jack said, and, offering out a hand to his muzzle, "What are you up to tonight, McMahon?"

He'd expected Paul to be there with him when he looked over his shoulder. *Gone, then*, he thought. His brother returned to the dark and away of death. There had been a time early on when he thought his brother really was alive, that he'd faked it, put some nameless body in his place. Such a made-for-TV idea would have fit his personality. A man of shade and mystery, always up to something, hard to trust. And now, with his reappearance, Jack worried where this was going, whether he *was* losing touch. He worried what Opal thought of him, too, if she could stand another day or week of this.

He stroked the foal's long, uncertain head, and when he'd apparently given him enough attention, Bertha, looming in the wide open barn doorway, half in light, snorted and coughed. "All right, all right," he said, and passing her, he reached up and rubbed her long snout. "Y'all tuck in for the night, okay?"

Walking back along the dirt path and then the gravel, he heard the faint howls of coyotes answering one another off in the woods. The Choir, he called it, though Opal didn't like him giving them anything close to human qualities. They were, she told him, devils in fur coats. At the patio, he breathed out a long sigh. His brother had moved on. Whatever had brought him here, whatever had returned him, had passed. Then in the hall he heard a snuffling noise. There, in the boys' old bedroom, his brother was stretched under the covers, sleeping uneasily, his face twitching like a fly had landed on his nose.

Not long after the traveling man had arrived and taken with him the next day their mother and father, Jack and Paul had turned in opposite directions. They had stayed on the farm two more years, but in that time he'd met Opal, who softened his hard edges, laughed at his closed-minded ways, filled him with dreams of some better life back where she was from in

Oklahoma. Paul, on the other hand, nursed his mean streak. It was him, the older brother, who said they should sell the farm to the bank in Boise, and not for any dreams of far-off Oklahoma but so he could track down those damned parents of theirs and give them a piece of his mind. Jack couldn't have cared less. But he welcomed the money, a young man turning twenty, ready to marry, his eyes on a used Ford he'd seen in town buying feed a week earlier. In no time at all the deal was done. He and Opal were hitched at the Baptist church and on the road the next morning. In Stroud, they lived with her parents and he worked at a little machine shop west of town, studying radio and television repair by mail in the evenings. Then came Meeker and the plan for his own shop, and then, after a month in business, his brother had appeared for the first time, and then with news that Dad had died in some kind of accident up north, in a town Jack had never heard of. Paul had been there, he said. He'd seen it. The boys were still little then, just starting grade school, and the month-long visit from this mysterious uncle knocked them for a loop. The three of them were fast friends, together every minute. By the time Paul packed up and left, assuring him that Mom would be well taken care of, he'd become a member of the family. It was the happiest Jack remembered ever seeing him.

Thirty years went by, selling and fixing appliances, the boys growing up and out, and over the last five, Jack had started renting out videocassettes, and in the end that's what the buyer had wanted out of Penrod TVs & More. Taking the risk on the VHS rental market had been gold. That alone had paid off their mortgage, and with the sale of the shop this spring, he and Opal wouldn't have to worry for money. Only a few weeks after this early retirement, news had come that Paul had died, an undiagnosed heart problem, blood pooling in his chest, gasping for breath in an airport lounge in Minneapolis and then gone. They had paid to bring him to Meeker, to the cemetery over the highway, and then had come the visits, the long conversations, the sudden appearances.

Originally he'd pictured retiring at fifty-nine to be filled with travel and projects around the house. Instead he'd spent most of his time puttering from room to room and getting on his wife's nerves. She wasn't used to him being around all day, she reminded him again and again. Maybe it was time he made some friends and got out of the house. "Friends," he liked to say. "So I can sit at the Corner Café all morning reading the paper and talking about younger women?" But what he really wanted to tell her he couldn't put together in words. Something about how he missed her so desperately, how it seemed anymore they were strangers passing on a sidewalk, how he'd started to itch with this feeling that he'd wasted all his life doing next to nothing.

At first he thought the return of his brother, no matter how strange his attitude, would turn out to be a relief from these troubles. Instead the man sat in a chair looking at the back field most of each day, getting up only to come to the table or to use the bathroom. Jack asked him every afternoon if he wanted to go tend to the horses with him, as they'd once done as children, but Paul only shook his head. Opal tried ignoring the subject, acting as if she wasn't troubled when Jack brought up their visitor. Now and again, just as it seemed they were alone, Jack would hear his brother talking to himself, muttering, complaining. The few times Jack called to him from the other room to ask what he was saying, he'd go silent, and Opal in turn would busy herself with a magazine or something, her face burnished with shame. After a few days, he made peace with the idea that his brother would haunt the guest bedroom for the remainder of time. Opal, too, seemed to resign herself to the situation. He overheard her on the phone talking to a friend in town, saying something about old age and the brain playing tricks and how there was nothing to do, was there? "Probably nothing," she'd said after a pause, and the sink in her voice had sent him out into the dry wind, feeling like a lost child.

In bed that Saturday night, her Dick Francis book open on her chest, she said, "I guess he's staying? I guess you won't make him leave?"

"I only wish I knew why he was here this time," he said. "If I understood the trouble—"

"You need to get out of the house," she said, turning to the wall. "Go to a football game or something."

Later that night he woke to what he thought was her shivering. When he turned on his side he saw that she was sitting up in bed, facing the closed window, her hands gripping the mattress. Her shoulders moved in a strange rhythm. Her face aimed at the floor. She was sniffling. Crying. He reached to grip her arm, felt the softness of her skin and instantly the hard tightness of her fear. "It's too much," she said. And then, after another sniffle, "Oh, this can't happen to us."

"I'm fine," he said. "Everything's okay."

She stood, free of his hand, and shuffled in her house shoes around the front of the bed. "It isn't," she said. "And we both know you aren't."

. . .

Fall came on hard the next day. A cold, stiff wind and driz-
zling rain.

Jack took the four-wheeler to the back forty in his thick
denim work jacket to feed the horses. But after stopping to
close the gate, he saw the foal down in the grass near the
south fence. Immediately his chest strained. He sped over the
uneven turf. Off the four-wheeler, he ran to the poor child
and dropped there to his knees. The foal's legs and haunches
were all torn up. Blood coagulated in dark wet streaks and
still siphoning into the grass blades, cool to the touch. Eyes
open. The pink innocent fat of his tongue stuck out just past
his teeth. Tears and bite marks. Coyotes. The whole picture
came to him at once, not only what lay before him but also
the terrifying final moments, the fear that must have seized
up his weak thin legs, the bleating from his damp new lips.
How had Bertha not heard his calls? How had the others? He
twisted around to see only the hillock field leading up to the
run of trees that bifurcated the back half of the property. A
miserable cursing rage welled up in his gut and spilled out
his eyes, and for a solid minute he knelt in the rain next to
the foal hating with all his heart every last living thing in the
world.

Then he left the foal there and, without returning to his
chores, parked the four-wheeler in the shed near the house.
From the open door through the rain he could see into the
field, the other horses, grown and alert, ambulating in the
orange dawn. He spat. They'd disappointed him. They'd failed
to come to the little one's aid. Only when he had gathered

himself back together did he return to the house, determined
to keep all of this from Opal as long as he could.

Paul, to his surprise, was at the table when he came in, wearing the brown suit he'd arrived in five days earlier. "I need to
go into town," he said.

Jack looked from his brother to his wife and back again.
"I'm too busy today to go into town."

Opal's eyes lit up. Shaking cornflakes into a bowl, she said,
"You do need stimulation, hon." Then she looked around the
room as if trying to place something. "Maybe the two of you
ought to go in. Waste a little time?"

"That's right," Paul said, smiling. "That's exactly what we
should do."

Jack didn't like the change, not today. That foal, tan and
white-legged with a skirt of white around its black snout, had
been a favorite. A sweet child, always nubbling at his elbow
when he came around. He'd done something wrong to let it
get attacked by those damn coyotes, had made a terrible mistake, and seated at the table now, he remembered that he'd
closed the side gate. He'd closed the damn side gate, leaving
the foal alone and split from his mother. Why in god's name
had he done that? How hadn't he noticed they were parted?
He tried to remember. But really it didn't matter. One way or
another he'd failed.

He took a deep breath. "Just where are you planning on
going?"

"Into town," Paul said. "Into Shawnee."

"Would tomorrow work?"

Opal tapped the back of his arm with her knuckles, her

smile as uncertain as someone testing a face in the mirror. "The man wants out of the house, hon. Even I can see that."

There may never have been a day in his life he less wanted to go to Shawnee. "All right," he said. "First we got to take care of a couple things."

Outside, the rain had stopped but everything held its damp under the long gray sky. A canal of red mud ran along the gravel path. He made his brother sit behind him on the four-wheeler, side-saddle, holding him by the shoulders like some 1950s girlfriend. With the cart attached empty behind he wouldn't let him sit there. "You're in a suit, goddamnit," he told him. "Just sit still and hold on."

Then he took him beyond the chained gate to the back forty acres, a single rolling hill that slid up to the northwest corner, where on the other side of the line of trees his tractor and the horses and the barn had been assembled over time, ostensibly the purpose of his retirement years. Three mares, a filly, and after that first successful breeding, Bertha had produced the foal, whom Opal had wanted to call McMahon after the fellow who sat next to Johnny Carson and sent all those ads for million-dollar prizes. Up the rut path bouncing back and forth he half expected his brother to leap off and start back for the house. But he didn't. He was still there holding on when Jack pulled to a stop on the flattened grass where McMahon was stretched, his legs parted as if frozen in mid-leap, his eyes staring ahead, anything but at peace. Paul, sliding off in his ridiculous clothes, said, "He's been hurt."

"That boy's dead," Jack told him. "Just about the worst news I've had."

His brother hunched down into a squat like a body much stronger than he'd expected. With a flat hand he combed back the foal's ears. Nearing the fence along the tree line, Bertha was all snout, snorting and neighing. "Girl, I'm sorry!" Jack shouted, though he knew she wouldn't be consoled. "Girl, I'm so sorry."

Bertha seemed terrified and wild, her eyes bulged, her front hooves punching the earth, her knees punching at the barbed wire. Behind him, as a miserable silence fell onto the field, Paul grunted. He was hefting the foal up into his arms, carrying him to the little flatbed trailer. Now Jack could see the mortal wound, the silvery insides drooping out a sad and jagged hole. They'd done this for sport or something had scared them off in the midst of the kill. Paul dropped the foal into the trailer like a sack of bones and then brushed at the lapel of his suit. Blood streaked down the left side, darkening a whole arm. "She's scared of you now," he said. "Likely thinks you killed him."

"I did kill him." He looked at the stain in the grass. "I may as well have killed him."

Back on the four-wheeler, Paul said, "Remember that time we came up on that buzzard eating a dead possum?"

Of course he did. The image had burned deep in his mind. One foggy morning the two of them, Jack likely no more than eight, had been adventuring through the fields behind their parents' farmhouse when they heard rustling near the creek bed they were following. Through a part in the tall grass they came face-to-face with a red-faced buzzard nearly Jack's height, his beak stretching the bloody meat out of a splayed gray corpse. The possum's face seemed peaceful, like it was a sleeping lapdog, but for the single red drip of blood streaking down between its eyes. Thinking on it now, Jack knew that buzzard had set him forever against death. Blood turned his stomach even when he'd been made to pretend otherwise.

Paul, on the other hand, had taken scientific pleasure in the sighting, telling the story to anyone who would listen, the gore of that experience a passed test of his burgeoning manhood. What had that buzzard meant to him? Jack had never thought to ask.

On the house side of the back fence curled a dried-up creek where Jack and Opal burned their trash in big oil cans and where, in the narrow red-dirt canyon, they had over time dumped a broken-down dishwasher, an old refrigerator, the rotted studs from their first carport, and anything else bigger than a garbage bag. Jack parked the four-wheeler alongside the dry bed. He'd brought a gas can and matches, items Paul only now seemed to notice. "You're not going to burn that creature, are you?"

"What else?"

Paul grimaced. In the bloody suit, deep in the field so far from civilization, he seemed like a man who had walked off a movie set. "It's monstrous," he said. "You bury a thing like that, not burn it."

"What about the coyotes?" Jack said. He didn't like this brother of his telling him how to run things, especially now, after days of muttering quiet. "They'll dig it up."

"That's idiotic," he said. "They'll do no such thing."

So Jack rode up the drive to get the shovel and post-hole digger from the garage, leaving his brother downhill with the foal. When he returned, Paul had put his suit jacket over Mc-Mahon's head and rolled up the sleeves of his shirt. Half his tie was tucked between buttons at his sternum. Jack took the post-hole digger for himself and handed the shovel to his brother. Then he began clawing up the perimeter of the grave. Alongside, Paul slung the shovel's blade into the red earth and snuffed it in farther with his shoe, making a pile in the scrubby grass. After a half hour they had a rectangle three and a half feet deep and both men had sweat running down their faces and arms even in the chill wind.

"That's good," Jack said. "That'll work."

Paul lifted the veil of his suit jacket from the foal's head and dropped it into the bottom of the hole, then reached down to spread it toward the corners like a silk liner. Jack came behind with McMahon's body. When he stood again, his brother was just finishing an awkward gesture like crossing himself. "You Catholic now?" he said.

Paul looked him in the eye, troubled. "I've come to respect life," he said. "If that's what you're asking."

Jack picked up the shovel and lifted a pile of clay. "Not exactly."

After those morbid duties, they washed their hands at the spigot next to the garage, hopped into the truck stinking of sweat and dirt, and started off down the county road toward Shawnee. "Listen," Jack told him. "Don't tell Opal about all that. I'll tell her on my own. And for god's sake, nothing about that side gate. Got it?"

His brother was staring out the window at the flat plains and the towering white clouds. "Got it," he said. And then, without any prompting, he said, "Jack, I need you to go to her. To go to Eileen."

When this was followed by a long silence, or only the sound of the road and a country song faintly whispering from the radio, Jack said, "You know I called her again. I told you that."

He had called her, had called Eileen, the woman his brother had told him about by phone in the weeks before he died, the woman his brother had been on the way to see when his heart seized up in the lounge at the Minneapolis airport. He'd told her then about Paul's death, the funeral, and how he knew that she was someone important to him. He hadn't told her about what a mystery she was to him, or how Paul had said that he owed her something, that he'd said he'd thought he was finished with all this in '82 and only now saw he wasn't. "I never even knew her," Paul had told him over the phone a couple of days before leaving for the trip. "She was a sort of muse for all this, the source. I made all these mistakes. Hurt people. I've got to make good with her. I blamed her brother, see?"

"Uh-huh," Jack had told him, though really he didn't see much of anything through the ricocheting pellets of his brother's scattershot rambling.

Paul had been like that in the weeks before the heart attack. He'd wanted to come clean about everything, keeping him up late into the night on the phone, long distance, harping about unexplained details he'd said he couldn't share, convinced he'd wasted his life on the wrong side of events. This was not long after Paul's own shock, the sudden death of his only son,

Theresa his second wife's son, Bradley, killed by a car going the wrong direction on a California freeway. Twenty-two years old. About to finish college. April of '85. That grief had stripped him in what would be his last months down to the bitter rack of his bones, where he could measure out his sins and make plans for absolution. Jack had learned to weather whatever his brother threw at him over the phone then.

"Can I ask you about your job?" Jack said finally, at the tail end of one of those long talks. "About what you did all these years?"

He could tell by the long sighing pause that Paul would talk, that he wanted to talk, and he'd been waiting for permission. "There was an interested party," he said. "He had work for me to do. Keeping an eye on certain types. Checking in. You'd be surprised what the fucking communists have been up to all these years."

"So it's government," Jack said. "I always told Opal it was government work."

His brother seemed to consider this, to weigh it on either hand. "Yeah, why not?"

Then his brother told the story of a man of great wealth, a man with a public face and a private one who'd been determined to stamp out Reds anywhere they appeared. This man, this interested party, as Paul called him, had heard about a commune led by some guru out in California who had pooled all his followers' money and partnered with a developer to build nearly a whole town up north somewhere, a place called Eden Gardens. This commune included a number of blacks and Mexicans and even a few Asians, so the job was easy. But things got out of hand. He'd wanted—he'd been paid—to scare them off. He did that, but people were hurt. And to his surprise—or maybe not surprise, maybe he'd actually expected it—Mom and Dad were there. That's where their father had died, along with a little girl. This circumstance had in some respects been the fault of Paul. No, maybe it just was his fault. He couldn't say for sure, but he wanted to come clean about it. Wanted Jack to know.

After that, he'd kept working for the interested party, writing a monthly pamphlet attacking the American government as a socialist dictatorship, putting down civil rights protesters as Soviet thugs, calling for the use of the atomic bomb in Cuba and Vietnam. By the Nixon years he helped push theories of government conspiracies behind everything, placing ads in the backs of magazines and local newspapers, ghostwriting a book on the Kennedy assassination, pushing the Watergate thing into hysterics. He gave info, was an informer. To radio shows, to newspapers. The goal was to cause mistrust and disillusion. Burn the village to save it, they used to say. He was, he explained, in the vanguard of a vast defensive action that would one day put a stop to all this garbage about blacks and queers and women having special rights. America would go back to being America.

But he had made mistakes, as he'd said. He'd hurt people. There had been a woman, a radio personality, he claimed to have buried in the desert, a woman with some connection to that drifter, to Eden Gardens, to the fuzzy story line of Paul's obsession, though Jack had never believed Paul capable of such things. And as to what had happened with this woman Eileen's brother, Jack couldn't get a straight answer out of him. On that he seemed afraid to expand.

In Washington, Paul had become an invisible legend, and for a while worked with a firm of brash young lobbyists, real cutthroats. The work he did with them was mostly petty. Leaking pictures of politicians with young women to the press. Spitballing ways to fund the Contras with military folks who should have known better. Bringing down a sad drunk who thought his nomination to a big post was a sure deal by telling tales of a young man who used to live in his pool house, never mind there was no young man, no pool house. Aside from that it was scaring the bejesus out of corporate leaders and neophyte congressmen, and occasionally putting them together in a room to make a deal that would lead to legislation. A filthy job, really.

He'd said all this before, over the phone, but still Jack had a hard time responding. The whole speech sounded to him like the sort of malarkey they dream up for James Bond movies. And he'd never liked his brother's bigoted side, the ugly way he looked at anyone who'd been given an unfair shake in this life. "Is all this true?" he said. "Are you just pulling my leg?"

"Jesus, Jack," his brother had said.

"Well, I don't know. Don't you understand how this all sounds?"

"Don't worry about it, then," Paul said, clearly angry. "Anyway I'm going to see Eileen. We'll see what happens."

But for the radio the ride to Shawnee had sped by in monologue, his brother telling his story like a spy being debriefed by his superior. Soon they were in the parking lot of the Kmart on Harrison, and Jack knew he had to tell him about the other call, the one he'd made to Eileen that summer, when he had wanted his brother to disappear. "She's sick," he said. "Cancer. That woman who lives with her, that Claudette, she says she's terminal."

"You mean she's dying?" Paul said. "Why didn't you say anything?"

"I'm saying it now."

Paul looked hurt for an instant and then just angry. "You've always been a son of a bitch," he said, and opened the truck door.

In the parking lot headed for the store, Jack tried catching up but felt mysteriously winded. "I'll call her again!" he shouted. A woman pushing a child in her shopping cart looked at him with alarm as he rushed by. "I'll see how she's doing."

He found him in the back left corner of the store in the men's clothes, trying on a simple beige jacket in front of a mirror. "Listen," Jack said, "I'm trying to help."

His brother shot his cuffs and began tilting his newly shaven chin this way and that. The jacket, plain as anything, looked awkward with slacks and a bloody dress shirt. "All right," he said. "Then help."

Jack followed him in a vague eight-pattern as he picked up trousers and a couple of T-shirts and socks and underwear. "I don't understand," he said finally. "How am I helping?"

Standing in front of the mirror, Paul seemed a decade younger, meaning younger than Jack himself. His eyes had a brightness to them he didn't remember and his splotchy shiny head appeared now to be a fake, his loose neck and sagging cheeks the shifts and settlements of a mask. "You're taking me to her," Paul said.

Over the intercom, a crackling voice announced a Bluelight Special in housewares.

"I don't think I can do that."

"She's in Lawrence. She's sick, Jack. This is my one chance."

With that, his brother swung around and started for the checkout. Again, Jack found himself struggling to keep up, though now in his hands were the clothes Paul had picked up. "When the hell am I supposed to go to Kansas?"

"Today," Paul said over his shoulder. "Right now."

Maybe it was seeing his brother suddenly so alive, so energized, that put him behind the wheel a few minutes later, pushing a mile an hour over the speed limit on the interstate toward Oklahoma City, where they could hit I-35 northbound and be there by evening. He trusted Paul to find their way, though thinking on it, he'd never done such a thing before. It had been Paul who had lost him in the Sears in Boise all those years back, who'd gone running ahead, weaving in and out of the displays, leaving him to collapse on the ice-cold floor Indian-style, weeping, sure he'd never find his family again. Yeah, he held that against Paul even some fifty years later. Thinking on it put a tremble in his eye, a silvery quiver. He rubbed it with his thumb.

"This woman," Jack asked, "was she an ex-girlfriend?"

"Eileen? No." His brother stared out the window at the flat expanse west of McLoud. "She started all this. I wrecked her brother's life. Wrecked his whole life's work. This whole idea he had to better people's lives. All to hunt down Mom and Dad, and then it didn't stop after that, either. I told you all this." He worked his fists on his thighs like he was trying to rub something off his knuckles. "But if I can talk to her, I think I can sort it all out. I just got to tell her."

They drove awhile without speaking. He reached for the radio knob and then thought better of it. "Tell her what, exactly?"

Paul turned toward him again. "I'll prostrate myself," he said. "I'll beg forgiveness."

Just ahead was the exit for the Choctaw Love's station. Jack tapped the brake. "I say we get a little coffee," he said. And when he stopped, he was pleased his brother wanted to wait outside. In the hallway next to the restrooms he rang Opal on the pay phone. "I'm taking him to Kansas."

"What?" she said. "What are you *talking* about? Jack, just come home."

"I'm taking Paul up to some woman in Kansas."

She gasped. "I thought you were going to the Kmart."

He tilted back to look out the wide dining-area window. Paul was still there, staring forward, as lifeless as he'd been in that room for the last week. That room. The boys' room. The extra room. "We went there first, honey," he said. "But I think he needs to go up and see this woman. He's got something to get off his chest. She's real sick."

"It's ridiculous," she said, and he knew, deep down, that he was embarrassing her. "No woman wants to hear what he's got to say. Jack, he's not real. You know that, don't you?"

On the phone box someone had scratched the word *FUCK* in angular geometric cuts just below a half-finished phone number. He knew that she didn't see him, that to her, Paul was just a figment of his imagination. She had only been playing along, and really, lately, not playing along at all. But that conversation was for another time.

"Well, he's got to do this," he said. "And I don't know what else to do but take him."

"Jack, please just come home, will you? We can talk about it. I'll go with you if you still want to go."

He considered this a moment. Opal there in the truck with Paul, the two of them fighting over who sits next to the window. "No," he said, "I'll take care of this first."

A humming silence filled the gap between them. "Oh, just go," she said frantically. "But I've never heard a dumber idea in my life. Jack, you're sick. You need help. This has got out of hand, don't you see?"

"All right," he said. "All right."

Across the store, a fat man in overalls was filling a giant Styrofoam cup with a squirt from each soda on the fountain, going back and forth like some fleshy typewriter. "Jack," Opal gasped, "whatever you think you're doing? Don't you dare get yourself hurt."

"Of course, honey. There's nothing to worry about."

He kept Eileen's phone number on a folded piece of paper in a pocket of his wallet, away from where Opal would ever see it. He'd hidden it there when Paul first gave it to him, as a number to call if he needed him on that trip he never made. When a woman answered, he could tell by her singsong voice that it was Claudette, her friend. "She's got a room at the hospital," she told him. She was, she said, on her way up there. "Just packing a bag to stay overnight. We're nearing the end."

"I'll be there today," he said.

"You really don't have to."

He didn't want to, of course, and had no idea what he'd say when he arrived, but he was determined to do what Paul wanted. "I'll be there," he said. "See you soon."

He really did buy a coffee, as well as a Reese's Peanut Butter Cup, eating the latter still watching his brother out the wide front windows. Ten years ago he'd quit drinking, and never before did he know of his sweet tooth. Now in this dumb trouble, he leaned on the faint tingling release of sugar in the blood and wondered if he was in danger. He'd failed to tell Opal about the woman having something to do with his brother's hunt for their parents all those years ago. Maybe he should call her back. But then a family wanted the table he stood near and his throat leaped and his coffee had cooled and he was outside in the gauzy fall midday, striding like a criminal toward his truck.

"Okay," Paul said as Jack was gunning up the highway ramp, "I know what you're thinking, and I'm making no trouble."

Jack felt stupid saying it, but thought he had to. "Who's making trouble?"

Paul was looking out the window again, now at the whopping tan rectangles of the Crossroads Mall. He'd changed into his new clothes while Jack had been in the Love's station, and in the tennis shoes and beige jacket, he looked like a stranger, an old man taking up jogging. Or a bank robber. Maybe the kind of man who could do those things he'd said. No, no. Better to put that nonsense out of mind. Still, he kept glancing over at him. "I just told you I'm not making trouble," Paul said when enough time had passed that it seemed disconnected from their conversation. "The woman's seriously ill."

Jack turned up the radio and glided north, through the interchange downtown and up past Edmond into the rolling tan fields toward Guthrie. Time rolled onward, the land around them receding on either side in humps and sawtooths of red exposed earth and straw-colored grass. On the plains, George Jones's voice joined the cleared sun and dry land, telling of a lie told to a lover. When the song ended, a man came on screaming about cars. The Stillwater highway flew past. Jack killed the noise. "So what is it I'm going to say? What am I supposed to ask forgiveness for?"

For once Paul didn't hesitate. "Everything," he said. "Just about every fucking thing."

The boys, his boys, had gone off in their own directions like people they'd known only at church, friendly neighbors, two young men who had at some time in the past played in their yard and eaten at their table. Before that—oh, before that—had been the best of times. When the boys were old enough to spend time at the shop, walking over after school, telling him about their days as he finished paperwork and checked over the stock. Together they'd ride in the truck, that very truck, down and up and down and up those hills south of town, to dinner, to their mother, who back in those years came to the shop for lunch, telling him everything she'd heard on the news radio since he'd left for the day. It had been Watergate and Nixon and gas troubles and the Middle East and then Iran. It was Joshua who said by phone from college they should vote Reagan, and the only one convinced had been Terry, who'd taken to wearing his football jersey with no shirt underneath right there at the dinner table as they handed the receiver around. A month later Jack had begrudgingly helped the boy register to vote and stood in line with him in the Baptist church basement. A year later Terry was gone to school as well. They had become, in small ways, what Opal had taken to calling yuppies, just as the folks on TV did. This generational difference to him now seemed small. What mattered, especially with time on his hands for once, was how he'd lost all that had made him happy with life. Sobriety was good, but in the fog of his long drinking, he'd let the years of joy go by like a flitting dream. The present had the boys gone so far away and Opal gone even if she was close at hand. "You know she stopped even coming to see me at the shop," he said as they waited for their chicken-fried steaks at a diner outside Wichita. "It's like she started living another life without me. And with you showing up, I'm driving her up the walls."

Paul gave him a sour look over his mug. The late-afternoon sun reflected gold on the surface of his coffee. "And you've talked to her about this?"

"About what?"

"With the other life," he said. "With the lunches alone."

"Oh, Opal," he said, but he didn't really have any way to explain the elated terror he felt in saying her name. "She'd think I was crazy talking about it. She already does."

"Maybe you ought to get a divorce," Paul said. "Seems about the right age to start over."

"Shit," Jack said. "I didn't say I'd lost my mind."

"Who ever does?"

He tried to picture himself telling Opal how he'd felt so alone these last years and how being home had made it so much worse. Maybe in their chairs with the television playing in front of them, where he could look at someone else's face when he spoke. Or in the kitchen with the coffeemaker gurgling, just as she reached up into the cabinet for a box of cereal. He could take her out to dinner, even to a place in Shawnee, maybe the new Red Lobster. But each of these images sunk into a muddy fog, Polaroids in reverse. He hadn't been able that morning to tell her about the foal.

"I'm only kidding," said Paul. "You're talking sense. But these are Phil Donahue years. You watch his show?"

Jack had. On the televisions in his shop, he'd seen that foppish character walk around with a microphone and note cards, by turns interviewing and inciting. What he hadn't ever done is turn on the sound. "I'm aware of it," he said.

"A man's got to share his feelings. That's the message." He pointed a crooked finger at him, smiling, toothy. "You don't share your feelings, you get cancer of the balls now."

The food came, and when the waitress offered to box up Paul's untouched food, he told her to leave it. He ate, feeling the sharp twist in his gut cinch and loosen, cinch and loosen. He missed Opal. A young man's lifetime had passed since he'd been this far away from her. Not since the day they'd met. Finally, to change the subject, he said, "I'm sorry about your boy. About Bradley. Have you seen him?"

His brother gave him a dull look. "Seen him?" he said. "You've got a mistaken notion of what's going on here, don't you?"

He looked around the little diner. A younger man in a ball cap and mustache eyed him suspiciously. "I only thought since—"

"There's no one for me to talk to but you."

"What about Dad?" he said. "You never really told me what happened to Dad."

"Forget it," Paul said. "You're taking me to Eileen and then it'll be all done."

All done? What, exactly? The visits? This, well, haunting? Or was it more than that? His brother flustered him, really. Put him on edge. It had been like that all their lives. Nobody could go around asking Paul what his problem was, or advising him to seek a shrink, or just come out with it and say he was loony, mostly because of the generally threatening demeanor he carried around in his little body. He was like a small old dog everyone put up with snapping and growling at them, all for the brief moments of recognition in his saddened eyes. And here it was, too, Jack's big chance to talk to his brother. In a way, their relationship had always worked this way. Paul remained his elder, spinning off advice, acting as his confessor, and always maintaining this awkward power over him.

Years before their parents left with that drifter, back when Jack was fourteen, a rumor got around that he'd been caught by other boys kissing a girl everyone called Dog-Face Betty behind the school gymnasium. Paul sat him down in their shared bedroom and asked him if it was true. Jack said it wasn't, of course, but Paul pressed him on whether he had something for Betty, if he thought it was right for the other boys to call her such a name. After fifteen minutes of this wrangling, Jack confessed everything. He'd thought no girl would ever kiss him, so he'd tried with Betty, writing her a poem even, making her promises, and when they'd kissed, he'd thought she was the most beautiful girl in the world, but when the rumor surfaced, he said he'd never, he'd dodged past her in the halls, he'd treated her like no one should ever treat anyone. "Like an ant under your heel," Paul had said as Jack blubbered and sniffled into his sleeve. "That's no way to be a man in the world, Jack. Now go to the telephone and apologize to her."

He'd been that kind of brother before the folks left. Maybe only Jack understood this. So here, decades later, sensing he might not get another chance, he couldn't waste the opportunity to spill his guts. "I don't know what all this has been about," he said.

"About Opal?" Paul waved a hand between them. "About this?"

"Sure, about Opal and you and all of it. Life. Being here. That store of mine. The years I poured into it thinking it was taking me somewhere and I was going to be rewarded. You know what it amounted to? Some money. Most of it out the door before I could even put my feet up at night. Every day was like climbing on the same roller coaster, thinking eventually, with all evidence to the contrary, that this was the night train to Hong Kong."

"You want to go to Hong Kong?"

"I meant figuratively," he said. "I mean I went nowhere. Work, sleep, work, sleep, and then my name taken off the front of the building and a wad of somebody else's money in the bank. I missed something, is what I'm saying. I missed life. The boys are different people now and Opal doesn't even want to look at me and here I am sixty years old, worse off than when I started."

Paul pushed away his food and licked at his lips. Then he said, "This is about the pony, then?"

"What pony?"

"Today."

"That was a horse," he said. "A foal. That wasn't a pony."

"I thought—"

"Two different animals," he said. And then, registering his brother's little smile, "Well, you know that. But no. It isn't about the pony."

In truth it was, though, and he knew that. The poor foal dead in the grass, murdered by unseen culprits, the bleak meaninglessness of it all. That small life taken in the night, and him to blame. It was like a scab pulled off him and now out tumbled all his doubt and trepidation. He took turns with his brother looking out the slat-blind windows at the shushing highway. The waitress came by with the check and took their plates, asking again about a box for the food.

"You just need to talk to her," Paul said finally. "You need to look her in the eyes and talk to her. Just like you'll talk to Eileen."

There was something to not telling her about that foal that had gotten him on this line of thinking, missing her and the horses and their home, and now he could see her again, Opal, gazing back at him, expectant. She was such a decent person. A good wife. Nobody knew him better, but then again, no one knew him less. He couldn't quite get his head around what he meant by that thought. Maybe that they'd been playing parts on the same stage so long neither one of them remembered their real name. "I couldn't," he said. And then, deflating, "I'll try."

Lawrence, before this trip, hadn't even registered for him as the name of a city in Kansas. He just hadn't given the place much thought north of Topeka, and the one friend of his who'd been to Kansas City, Herb Stelig, had returned with tales of criminals lurking down every street, drug dealers mumbling in bathrooms, women in fishnet stockings fluttering their eyelashes at him like slutty characters in a crime novel. The tree-lined downtown and grand buildings of Lawrence struck Jack as familiar, like the photo spread of an old *Time* magazine story on American civic virtue during the heyday of the Cold War. Paul had him stop at a newsstand to get directions to the hospital. It wasn't until his brother jauntily made his way back to the truck, smiling like an overheated dog, that Jack wondered how he'd behave at the hospital once they got there. "We're brothers," he said as they crossed town. "I'll tell you what to say. But really you already know what to say."

"And what's that?"

"That her brother was a good man. It's too late for him, but I can tell her." He rubbed his hands together expectantly. "Maybe it's not too late to make it all right?"

Ahead on the right, a modern-looking brown rectangle rose

above the trees. He felt like a man about to give a speech at a wedding, all sweat and nerves. "Who was her brother?" And then, something sharp moving in his gut, he thought of the woman in the desert, the one Paul said he'd buried. Suddenly he believed that story, something he'd once thought was a sick joke. "What did you do to him? Did you kill him?"

"You know I didn't tell you that."

"You can tell me now."

"Jack," his brother said, "I'm dead."

During that last phone call before he died, what he had told him should have been enough to know. Paul had said then the woman's brother was the same drifter who had come to their home one chilly evening in Boise and left the next morning, left with their mother and father, none of them to return. Maybe Paul's vengeance on that count had never abated. And in a single breath it all unraveled before him: his brother infected with an evil he couldn't control, leaving a trail of hopelessness in his wake. He felt like Abel, snuck out the door before he could be sacrificed to Cain's hate. And look what suffering manifested in his stead.

He was uneasy. He had to change the subject. "What was so good about him, this man?"

"Oh, get off it," Paul said. "You understand what you're doing. This is you, Jack. Don't pretend to be a fool."

Up ahead, a sign guided him toward visitor parking. "What did you ever do to them?" he said. "Why's it any of my business?"

But he'd just stopped the truck and his brother was out the door, hotfooting it toward the glass entrance. He cut the engine and watched him, a rail-thin little man with a bony face and half his white hair combed over the top of his spotty head, this itinerant and moody character he'd never really understood, four times married and four times divorced, who had rushed him here to Kansas after insisting he carry that foal and bloodying up his clothes. This brother who had lost his only son and then lost himself, who had appeared at the end of the driveway like a kidnap victim and haunted him not only these last two years but every year since they'd parted ways. What had his life been, this older brother of his? Had it all been hate and seething? He remembered a visit from him back in the sixties, a game of pool over in Shawnee, the easy way Paul had smiled and laughed. And why take him to this dying woman? The thought of her, the abstraction of her, seemed now to correspond to an actual human being, right inside that building, tied up to god knows what machines, some other woman weeping at her side, a white-smocked doctor grimacing over charts.

Jack was sure he wouldn't follow. He wouldn't go inside. Instead he would turn back over the engine, he would pull free of this place and rush into the falling night, back home. All the way back to Opal, his only faith. Back home and to Opal.

But then he reached for the door handle. He stepped out. And as if a string pulled him forward by the belt, he sauntered along to where he knew his brother had already disappeared and where he knew he'd never really been. He recalled the pair of horses their parents had left behind, two healthy paint mares, Dipsy and Sunflower. He'd let Paul sell them all those years ago and never felt good about it. He should have done otherwise. His heart should have been big enough. Just like now, even in death, Paul got what he wanted. He was thinking of those mares, of their proud silhouettes in the field, wishing they were alive now along with that foal, not passed into the forgetting of death but right here in the undeniable moment of life, when the electric doors whooshed open and the heavy clinical air swept his mind empty of all but the task at hand, the undertaking.

The woman was old as dust, her face a blotch of skin hung on a toothless skull. Her eyes glowed with life in spite of this, and when they landed on Jack standing next to the half-open accordion door, with the bustle of intensive care at his back, he sensed her recognition. Paul wasn't there, or at least he couldn't see him, and she'd never met him in her life, they'd never seen each other before this instant. But the recognition was there anyway. "Ma'am," he said, "I'm Paul Penrod's brother."

One of her arms rested under the green blanket, a wad of tubes and wires feeding into her there, but with her free arm she raised a veiny hand and gestured him in, where he discovered the other woman, the one he'd spoken to earlier on the phone, Claudette. She was asleep in a boxy hospital-room recliner, a copy of *Newsweek* splayed over her chest. Jack went to the old woman's side and took her proffered hand. She appeared to be speaking, her in-turned lips working up and down, the jaw moving. But when he leaned down to her, not even a whisper issued forth. She hadn't once stopped looking in his eyes.

"He made a mistake," he told her. He knew then, like a pane

of glass lifted from a window, that his brother really was gone for good. Whether Paul deserved to be forgiven and what he'd done, that was another question. "Paul wanted me to tell you. He made a mistake, ma'am. He wanted to say your brother—"

Just then the other woman woke with a jerk. "Hello?" she said with a note of alarm.

The old woman, Eileen, squeezed his hand weakly, then rested her head back and closed her eyes. A nurse in pale green scrubs had entered, and instantly Claudette was on her feet, smiling, telling him they should get out of the way. "I'm Jack Penrod," he told her as the nurse closed the accordion door behind them. "We spoke?"

She was a broad-faced, slim-hipped woman roughly his age, her hair dyed a dull brown. In her Spuds MacKenzie sweat shirt and blue jeans she looked like someone's mother at a high school football game. She gave him a warm smile and, with an effortless gesture, patted his elbow. "Of course," she said. "Let's go get some coffee."

In the elevator he asked her about Paul, about what he could have done wrong to her friend. Instead of answering the question, she told him a story about many years ago, how she tracked Eileen down in Indiana where her family lived. She told him about Eileen's life as a schoolteacher for twenty-some-odd years, initially in St. Louis, where the two of them had first lived in a little ranch house, and then since '78 here in Lawrence. "She taught English and a little social studies now and again. Loved Shakespeare. Her ex-husband . . . well, that was his whole thing, you see. Shakespeare is what brought them together."

"And you two?" he asked as they stepped out into the basement, the scent of fried chicken and burnt coffee mixing with all the other hospital smells. "What brought you together?"

She laughed. "Same stuff that brings anyone together," she said. "You ever loved anyone before?"

"One," he said. And it was all he could do not to stop her there and expound on the subject of Opal Keating, the prettiest girl to ever step foot in Boise, Idaho.

"Well then, you know," she said. "Anyway, Eileen kept busy. Her life was her students. She touched a lot of people over the years. A bright light." She patted at her eyes with her fingertips, took a sharp breath. "Together we went everywhere but Antarctica. We've been so blessed."

They stood in line with gray trays, waiting their turn at the coffee. He told her about his parents running off one day with a strange drifter from Chicago, how he and Paul were left to live with their grandparents, and about the building rage of his brother, the long mass of life when they didn't much talk. "It's funny," he said. "It was Paul's death that brought me and him closer. We may never have talked so much before."

She gave him a funny look. "That's an odd thing to say," she said. "But I think I follow."

"He had some things he needed settled," he said.

A little later, huddled at a wonky table with Styrofoam cups of steaming black coffee between them, she spoke about a town dreamed up by her beloved Eileen, a thing she'd thought of one day and drawn up for her brother, a little pinch of utopia snuffed out in an instant by fearful men. As she spoke about all it would be, he began to see it in his mind, and as it formed, he felt a warm glow at the base of his neck. Here was a dream, yes, and the two of them, connected to it only by hearsay, frolicked in its possibilities. A town that was more like a family, spreading out in all directions, changing its neighboring towns like falling dominoes. The vision of this better place seemed so easy to make true, and he had to stop himself from reaching out and taking her hand in his. To his surprise, they had already become friends.

He wished for a moment that he could have known her before, that they all could have known one another. Maybe things would have turned out differently. "I found Eileen only after it went bad there," Claudette said, her voice graveling out. "I'd been looking so long, and then I found her."

"And in the town," he said, trying to bring her back to something he needed to understand. "My brother was there?"

She sipped from her coffee. "Oh, he was always there. His kind is."

And then, from the edge of that imagined town in his mind, he registered them, their coyote voices calling back and forth, howling and wavering into the night air, telling their story he didn't want to hear. That inhuman choir. And did he see their eyes there, glowing in the scrub, or were those only trick lights playing in the night distance, the reflections of unnamed stars? It didn't seem to matter, because anyway he was afraid. He gazed across the half-empty basement cafeteria, all gray and paper flowers, and felt the whole world around him curling up like a poked grub. A couple of seats over, the remains of a crumpled newspaper announced something about Gorbachev. He looked back at her, at Claudette. He was afraid to ask more, and maybe he didn't want to know.

Time passed. They finished their coffee. In the open elevator door, they hugged awkwardly, and then he was alone again in the high-tech lobby, an armed guard nodding at him as he neared the sliding door. Outside, at the truck, the wind had gone cold. He reached inside for the jacket he'd bought, foolishly, for his brother, and stood in the parking lot a moment, snapping it on. He looked up into the deep vastness above, hoping for a shooting star to arc earthward, something he could take home as a sign. But there was only the chill in the air and the big country around him, floating loose, unmoored, starved for meaning.

ACKNOWLEDGMENTS

For their early inspiration, I have to thank Toni Graham and Ed Walkiewicz, two of the greatest teachers in the business, and my parents, who raised me in a bookish household and filled my brain with old sci-fi movies. There would be no book at all without the unstoppable effort of my agent, Chad Luibl at J&N. And I wouldn't have understood the book I'd written without the incredible editorial eye of Geoff Shandler. Much thanks to the entire Custom House team. And most of all, thanks to Crystal, obviously, without whom I'd be nowhere, and who has watched this book and others form and fall apart and form again, somehow without losing faith in me. And to our dogs, who don't know any better.